LOST AND FOUND

LOST AND FOUND

WILL LOST TREASURES FROM THE PAST BE
FOUND IN THE TRAGEDIES OF THE PRESENT?

Jeff LaFerney

Copyright © by Jeff LaFerney 2015

Publisher: Tower Publications

ISBN-13: 978-0692424674

ISBN-10: 0692424679

Cover and interior design: Ashley Fontainne

Visit Jeff's website http://jefflaferney.blogspot.com/

BOOK DESCRIPTION

In 1939, a sole Jewish smuggler immigrates to America to preserve a heritage Hitler hoped to erase. In 1944, two spies enter the United States on a mission to track down one man and a treasure of missing Spanish gold. In 2014, the immigrant's son, his mind deteriorating from dementia, disappears, but not before he leaves his grandson clues, thrusting him into a mystery seventy-five years in the making. Blake Nolan and his girlfriend set out to unravel clues that could not only set secrets from history right again but also lead to two priceless treasures. With his grandfather's life in the balance and suspects hot on Blake's trail, will what was lost be found in time?

DEDICATION

I'd like to dedicate this book to my wife's parents. Her mother, Bonnie Smith, currently resides in a convalescent home, suffering from severe Alzheimer's. We watched her deteriorate from a talented, smart, energetic woman to someone who needs care 24/7. My wife's father, Darwin Smith, had his own unique issues after suffering a stroke. He left his living facility, never to return. We spent six days searching with no results, only to have his body discovered three days later, deceased in the woods. I was blessed to be included in their family, and I think of them often. This book will forever be in remembrance of them.

PROLOGUE

Monday, May 1, 1939

Internment didn't require a trial, so release didn't require compensation or apology. All it required was for the electrified, barbed-wire fence gate to be swung open. Out stumbled Yosef Bloomberg, shielding his eyes from the painful, glaring sun. His tortured, malnourished body barely resembled the young man who entered the German concentration camp six months before. A man of only twenty-one years of age, Yosef exalted in his exit, but he knew his happiness would be short lived. If he had remained in custody, he would have surely died. There wasn't much likelihood beyond death in a place like that. He had witnessed more than ten thousand men brought into Dachau. A few were executed, others were moved to different camps, but most were like Yosef—Jews who were worked to the bone building roads, digging in gravel pits, and draining marshes. Nearly all, including Yosef, were physically abused and used in medical experiments. After demonstrating proof of their impending emigration from Germany, most of his fellow captives were released, but Yosef was one of the last to leave from his initial, physical confinement. His emotional suffering, however, would continue. Chaim and Freida Bloomberg rushed to hold their son in their arms.

"Yosef, you're free! Jehovah be praised, you're finally free!" Chaim's voice cracked as he fought to hold back tears.

Yosef winced. The painful embrace aggravated his broken skin from the flogging he had received in "celebration" of his exit. His mother pulled away from the hug and scrutinized her son more closely. Shocked, Freida swallowed her panic. "You don't look well."

Of course he didn't. He had been overworked and undernourished. Scientists rendered him unconscious three times in experiments with extreme hypothermia, only to revive and treat him. They used him in medical experiments, testing methods of making salt water potable. The many times he was dehydrated from a heavy work load and then given salt water to drink had caused his blood pressure to rise, his heart rate to increase, and his kidneys to deteriorate. He had physical scars from whippings and emotional scars from nearly six months of suffering.

But now he was free. His prayers had been answered, yet his release would bring with it a new pain. After a half year in Dachau, he would be sent to America...alone. His family would be left behind. His sister was already dead, a victim of Kristallnacht. She died in the early morning hours of November 10, 1938, a victim of a brutal rape and a gun barrel to the temple. Naked and bleeding, she was left sprawled on the shop floor while glass and destruction littered the streets. Assault detachments of the Nazi party wreaked havoc to his parents' business in Berlin along with more than seven thousand other businesses.

The Bloombergs knew they were coming—stormtroopers, security police, Gestapo, and Hitler Youth. Yosef and his sister, Bayla, gathered the lightweight bedroom furniture their father had assembled and stowed it in the hidden space below the floor. They had barely finished moving carpeting and the main workbench of the cabinetry shop back overtop the crawl space as the SS arrived, smashing windows and destroying their father's precious workmanship in his shop. Chaim and Freida were gone during the destruction—making the final arrangements to get

Yosef and Bayla's grandparents safely out of the country. The Bloomberg family had planned to leave together—mother, father, sister, and Yosef—for the United States once Chaim's parents were safely away, but things had changed.

Exhausted, Yosef groaned and sat in his father's vehicle.

His father got right down to business as the car pulled away. "You will be a passenger on the S.S. *St. Louis* in twelve days. In order to get you out of the internment camp, we had to promise you'd be out of the country within the next two weeks."

"You mean *we*, don't you, Father?" His stomach felt sick. "*We* will be leaving the country."

"We cannot afford to go with you. Things have changed, Son. We no longer have enough money to pay our way."

"We need to get you some food and some rest, Yosef," his mother interjected. "You need your strength. We can talk about this later."

"No, Mother, we need to discuss this now. You *must* come with me." All relief he felt when he left Dachau had flown away. Fear and concern replaced it. "You would die in a place like that," he said as he looked back over his shoulder. "There must be a way."

"Yosef," his father said. "Things are different. Worse even since Kristallnacht. Insurance didn't pay for the damages to the business. *We* paid for the repairs. The price of visas has risen as well as the passage fees. They're now charging a 'contingency fee' to cover expenses in case of an unplanned return voyage. Also, there is now a fee for a landing permit in Cuba."

"Cuba? Why Cuba?" Anxiety cursed through his battered body.

"That is the destination of the S.S. *St. Louis*," he replied. "From there we had to pay to get you to the top of the waiting list to enter the United States from Cuba. There is a passenger fee for your voyage to America as well. And there are other costs that take precedence over my life or your mother's...."

Because of his hesitation, Yosef knew what he would hear next was important beyond a simple emigration from Germany. "What, Father? What is more important than your safety?"

"We must pay to ship the furniture and many, many artifacts with you. We've had to arrange to change your identity when you land in America and get you a vehicle. Then you must disappear with all of the items you smuggle into the country....and you must have money to begin a new life. You are charged with the responsibility of protecting our heritage."

Yosef's jaw hung open as he sat, speechless, the pain of leaving his parents and the fear of the unknown weighing on his mind.

"Hitler is confiscating evidence of our culture and history, Yosef," his mother said. "The art and the artifacts must never be discovered. It's our history and should never be stolen or destroyed. It should be held up and admired. Because you are young and strong, you're better equipped to survive and preserve our heritage than your father or I."

"Why me? Why are you taking me from one life of torment and sending me away to another life of misery? Why me and not someone else?" Yosef hands shook, and his voice groaned in desperation.

"We've been making arrangements from the moment we got your grandparents to safety. That's one reason why we couldn't get you out. We couldn't free you until we were able to make the emigration plans and to collect the rest of the items now hidden in the furniture. We are ready now, and it is *you* who has been selected. You have your whole life before you. *You* must be the one to do this. There is no argument. This is bigger than all of us."

Monday, May 29, 1939

The S.S. *St. Louis* from the Hamburg-America Line had sat in the Havana Harbor for two full days. After Dachau, the "first class" lodging for sixteen days on the passenger ship seemed like a pleasure cruise to Yosef. His strength returned after close to a full month of freedom, and with it came his old confidence and strength. Captain Schoeffler was a good man. With 231 crewmen on board, the captain had ordered and maintained respectful treatment of the Jewish refugees—400 first-class and 500 tourist-class passengers. Except in their treatment by Otto Rechtsteiner, a Nazi party local group leader—an Ortsgruppen-leiter—Yosef and the others had experienced a pleasant voyage.

"Yosef," Captain Schoeffler said, "have you not been comfortable? You've never interacted with the other passengers much, and you are sad."

"Nearly six months at Dachau, Captain..."

"I've heard it is a hard place to be," Schoeffler interrupted.

"Yes, but this voyage has been most pleasant. Thank you."

"I assume you were forced to leave. What of your family?"

"They've lost just about everything since the Night of Broken Glass. They couldn't afford to leave with me."

"Now I understand your sadness." He hesitated. "I'm not in agreement with what is happening in Germany, Yosef. It is wrong. I do my best to assure the Jewish refugees are treated with respect as all men should be. I fear for your family, however. There will be war, and there will be horror for the Jews. If I had my way, I'd leave with my wife and child to avoid it all. I have relatives in America. Family is what is most important. Do you know where you're going?"

"Virginia, sir. I don't have family in the United States. Where are yours?"

The Captain beamed. "I'm from Bremerhafen, Mittelfranken, in Bavaria. It's a beautiful place. Many of my ancestors have moved from there to a state called Michigan. They're good German Lutherans living in towns called Frankenmuth and Frankentrost. They're Bavarian towns just like home. I'm certain I'd go there to be with my family."

"That sounds nice."

Captain Schoeffler paused to think, sighed, and then changed subjects. "I've heard they're allowing you off my ship today."

"Yes, sir," Yosef said.

"I wish you well. Unfortunately, I see my future as a navy captain in a war. I think I would trade my fate for your sorrow."

As a courier for the German Secret Police, the Abwehr, Otto Rechtsteiner was to deliver a sealed, secret document at the port in Cuba. The mission was code-named Operation Samland, and Rechtsteiner was to pass the letter of instructions to Roger Norman, the official from the Hamburg-America shipping line in Havana. Norman would then pass it on to German spies in America, who would see to it that the message made it into the right agent's hands.

However, as political negotiations for the prisoners continued, and as the vessel's detainment was prolonged in the harbor, Rechtsteiner hadn't been able to get off the ship, and Norman hadn't been able to get on. The latest word was that twenty-nine passengers with appropriate visas were going to be released. The 250 passengers waiting to board the ship for the return voyage to Europe were not going to be let on, and Captain Schoeffler was being ordered out of the harbor.

"Bloomberg!" Otto Rechtsteiner eyed Yosef with typical animosity. "What do you think you're doing?"

"I'm setting ashore, sir." Yosef wiped dust from a wooden dresser. "I'm gathering my belongings and getting off the ship." Yosef looked the officer in the eye but did his best to feign the appropriate amount of intimidation that had kept the hateful Rechtsteiner off his back for sixteen days.

"What is it with the furniture?" he asked. "Since when are we shipping junk across the sea?"

Yosef recited his well-rehearsed story. "It's hand-crafted furniture from my father's shop, designed to General Field Marshall van Leeb's specifications. It's to be delivered to his granddaughter in America in time for her wedding."

"And you are his hand-chosen messenger?"

Yosef didn't trust Rechtsteiner. "In a way, I guess I am. I helped to build the furniture, so after my detainment in Dachau, when I was ordered to leave the country, I volunteered to deliver it myself. The Field Marshall's daughter lives in Miami where her husband-to-be is a medical doctor. I've been instructed to deliver it undamaged before meeting some family in the state of Virginia," Yosef stated as sincerely as he could manage. What would happen in reality, however, was a man named Daniel Greenberg, the director of the Relief Committee in Cuba, which was financed by the American Jewish Joint Distribution Committee, made arrangements for Yosef to get off the ship. Greenberg booked passage to St. Petersburg, Florida, and purchased a truck for Joseph Bloom to take to a destination unknown. Yosef Bloomberg became Joseph Bloom, German immigrant to America.

As they spoke, Solly Wernher, a crazy man who had threatened suicide numerous times since the ship put in to the harbor, ran his way across the starboard bow. "Get me off this ship...now!" he yelled. He claimed the Gestapo had managed to board the ship with potato peelers and were planning to skin him alive. "Let me off! I'll jump. They're everywhere!" Rechtsteiner made his way after the loony passenger, and Yosef headed back to steerage to help with another piece of furniture.

Once Rechtsteiner detained and delivered Wernher to his wife in her cabin, he headed for the forecastle where he took the sealed envelope and some tape from his locker. While Bloomberg had his dresser carried off the ship, the courier for the secret police snuck up and slid open a night stand drawer. He affixed the envelope and its message to the underside of the plywood bottom panel on which the top drawer rested. Later, he radioed Roger Norman in Havana. He attempted to tell Norman that Bloomberg was headed to Miami to Field Marshall van Leeb's grand-daughter's home. Unfortunately for Rechtsteiner, while Norman negotiated terms with Cuban President Bru in an attempt to get on board the *St. Louis*—and before he ever received Rechtsteiner's message—Yosef Bloomberg had become Joseph Bloom, and the furniture along with the message sailed in a vessel toward St. Petersburg.

As the *St. Louis* sailed around Cuba awaiting a final decision on its fate, Rechtsteiner received two messages. The first said President Roosevelt had announced his refusal to accept the refugees on American soil, but also he learned President Bru had put an end to the negotiations to let the passengers disembark in Cuba. The ship had no choice but to return to Europe. The second notification explained Norman had received the message from the *St. Louis* when he returned from his negotiations, but no Yosef Bloomberg had boarded a ship to Miami. There was no furniture, and Field Marshall van Leeb had no grand-daughter in Miami. The sealed message had been lost. Within two days, Rechtsteiner, who had failed in his duty, leapt overboard and was lost at sea, and with his death, it assured that the Secret Police back in Germany would have no knowledge the message was never delivered.

Friday, December 15, 1944

"Happy Birthday, Robert," Gunther Metzger said to his friend, Robert Coleman. He slapped his comrade on the back and handed him a drink. Two seats opened up at the end of the bar, so the men slid into them.

"*Danke*, Gunther. Merely one of many more to come," Robert replied with a smirk. "A lot more than you'll have, old man, since you have ten years on me."

"*Ja*...I suppose we ought to find Hirsch soon, then, or I'm likely to keel over and die before we locate the traitor."

"Yes, your days are numbered, *freunde*." He laughed and took a drink.

"Seriously though...today's your birthday celebration, but we've been in America two and a half weeks already—three days camped out in this bar—and we've made no progress in our search. I never knew of this place called New Jersey, but now that you've made headquarters of this tavern with no result, I think it's high time we made our way to the state you call Pennsylvania and its famous Lake Erie. It's the last location Detlef Hirsch was known to have settled."

"We will, Gunther. But this is where the snobs from Princeton turned their noses up at me. My roommate came here often. He'll show up sooner or later, and since I'm here with a fortune in cash and diamonds, courtesy of the Nazi party, I want to flash some of it around. He was a friend, but he never looked at me as an equal because I wasn't born into the right family."

"That's how life is, and now it's in the past. It's time to move on and complete our mission."

"I was smarter than him." Robert was not to be sidetracked. "And I proved it when I left this miserable country. I chose the right side when I left to become a spy, and you and I will be wealthier yet when we find Hirsch's Spanish gold and the Germans win the war."

Robert motioned for the bartender to bring another round of drinks for the birthday celebration. Gunther scanned the bar. He'd made his suspicious nature and nervousness about Robert's intentions clear to his friend on numerous occasions. A man plodded into the bar, hair disheveled and tie loosened. Alone, he found a table for two and motioned for a waitress to attend to his obvious desire for a drink. He looked overworked, exhausted, and disenchanted with his present circumstances.

As Robert slid the drink to Gunther, he followed his friend's gaze. It was the roommate. Finally. "It's him, Gunther. The gods have seen fit to give me my moment of recompense. Look who's doing better now."

Robert sauntered over to his old friend's table. "Tsk, tsk, tsk. If it isn't the great MacAllister Cornwall. You don't look well, old friend. Life getting you down?"

"Robert? I haven't seen you in nearly two years. What happened to you?"

"I'm doing quite well, I must say. Let me buy you a drink. I have a big pile of cash burning a hole in my pocket." He made a show of extracting a thick wad of one hundred dollar bills. He licked his fingers and peeled off a bill for the waitress.

MacAllister glanced at the bills, envy in his eyes, but his words were calm and collected. "What are you doing for a living, Rob? I'm working my way up the corporate ladder, but the going seems to be slower for me than it is for you."

He hesitated before saying, "Um...I work for the government."

MacAllister found that to be funny. He laughed as he gulped down a shot and then sipped from his beer. "You? You were a good friend, Robert, but I never heard you say a positive word about our government. Seriously...Did you rob a bank? You were always looking for a shortcut to success. There's not a chance you're working for the American government." He laughed again, louder than before.

Robert seethed. His "friend" was supposed to be impressed. Instead, he laughed. "Who said it was the *American* government, Cornwall? I prefer to be on the winning side. This money comes from the *German* government, and there'll be plenty more when my comrade and I complete our mission and the Germans win the war." He had said too much, but his anger boiled.

"Yeah, right. I don't know how you're rolling in cash, but you must be putting me on. I'm supposed to believe you're some sort of German spy? Who would ever believe that?"

"Do you think I care what you believe? I suppose the fact I trained in Berlin and crossed the ocean on a German U-boat doesn't impress you? My comrade, Gunther, and I entered America off the coast of Maine only two and a half weeks ago with a pile of cash, a stash of seventy diamonds to sell when the cash runs out, and a mission to find a Nazi traitor and his stolen Spanish gold. I came to this bar to show you how stupid your journey up the corporate ladder is. This whole country is reeling. Look at you. Hitler will win the war, and I'll be rewarded. What'll ever happen to you? Do you suppose your daddy will be able to protect you then?"

MacAllister snorted again. "Nice practical joke, guy. I don't know where you got your money, but you're no more a spy than I am."

Angry and disgusted by MacAllister's reaction, Robert grabbed his drink, scowled, and stormed back to his friend, disappointed he hadn't been treated with the respect he felt he deserved. Gunther, still seated at the counter, focused on a small, black and white television screen behind the bar. Programming had been interrupted, and the bartender turned up the volume.

"...Canadian freighter, Cornwallis, has been sunk in the

Atlantic by the German submarine U-*1230*. The freighter was carrying sugar and molasses from Barbados to Saint John, New Brunswick. Only six weeks ago, the German sister ship, the U-*1229* was sunk in the North Atlantic, close to the shores of Maine. This is the second known verified German submarine activity near Maine in less than two months, causing alarm with the FBI who is concerned the U-boats may be dropping off enemy agents onto US soil. The Frenchman Bay near Bar Harbor and Sunset Ledge near Hancock Point are areas considered to be possible drop-off points in the Northern Atlantic. The Boston FBI office has sent men to Northern Maine to investigate...."

Gunther's face went white. He leaned in close to Robert, keeping his words private. "That's our U-boat, Robert. It's where we were dropped. Your United States FBI may be onto us. We need to be on the move before our mission is compromised."

Robert turned for one last look at his old roommate who leaned forward and squinted at the grainy, portable TV, straining to hear the reporter. "I believe you're right, Gunther. I think it's best we leave right now." He threw some cash on the counter and without hesitation, the two men walked out.

CHAPTER 1

Saturday, December 13, 2014

For the third time that day, Blake Nolan watched his grandfather, Matthias Bloom, stand at the front picture window, a curious expression adorning his stubbly face. His gray-haired head tilted to the side as Blake's mother parked a silver Volkswagen Touareg in his driveway.

"I'm exhausted, Blake," said Deborah Nolan as she climbed out of the driver's seat. The car, packed to the roof, held their final load of possessions they'd moved. "Let's get this last batch of things into the house, and we can call it a day."

The front door swung open, and the elderly man, wearing black socks, boxer shorts, and a cardigan sweater to ward off the cold December Michigan air, stepped shoeless onto the front porch. "Deborah! What are you doing here?" he asked.

"Dad, don't come out here in your underwear! We're moving

in with you, remember? We've already been here twice today, dropping off our things."

"You have? Oh, yes, the snowstorm. You were here for the snowstorm."

Frowning, Blake said, "It's cold enough, but it never snowed today, Grandpa. You must be thinking of something else."

"Be respectful of your grandpa, Blake," his mother said quietly. "He doesn't remember."

"I am?" Matthias pointed. "I remember your mother playing right over there with the Marquardt girl, eating icicles, but you weren't here, Blake."

Blake took a deep breath and tried his hardest not to roll his dark-brown eyes. Moving the sixty miles from Clarkston to Frankenmuth in the middle of his senior year was hard enough. Doing it without his dad, who had been called into duty in the Army reserves made it even harder, but doing it with a grandfather who had dementia would be the hardest yet.

"Speaking of eating, Grandpa, I'm starving. Is there anything for dinner?"

"Sure, sure, we have plenty of Marquardt. Let me get my pants on, and I'll get you some, Blake. Why did you say you're here?" He turned and went back inside without waiting for the answer.

"Marquardt? This is gonna be difficult, isn't it?" Blake commented to his mother.

"Not as much as it would have been in our old house. At least here, I won't have ghosts from the past stalking me."

He could see that his normally energetic mom was cold and tired, so when she turned away to begin unloading, Blake let her comments drop. When he stepped his six-foot-two-inch frame inside with the first of the latest load of his things, his grandpa sat in his underpants looking at an art book in the living room. There was no food in sight.

Two hours later, after eating three grilled cheese sandwiches and almost a full bag of Bar-B-Q Fritos, Blake had managed to arrange his things in his new bedroom where he collapsed onto the bed. Less than twenty-four hours before, he led his eleventh ranked Clarkston basketball team to a come-from-behind victory over Bloomfield Hills. He lay on his back and shot a spinning shot up over his head, letting it settle back into his shooting hand. The ball, signed by each of his teammates, was a parting gift from his coach. Blake was an honorable-mention all-state player his junior year, yet apparently, Frankenmuth's coach saw no reason to add Blake to his team to finish out his senior season. It looked as if Blake's basketball career had ended.

In addition to being at a new school—*not* on the basketball team—his father was now deployed in Kuwait, and he had to help take care of a grandfather who couldn't remember to get dressed. It was going to be a horrible senior year.

His bedroom door opened as another shot floated toward the ceiling and fell again perfectly into his right hand.

"Can we talk, Blake?"

His grandfather stood in the doorway. Dressed in khakis, his face smooth from a shave and his gray hair combed into place, he didn't look like the lost man in the picture window any longer. "Sure, Grandpa."

At sixty-five years of age, Matthias Bloom had a full head of hair and a few wrinkles that simply made him look distinguished, but it wasn't his outward appearance that aged him. It was his mind. He'd been diagnosed with dementia, stemming from two obvious causes. The first was concussions. In addition to being a boxer in his youth, he'd also had concussions from a tire hub cap to the cranium—received while foolishly chasing a tornado—and from an imprudent head-first dive into a wading pool, which was generally explained in part from the brain swelling caused by the wheel cover to his forehead. In addition, he'd had a minor stroke less than two years past that accelerated his symptoms. He looked coherent at the moment, however, so Blake sat up to give him his attention.

"Did you get enough to eat?"

"Yes."

"Do you like your room okay?"

3

"It's fine."

"Are you worried about your dad?"

"A little."

"Do you know why your mother is treating me like a child?"

"Well, I guess your memory isn't so good."

"What? That's preposterous."

"You forgot to put on your pants."

"I only wear pants when I need them, son. Like when I need to put things in my pockets. Like litter. One should never litter, and pockets prevent littering. Also, I think better with my legs spread out so air can get to my private parts. The family jewels need to breathe. Do you have any use for *your* pants right now?"

"Um, not really..."

"Then take them off. We need to talk."

"Seriously?"

Instead of answering, he stood up and yanked off his pants again. He nodded at Blake and raised an eyebrow as if to say "What are you waiting for?"

So Blake took his pants off too.

"Feels better doesn't it?" his grandpa asked. Uncomfortable, Blake shrugged his shoulders and ran a hand through his short brown hair. It was a little weird in his opinion. "Kids these days," his grandpa continued. "They know too much about nothing. What they need to know is numbers and history...and puzzles and mystery. Hmmph. I'm a poet and didn't know it. Except my fingers are Longfellows. Throw me that ball."

Blake shrugged and tossed it to his grandfather who caught it with one huge hand, palming it and faking a throw back while the ball stuck firmly in his grasp.

"You like poetry, Blake?"

"Uh, not really. Nikki Giovanni's pretty cool, I guess."

"Well, one of my favorite poets is Shel Silverstein," he continued. "He's Jewish, you know. Just like my father and my grandfather and grandmother...and your mother and you. You didn't know that did you? Well, you're only one-eighth...an important number for you to remember. Silverstein had a poem that said you should listen to the don'ts, shouldn'ts, couldn'ts, impossibles, and never haves. And then he said you should listen even closer to me because I say 'anything can happen or anything can be.' Not bad memory for an old guy who forgets to wash his hands after he wipes his butt, don't you think?"

Blake scrunched his face up in semi-disgust. His grandpa held Blake's basketball in those hands.

"Kidding, my boy. I'm not serious. I just wanted you to know you can accomplish anything you set your mind to. Like me. I wanted to write a poem too, so I did it. It goes like this...." He tossed the ball back to Blake, and with a confused look on his face, he stared into space. He didn't say anything for several seconds. "Oh, yes, give me a minute." He bent over and retrieved his pants, pulling them onto his legs and over his hips. After he snapped them, forgetting all about the zipper, he patted his pants, front and back, before putting his hand in his front-right pocket and removing a piece of paper. "I love pockets," he said. Then he cleared his throat and began reading.

"I call this one 'Literally'." He cleared his throat.

"Rise and ascend the climbing tree;
Come and ponder...thinking free.
Notice the way the puzzle weaves.
Connect the branches up through the leaves—
The crooks and knots of the climbing tree,
Sprouting nails as signs for thee.
So come and think and know your history—
The only way to solve the mystery.
The king's star is what you'll see,
And in the center is the key."

Blake tilted his head as he looked at his grandpa, confusion on his face.

"I know. It's kind of cryptic, but it's the best I can do. My digits may remind me of that Longfellow poet, but my words are no Silverstein. Anyway...you can have it. It's a gift. The first of five—something a good numbers man won't forget."

He patted his pockets again as if wondering what to do next, his fly wide open and his face one of confusion. He looked back to Blake and said, "What are you doing here again? And why are you sitting there in your underwear? You should put on some pants." Then he walked out of the room.

CHAPTER 2

"So here's your schedule, and Mr. Parker's down the hall and to the left," said Ms. Hartman, the petite guidance office secretary who was far too perky for a Monday morning. "Welcome to Frankenmuth High School, Blake." She handed him the sheet of paper. "If you need anything, let me know." She winked at him like her helpfulness was their personal little secret.

"Thank you, Ms. Hartman." He considered winking back but decided against making a bad first impression. Blake's mother volunteered to come in with him to school, but he couldn't imagine showing up with his mom, so he told her he could take care of things himself. Getting a parking permit for his grandpa's car was thing number one checked off his to-do list. The schedule was number two. Discussing basketball with the A.D. was item number three.

He headed down the hall to see the athletic director before his classes began and knocked on his open door. Mr. Parker looked up but didn't say a word. He wore a loosened neck tie, exposing the unbuttoned top button of his shirt. A Yahoo sports update occupied his computer screen.

Blake cleared his throat. "Um...I'm Blake Nolan. I'm a new student here, and I wanted to talk to you about the basketball team."

Mr. Parker stood and reached out his hand for Blake to shake. "Oh, hi, Blake. Your coach from Clarkston called me. Welcome to Frankenmuth."

"Thanks." Blake's lack of enthusiasm was most likely apparent. He squeezed the bridge of his nose, already possessing a headache, though the day had barely begun.

"Go ahead and have a seat."

Blake looked at the clock on the wall, concerned he'd be late for his first class, and then sat in front of Mr. Parker's desk. "It's just that..." Blake began. "Well, the coach here told *my* coach there was no place on the team for me, and I guess I hoped you'd say something to him so he'd give me a chance."

Mr. Parker readjusted himself in his seat and began to look quite uncomfortable. He yanked his tie even looser and cleared his throat. "I already talked to Coach Hahn, Blake. He's not so easy to reason with."

"So you're saying all he has to say is he doesn't want me, and there's nothing you can do about it? Not even get me a tryout?"

"Well, when we hire our coaches, we let them choose their own rosters. Coach says his roster is full and there's no more room. I guess he wasn't as impressed by your credentials as I was."

Silence pervaded the office as Blake tried to suppress his anger and Mr. Parker tried not to give eye contact. Though upset, Blake calmed himself enough to ask, "Does he know I can play?"

"Uh, yeah. I told him. After your coach called, I looked you up and told him all about you, but Mr. Hahn is a stubborn man. He showed up out of the blue from Pennsylvania two years ago when we needed a varsity coach. He works hard, but he's a private man who avoids distractions like a plague, and you, Blake, he considers a distraction. Anyway, it's his call. I don't know…maybe you could talk to him yourself. They practice right after school."

Blake simmered in silence for a moment before Mr. Parker said, "I heard your father's been deployed in the Army reserves. Sorry to hear that, but I respect the man for serving. Army offered me a scholarship for basketball…"

"I'll bet it was because of your great senior season in high school." Blake rose to his feet and fought the urge to punch the wall on his way out. "Unfortunately, I'm not going to get the chance *my* senior year." He took a deep breath and composed himself. "It seems to me, since he knows I have talent, he'd at least consider me. It doesn't make sense that he wouldn't." After taking a step toward the door, he turned back toward Mr. Parker. Parker shrugged with his palms in the air as if to say it was out of his hands. "Seriously? There's *nothing* you can do?"

The athletic director sighed deeply, rubbed his temples, and went back to work. Disgusted, Blake walked out and headed for class.

School was exactly as he expected. A handful of kids said hi. Lots of kids seemed to be looking his way and talking about him. His teachers introduced him to their students, but only a few of them introduced themselves to him. He shuffled through his schedule: English 12, Calculus, Physics, World History, lunch at a table with kids who were talking about a party they went to over the weekend, Economics, and last hour, Advanced Fitness III. He took a pre-test in the sixth hour physical education class to form a fitness plan, and then school ended.

Kids streamed by on the way to buses, practices, or their cars. Coach Hahn entered the gym with a whistle and a stopwatch around his neck. He had man boobs with a thick neck and meaty arms. Clean-shaven and sporting graying, close-cropped hair and a receding hairline, he rolled a cage of balls out of a storage room and folded his arms onto his hefty gut, pacing and looking at his watch until his team began to arrive. Blake took a deep breath and made his way onto the court to talk.

"Mr. Hahn? My name is Blake Nolan." He extended his hand for a handshake.

"You're the new kid who wants to join my team," he said without reaching for Blake's hand.

Uncomfortably, Blake lowered his hand. "Yes. I moved from Clarkston on Saturday. I've been a starter on the team since my sophomore year..."

"My team is already set. We had tryouts four weeks ago."

"I wasn't going to school here four weeks ago, Mr. Hahn. Could you maybe let me try out now?"

"We got a game tomorrow and only one practice to get ready. I already have more guys than I can play. We have a good team, and I don't need no other discontented players on my bench. Sorry to turn you away, but I don't need to be dealing with a problem I can avoid right now."

"What would be the 'problem' if I can help the team?"

"It's *always* a problem when a new kid joins a team in the middle of the year."

"You've never brought a kid up from the JV?" Blake clenched his fists, fighting the rising anger. "I could help you."

"I see you got a attitude problem, son. Sorry your life sucks, but I like mine precisely as it is. Best of luck to you. I got a practice to run."

By then balls were bouncing and players were staring at Blake. He felt like slugging something but instead took a deep breath and walked to the gym doors to leave. One of the players laughed at him and gestured with a thumb pointing up like an umpire calling a baserunner out. Blake stopped to get a good look at the kid.

"His name's Kevin Hahn...the jerk who's laughing at you."

Blake turned to see a girl about five feet two inches tall with a crazy mop of wild, curly brown hair and thick-framed eyeglasses balancing on a slender, freckled nose. She had a baggy North Carolina Tar Heel sweatshirt hanging practically to her knees, which were hidden under gray leggings.

"'Star' of the team." She made little quotation marks with her fingers. "You may have noticed him in P.E., bullying everyone else in the class."

"Mr. Geyer tested me in gym class today, so I didn't notice. Did you say 'Hahn'? He's the coach's son?"

"Yep. My name's Julia Fischer, by the way." She held her hand out for a handshake. "Talk is you're quite a ballplayer."

Blake slipped his hand around Julia's, surprised at the firmness of her handshake. "I'm Blake. Blake Nolan. Are you saying that short, chubby guy is the best player on the team?"

"We've had better teams, but he's our best player...I guess."

Blake turned to watch Kevin Hahn lean to his left and launch a three-pointer from about ten feet beyond the arc, coming a good two feet short for an air ball. "Hit me for my change!" he yelled at a teammate.

"You don't get change when you miss," said Blake. "Clearly, he's an idiot."

"Or a bully who needs to be taken down a notch."

Kevin got his return pass anyway from a skinny kid whose shorts were too long. He dribbled left handed for a layup, which he double pumped, shot with his right hand, and banged off the bottom of the rim. He took the skinny kid's ball and threw it down to the other end of the court. "The juniors shoot down there," he said.

"Why did Coach Hahn just tell me the team is good?" Blake asked.

"Hahn's a pretty good coach. Out of fear, they play tough defense, and the rest of the team is better than you'd ever know since Kevin shoots about half the shots, but regardless, *you'd* make them better."

"I don't know what you think you know about me, but it doesn't matter because Hahn says I can't be on the team."

"I've always believed things happen for a reason. Maybe there's a bigger purpose for your life than a few high school basketball games." Julia pushed her glasses higher onto her nose and shrugged her shoulders. "Tough day today?"

"It was all right. Aren't you in my math class?" Blake asked, remembering the sweatshirt from earlier in the day.

"Uh, yeah. And your English class and History and Economics and lunch and gym the same hour. You're very observant."

"Sorry. You sound like you know a lot about basketball."

"I know a little bit about a lot of things. Mostly, I'm an observer. People don't much notice me around here, but I notice them." She stood confidently in the doorway with a contented look on her face. "You didn't seem too interested in making friends today. You don't want to be here, do you?"

"It's that easy to tell? My mom and I had to move in with my grandpa who has some health issues. It's too far to commute to Clarkston from here. But at least this town has the largest Christmas store on Earth and an indoor water park."

"See there? You're already looking on the bright side. But we have *two* indoor water parks." She smirked, displaying a cute dimple on her right cheek. "And speaking of the Christmas store, Bronner's needs a muscly new guy in trees. I'm heading to work now. Do you have a car?"

"I'm driving my grandpa's for now."

"Follow me there. You can apply, and I'll put in a good word for you. You'll have to fake some Christmas cheer, though. Bronner's is a happy place."

Since the weekend move, Blake allowed a rare smile to escape. She sure was cute for someone dressed like a pillow with skinny gray legs...and hair looking like she just dried it with a towel.

The basketball team had begun stretching at half court, so there was no reason to hang around any longer. "Maybe it'll help if I sing Christmas carols on the drive over to improve my attitude. Lead the way, Julia."

"Great," she said. As Blake followed, she sang, "I Want a Hippopotamus for Christmas."

CHAPTER 3

Grandpa Bloom tapped his fingers and bounced his knees to "You're So Vain," a song from the Carly Simon album playing on his vinyl record player in the corner of the living room. Deborah worked away on her laptop at a desk she'd set up at the opposite wall to run her internet marketing company. Brown, shoulder-length hair framed her face, and she brushed it away from her eyes as she worked. Colonel Michael Nolan, her husband, loved her hairstyle, so she was determined to keep it the way it was for when he saw her again. She swept it from her face out of habit and accepted the annoyance.

"I love this song," Matthias said, bouncing across the beige carpeting as Carly Simon sang out the chorus.

Deborah's father seemed to fade in and out of mental clarity. At the moment, it pleased her to see the coherent father she adored.

When Blake entered his grandpa's house at about 4:00, Deborah held her gaze on her father and didn't appear to notice his arrival, but Matthias's face lit up. "Is it collection day?" he asked.

Cautiously, Blake stood in the entryway from the kitchen. He lifted his hands, and then dropped them, seemingly not knowing how to respond. "I don't know. What am I supposed to be collecting?"

"For the newspaper. You're the newspaper boy, aren't you? Let me get my checkbook."

The word *checkbook* snapped Deborah out of her trance. Disappointed that he'd faded back out, she shifted gears into her protective mode. "No, Dad, you don't need your checkbook. You don't even get the paper anymore. It's Blake...home from school."

"School?" he repeated. "Seems like a strapping young man like you," he said to Blake, "should be looking for a job. We could use someone to deliver the newspaper around here. How's a man supposed to know what's going on in the world without a newspaper? I remember one time when I was about your age," he said with a new moment of coherence, "I was trimming some bushes with my dad's hedge shears when the local newsboy almost took my head off with one of his papers. He was a friend of mine because he was a lot like me—'cept a lot more stingy. Even though I knew he was fooling around, I chased him down the street waving those giant clippers at him—all the way to the Cass River. I had to laugh when he dropped his bag and dove in headfirst. Swam to the other side of the river to get away from me. Not only was he a terrific swimmer, he's now the town historian, and as hard as it is to trust him, he's a good man. It's good to know that as you learn your history too. Don't forget it."

Blake shrugged his shoulders as he looked at his mother.

"How was your day, dear?" She rose from her chair and moved to the large front window to straighten the curtains.

"Six classes. No basketball. I got a job."

"Delivering newspapers?" Grandpa Bloom asked.

"No." Blake hesitated, crinkling his forehead before continuing. "Bronner's Christmas Wonderland hired me in the lights and trees department. I'll set up displays, fix lights, carry parcels...that kind of thing."

"I'm glad you got a job, but are you saying the coach *really* isn't going to let you on the team? You'd probably be his best player," Deborah said.

"More than likely since the best player is short, round, and full of himself. But the jerk coach seems to think his team is super and I'd be a problem he doesn't want to deal with. And the pansy AD isn't willing to help either, so as pathetic as the whole thing is, I've entered the working world."

"I'm sorry, honey, and your dad will be disappointed too."

"This dad of yours...is *he* out delivering newspapers?" Matthias looked curiously at Blake.

"No, he's in Kuwait in the Army Reserves, Grandpa."

"Of course. I knew that." The lost look in his eyes seemed to disappear, replaced by excitement, and Blake's grandfather began quoting trivia. "Did *you* know, young man, that Jewish actors Hal Linden, Gene Wilder, Tony Curtis, Mel Brooks, Don Adams, and Bea Arthur were members of the U.S. Military?"

"No...I don't even know who those people are, to be honest."

"You're kidding, right? I remember telling you how important our Jewish history is. Your mother is one quarter Jewish but her heritage never interested her." Deborah rolled her eyes. "You're one-eighth—an important number for you to remember—but it's no less your history than mine or your mother's. You were listening, weren't you?" The record crackled as the needle slid to the next song, and Carly Simon sang, "Anticipation."

"Well, you spoke to me on Saturday, Grandpa. In the past two days, I haven't had time to learn much."

"Hmmmm. Maybe so. You listen to music, though, correct?"

"A little. On my iPhone or iPod. Sometimes Pandora or Spotify."

"Who are they? Are they Jewish?" Matthias asked. "I'm talking about Jewish musicians like Carly Simon, Paul Simon, Bob Dylan, Barbra Streisand, Neil Diamond, Barry Manilow, Bette Midler, Neil Sedaka, and Billy Joel."

"That's quite a list of names you recalled, Dad," interrupted Deborah.

"I have a memory like a steel trap—rusty and illegal in thirty-seven states. You've heard of them, right, Blake?"

"Um, some of them."

"Well, here. I have another gift for you. Number two of five. He slid one of his vinyl albums from his record collection. It's Neil Sedaka. When you remember your numbers, this album will give you direction. And the newspaper boy will help you fill in a few blanks."

"Uh, thanks, Grandpa. I'll put it with your poem."

"You're a good boy, Blake. Now, Deborah? What time is it?" he asked as he looked out on the porch. "Why isn't our darn newspaper here yet? Kids these days. They spend all their time on their phones making texts and twitters instead of using their heads. You're gonna love Neil Sedaka, son. He sings like a girl, but he sure can make you want to dance." He wiggled his hips with his elbows sticking out like one would do for the "Chicken Dance" and shuffled out of the room while Carly Simon sang "Nobody Does It Better" on his record player.

Blake smiled about his grandpa as he put the Sedaka album on his dresser with the poem and sat on his bed to eat the dozen Deluxe Grahams he'd brought with him for a snack. His grandfather was gradually losing his mind and seemed to think his gifts were something special—like they were some kind of signs for Blake, used to impart some grandfatherly wisdom. Instead, they were two additional things to clutter up his dresser. It wasn't probable he'd be chicken dancing to the girly Neil Sedaka anytime soon.

After dropping his book bag in the middle of the floor and depositing his tennis shoes under his desk, he logged into his computer to write his dad an email.

Dad,

I hope you're safe. I'm proud of you, but I'm scared too. Please be safe. Mom's being strong, but taking care of Grandpa isn't going to be easy, and everything is easier with you around. The coach at Frankenmuth High is an idiot because he doesn't want the inconvenience of me joining the team, and the athletic director isn't much better because he isn't willing to help me either. My classes are okay and the kids are okay so far. One of my classmates gave me a lead on a job at Bronner's Christmas Wonderland, so I guess I'll work instead of earning a basketball scholarship. I suppose I can still play AAU and hope someone notices me. Grandpa seems to be a lost person one minute and totally cool the next. I try to be patient with his advice and history lessons and forgetfulness, but then he does nice things like give me gifts, and he makes me laugh. I feel bad for him, but to be honest, right now I feel bad for me too. I love basketball. I miss my friends. I'm worried about you and Mom, and Grandpa is only going to get worse, and I have to keep an eye on him. I'll admit, I'm kind of discouraged...well, maybe a lot discouraged. Love you, Dad.
   Blake

4

CHAPTER 4

The school day went by on Tuesday much the same as Monday except more kids seemed willing to say hi, and fewer teachers seemed concerned about how Blake would adjust. He nodded to Julia in first hour English, but she sat on the other side of the room. She sat right beside him in math, so she walked with him to class.

"I heard you got the job," she said.

"I have orientation today, so I work from three to six. Thanks for putting in a good word."

"My pleasure." She wore an oversized white T-shirt under an extra-large University of Louisville throwback basketball jersey with "Griffith" on the back. The jersey hung well down her thighs. She had skinny black jeans tucked into red, high-topped, unlaced Chuck Taylors. There was no telling what her body looked like under those clothes. She had gathered her curly hair into a ponytail, tied with a red, elastic hair tie. Strands of brown were sticking up from the hair tie in a couple of places, but the curly mess of the day before was far neater. "You must have managed a pleasant Christmas smile. They have a rule against hiring Ebenezer Scrooge, you know."

"I think they hired me for my physique rather than my smile." He flexed a bicep while also managing to grin. "But I'll do my best to get into the Christmas spirit. No bah humbug from me." He enjoyed the bantering with the girl who dressed like she had on a wind sock.

"Well, I don't work today, and since you're done at six, you can pick me up and take me to the basketball game. You'll enjoy Kevin Hahn and the wimps he bosses around. You drive, and I'll buy your ticket."

"Are you asking me out?" They entered the calculus classroom together, but Blake stalled in the doorway, waiting for an answer.

"No...just helping you adapt to your new school...and making sure I have a ride and don't have to sit alone."

The rest of the day crawled by without event until sixth hour advanced fitness. Once the class finished their scheduled workouts, the guys were allowed to shoot baskets in the gym. The PE teacher happened to be Mr. Geyer, the JV basketball coach, who willingly let the varsity players get some extra shooting in. Blake, in the midst of a long streak of made free throws, shot while the coach looked on, impressed. A skinny classmate named Roger rebounded. Kevin Hahn strolled toward them as balls bounced around the gym, tennis shoes squeaked on the floor, and clumsy ballplayers clanked shots off the rims.

"Hey, Nolan. You in for some two-on-two?" The chunky team captain had his six-foot-four-inch teammate to his left. The chaotic noise disappeared into silence. "You can have Roger Federer there," he said, nodding and pointing his thumb at the rebounder, "and I'll take Big Ben."

Ben Smyth rolled his eyes but didn't say anything, though all around the gym, people seemed to zero in on the conversation.

"Thanks for the opportunity," said Blake, "but I think I'll pass."

"You afraid to lose?"

Blake inhaled a lungful of air and breathed out a slow stream of air to calm himself as he continued to make free throw after free throw. "Seems like yesterday when I wanted to play, you were pretty happy your dad said no."

"You're an outsider, and we don't need you."

"I suppose the outsider rule didn't apply to you when you showed up two years ago?"

"I was here for tryouts, and *I'm* good."

"Of course. And your brilliant dad's the coach, so he's built the team around his short, plump son. You may think you're the big man on campus, but to me, you're nothing more than a chubby little bully, and I don't have time for you."

Kevin's face reddened with anger. "I don't let nobody talk to me like that!" His nostrils flared, and his eyes bore into Blake's.

"I'm surprised Big Ben puts up with you because it's easy to tell he's not your friend. I think I'll stay where I am and keep shooting free throws."

Kevin started for Blake, but Ben held him back temporarily. By the time he wrestled his way past his teammate, Mr. Geyer had stepped between them.

"That's enough, Kevin. Hit the locker room *now* before you regret it."

"He's the one who's gonna regret it," Kevin said, but he did as he was told.

When Mr. Geyer blew his whistle a moment later, signaling for everyone to put the balls in the bin, the class headed to their gym lockers. Everyone seemed fixated on how Blake stood up to Kevin and embarrassed him, but Blake was totally indifferent to the whole reaction.

"Your name's Roger Federer?" Blake asked the rebounder as they started away.

"Roger Fedler, but I *do* play tennis."

"Do you play basketball?"

"Uh...no," Roger admitted.

"It wouldn't have mattered," Blake said. "We'd have won anyway."

Blake dropped the ball in the bin and walked off the court.

"How many did he make in a row, Fedler?" Mr. Geyer asked.

"I don't know. Fifty? But he never missed once."

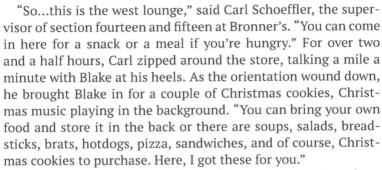

"So...this is the west lounge," said Carl Schoeffler, the supervisor of section fourteen and fifteen at Bronner's. "You can come in here for a snack or a meal if you're hungry." For over two and a half hours, Carl zipped around the store, talking a mile a minute with Blake at his heels. As the orientation wound down, he brought Blake in for a couple of Christmas cookies, Christmas music playing in the background. "You can bring your own food and store it in the back or there are soups, salads, breadsticks, brats, hotdogs, pizza, sandwiches, and of course, Christmas cookies to purchase. Here, I got these for you."

"Thanks," Blake replied before taking a bite. His new boss had been especially considerate and patient. Blake liked him the moment they met, and the past three hours hadn't changed his first impression.

"You're welcome. Grab a seat and let's review a few things. Maybe you have some questions." They sat at a corner table. "Do you understand what we're going to ask you to do?"

"I think so. Carrying things isn't too complicated, and I'm sure I can string lights and set up trees. I'll probably have questions once I get started, but right now I feel pretty confident."

"Do you understand how to punch in? Where to park? How to find your way around the store?"

"Well, finding my way around the store'll be a challenge. This place is gigantic."

"Largest Christmas store in the world. Fifty thousand different trims and gifts. The building covers over seven acres. Christmas music plays all day. Decorations and lights inside and out, 365 days a year. The whole place can be a little overwhelming for a new employee," said Carl.

"Lotsa things can be overwhelming. This job is only one of them."

"I know you've changed schools. What else is there?"

Blake hesitated because he didn't like talking about himself, but for going on three hours, his boss had been one of the friendliest people he'd ever met. "Well, winter without basketball is gonna bother me, especially when I know I could fit in and help Frankenmuth's team. The coach won't let me join...heck, he won't even give me a try out."

"That's too bad. You look like an athlete. I'm sure you would've helped the team. Why did you move here in the first place?"

Blake struggled to answer. "Well, after my dad headed off to Kuwait for the Army Reserves, my mom decided to move us here to watch my grandpa who's got some health problems."

"I'm sorry to hear that. Your dad'll be in my prayers." Blake half-smiled in appreciation to Carl's kind words. "I hope this job'll help you make an easier adjustment to Frankenmuth. I've lived here my whole life, so there's a good chance I might know your grandfather. What's his name?"

"Matthias Bloom. You probably wouldn't know him."

"Matthias Bloom?" he repeated. "Uh, yeah, I know him." Carl's eyes lit up with additional interest. "I didn't know about his health issues though. He's a really sharp guy, from what I know."

"Not so much now." Blake diverted his eyes and his cheeks flushed. "He has dementia."

"That's sad. I'm sorry. Your grandpa and his father before him were well-respected both around town and at the church I attend." He paused and then said, "It's funny. Most people in Frankenmuth pride themselves on the heritage and history of the town, but I've heard whispers about your grandparents because they've kept their own stories quiet. I don't suppose you know anything about that?" Carl fiddled with a napkin, wiping some crumbs off the table.

"I don't know much at all, but my grandpa's told me kids nowadays need to know about history, so it seems like he wouldn't be hiding anything. He's been talking about mysteries and puzzles and numbers too. He says totally random things though. I don't think he's all that coherent in what he says."

"Hmmm." Carl avoided eye contact while standing to throw his garbage in a trash can. "Maybe he'll say something more sensible sometime. I'd be curious about his story. I hate to see such a good man lose his faculties, though. It saddens me to hear about his illness."

Blake broke a piece off his cookie, holding it in his hand. "It's my mom who has to spend her days with him. Maybe she knows some things about his past, but I don't know much except my great-grandfather came here from Germany."

"Practically everyone in this town has relatives from Germany, but I think it's interesting your grandpa talked to you about history and mystery and puzzles and such. What did he mean?"

"I'm not sure. He says a lot of odd things. I wish he'd be more like the grandpa I grew up knowing." Blake looked at a clock on the wall and then watched as another employee entered on his break.

"What was he like?"

"I mean...he always had puzzles for me to solve...or riddles. He'd give me fun gifts when I figured them out. He set up treasure hunts on my birthday or on Easter. When I was little, he'd bring me *I Spy* books or *Where's Waldo* books. He said they'd hone my observation skills. He made it an adventure when he was around. And he was my biggest fan when I played sports. Whether I did well or not, I'd get a Slurpee or an ice cream to 'celebrate' the competition. And he was funny. He said there're always bad things happening in life, so I should laugh as much as possible. He said it would keep my mind sharp. It's kind of ironic that *his* mind is going."

"I didn't know about the puzzles and games, but I've known about his kindness and happy disposition. If I were you, I'd be curious if maybe the mystery he's referring to is his own. Who knows how long he has before all his secrets are lost."

Blake tilted his head and squinted at Mr. Schoeffler. His interest in his grandpa's "secrets" seemed odd, but the man had been nothing but kind and easygoing as he oriented Blake to his new work responsibilities. He liked him, and he felt comfortable and relaxed for the first time in several days.

As he punched his time card and headed for the parking lot where Christmas decorations sparkled and glowed, his thoughts switched to the basketball game and the sort-of date he had planned with Julia. Instead of being discouraged about watching the game, he felt excited about spending time with her. Shrugging his shoulders in confusion, he opened his car door, and set off for home.

CHAPTER 5

When Blake entered the house, he headed straight for the pantry. His mom's car wasn't in the garage, so he assumed he had the house to himself. He took out a box of macaroni and cheese and filled a pan half full of water. After he put it on the burner, he turned to get some butter and milk from the refrigerator, and his grandpa stood in his path.

"Holy cow, you scared me, Grandpa!"

"I'm like a stalking cat," he said.

"If you're hunting for macaroni, you've cornered your prey. Where's Mom?"

"Your mom's not here?"

"The car's gone...and I don't see her. Want some mac and cheese?"

"Deborah's not here? Hallelujah! Freedom. I can finally take off my pants and listen to Barry Manilow without your mother complaining."

"Please don't." Blake grimaced at the thought of another round of "I Write the Songs." Matthias, however, seemed conflicted about what to do. "Please, Grandpa. I like you better with pants on. And Barry Manilow's the Copacabana guy, right? I honestly can't have that song in my head all night. How about I make you something to eat? Are you hungry?"

"How about some Kohlroulade?" he asked.

"You want some Kool Aid? Seriously? I can look and see…"

"Kohlroulade is a German cabbage roll."

"Oh. That's a bit above my chef pay grade. Any other ideas?"

"Weihnachtsgans?"

"Why notskins? Uh…because I don't even know what a cabbage roll is."

"No, weihnachtsgans is a roasted goose."

"Do you see any geese around, Grandpa? How about a sandwich or some cereal? We have Cap'n Crunch." He removed a box of his favorite cereal from the pantry.

"When I see the name of that cereal brand, I can't help but think of the captain on my father's immigrant ship. He's the man who introduced my father to the town of Frankenmuth. Cap'n is spelled wrong though, but let me tell you; sometimes poor spelling can be a clue. As a matter of fact, it will be a clear clue to you one day."

"What…that someone's dumb?" Blake smiled at his grandpa and laughed.

"Maybe. Or maybe that there's more to some words than meets the eye. How about we skip the cereal? You boil your water, and I'll tell you a story."

Since Grandpa Bloom seemed coherent at the moment, Blake shrugged his shoulders, poured the box of pasta in the boiling water, laughed, and said, "Weinachtsgans?"

Matthias smiled. "You've always reminded me of someone special to me." He hesitated. "Oh, the story. Did you know today is the first day of Hanukkah?"

"No, I didn't. We've never much carried on your traditions, Grandpa."

"I understand. There's a good reason for that though." He

paused. Blake waited...turned down the burner as the water foamed and rose, threatening to overflow.

"My father was a German Jew, but when he came to Frankenmuth, he passed himself off as a simple German immigrant. He married my German mother who knew of his heritage, but, still, I was raised Lutheran. Only in the privacy of our own home did my father celebrate Jewish holidays and speak of his former years in Germany. Of course he taught me the story behind the Hanukkah celebration—a story I'm going to share with you today."

The timer on the stove counted down as Blake stirred the macaroni with a wooden spoon.

"It was in the 160's BC—which was before my birth young man..."

"A little." Blake winked and continued stirring.

"True...and the temple in Jerusalem had been seized by Syrian-Greeks and dedicated to the worship of Zeus. The Greeks desecrated the temple and soldiers forced Jews to participate in forbidden practices. After years of persecution and humiliation, a Jewish high priest by the name of Mattathias finally had enough, and he rebelled. With his five sons, he and numerous villagers killed some Greek soldiers and headed with their families to hide out in the mountains where they planned a successful revolution. The Maccabees—that's what they came to be called—succeeded in retaking their land from the Greeks."

The timer for the mac and cheese beeped, so Blake lifted the pan from the burner before dumping the pasta into a strainer in the sink.

Grandpa Bloom glanced all over the kitchen for the source of the beeping.

"It's the kitchen timer, Grandpa." Blake turned it off and moved back to the stove.

"Are you cooking something?" he asked, oblivious to Blake's dinner preparations. "I think you set off the smoke alarm."

Blake tried to hide his smile. "You were telling me about the history of Hanukkah," he said to refocus his grandfather. He dropped some butter and poured some milk into the metal pan before dumping the macaroni and packaged cheese on top. As he stirred the whole mixture with his spoon, the paper cheese packet fell from the counter onto the floor.

"I was? Oh, yes." But he raised his eyebrows to Blake as if he were asking for help.

"You were telling me how the Maccabees retook the land from the Greeks."

"Yes, of course," he said as he bent to pick up the fallen packet. "Litter isn't good. You should always pick up your litter. Anyway, as I was saying, once the Maccabees had regained control, they returned to the Temple in Jerusalem. It had been spiritually defiled, but Jewish priests were determined to make it ceremonially clean." He threw the garbage along with Blake's empty box into the waste basket. "A menorah was needed to burn for eight days to complete the ritual purification, but the priests were only able to find a single day's worth of oil. Tradition says they lit the menorah anyway, and a miracle occurred. To their surprise, that small amount of oil lasted the full eight days.

"In memory of the miracle, Hanukkah is celebrated for eight days and a candle is lit on each of those days. One candle is lit the first night, two the second, and so on, until the final night when all the candles are lit. Each of the eight candles is lit with the shamash. The shamash is a separate candle that's lit first and lights the other candles, and then it's returned to the ninth candle spot, which is set apart from the others."

"I remember you lighting some candles when I was little, but why does Mom never talk about Hanukkah?"

"Well, she's only a quarter Jewish and you're just one-eighth—a number you best keep in mind—and we raised her Lutheran. Plus..." he paused. "Plus, Hanukkah reminds her of her brother."

"She hardly ever talks about him." Blake's curiosity piqued. "All I know is he was younger than her and he died as a child."

Matthias didn't seem to know what more to say. Instead he reached into his pocket and held out what looked like a little wooden top. It had symbols on each of its four sides. "Here, Blake, I have another gift for you—the third of five. It's a dreidel. Each of its sides has a Hebrew letter corresponding to a word..."

"We've played this game," Blake interrupted. "We played it for candy after you lit candles on that candlestick thingy."

"The candle thingy is a menorah....Look here," he said, holding the game piece. "The Hebrew letters represent the first letter of four words. Once the menorah was lit, children for nearly 2000 years would remember the miracle of the oil burning for eight days. The letters stood for four words: 'great miracle happened there.' One day, the letters on this game piece will help you know what to do. When you remember your numbers, it'll give you guidance." Grandpa Bloom hesitated. He cleared his throat and his words seemed to catch in his throat. "It's because of the dreidel game your mother lost interest in Hanukkah."

"But why?"

"When I was your Uncle Samuel's age, my father began talking to me about mysteries concerning our history...about a life before America and a greater purpose for his being here. Deborah wasn't interested in puzzles and mysteries, but Samuel loved them, and you've always reminded me of him, Blake."

"What are you trying to say?"

"I'm saying the menorah...the dreidel...the stories and puzzles...they interested my son but not your mother. And then he passed away, and your mother became less interested than before."

"But why?"

A body stirred in the doorway. Deborah stood with a bag of groceries in her arms. "It was because of Hanukkah...because of dreidel...and because of me that Sammy died."

"Don't say that, Deborah," her father said.

"Why, Dad? It's true." She turned to Blake, tears welling up in her eyes. "We were playing dreidel. Sammy always won. It would make me so mad because he excelled at everything he did, even a game of chance. He was only eight years old, yet even as a child growing up, he was the sweetest boy. I was eleven. The day he died, he won the game like he always did, but that time, I took his candy. He chased me. We were in the living room, but I ran into the kitchen of the old house Mom and Dad inherited from my grandparents and headed down the basement stairs with Sammy running after me. I remember laughing. We both knew I'd give it back eventually—I was just being a bratty, sore loser—but the next thing I knew, Sammy had fallen. He tumbled all the way down the stairs. His head crashed into the cement near my feet. There was so much blood."

Tears ran down her cheeks. "He was the kindest, sweetest boy. He always gave me half the candy anyway. Why did he always win, Dad?" She sniffled and continued. "The blood pooled around my feet. I stood there...helpless...watching the life drain out of him."

Matthias put his arms around his daughter. "It wasn't your fault, sweetheart. God wanted Sammy to be with Him instead of with us."

"But it *was* my fault. I caused everything. And then when Mom died of a heart-attack less than a year later, I knew she died because of me too. She had a broken heart, and I'm the one who broke it. That's why I wanted to leave our old house...and why I never continued the Hanukkah traditions. It's why I didn't want any more to do with your riddles and history and mystery all the time. That was for Sammy...not for me."

"Honey, you know your mother never blamed you and neither did I." He turned to Blake. "I wrapped the menorah up, and it's still in storage in a box in the attic to this day, waiting for the day it's needed once again."

Macaroni and cheese no longer appealed to Blake. He watched his mother's tears roll down her face as she confessed years of anguish.

Matthias, who had managed to coherently verbalize several minutes of conversation, patted Deborah's back, giving her a comforting hug. He looked down at her and said, "Deborah? You're crying. Why are you crying, sweetheart?"

She leaned back from her father's embrace, her eyebrows knit in what looked like confusion before she said, "You don't remember what we were talking about, do you?"

"We were talking about cabbage rolls and roasted goose, I think. Is that what's in the bag?"

She sighed with a look of resignation, but eventually, she began to shake her head and laugh lightly. With a smile, she said, "I love you, Dad. I don't know what I'll do if I ever lose you too."

6

CHAPTER 6

As Blake drove to the game with Julia, his mind raced. He felt terrible for his mother and embarrassed by his own selfishness. She had moved back into a town—a town that brought up bad memories—to take care of the only person left in her immediate family, and she had to do it while worrying about her husband who wasn't there with her. It had to be sad to see her dad's mind deteriorating. He felt terrible for his grandfather too. He was a good man—fun and giving—who seemed to be trying for a relationship with Blake. The gifts and the stories seemed to have purpose for his grandpa, but Blake couldn't make heads or tails of them. And finally, he was on the way to watch a basketball game he should be playing in. And he was going with the most peculiar girl he'd ever met.

"You're quiet right now," Julia observed. "Is watching this game a bad idea? We can do something else if you'd rather."

"No, I'm intrigued. It's best I go.... I was thinking about my mom and grandpa." He changed the topic. "I didn't tell you about Kevin's challenge sixth hour today. I admit...I'm curious if he's any good."

"I saw it from the other side of the gym. You remember the silence that filled the place? Everyone watched. What'd you say that got him wanting a piece of you?"

"Oh...I recall using the words 'plump' and 'chubby' and 'bully'."

"That'd do it. All true, but I suspect you've made an enemy."

"So what? You're the one who said he needed to be taken down a notch. Do you think I care if he likes me or not?"

"I'm simply suggesting you might want to watch your back. As a person, he's not exactly the pride of the school."

The wintery wind whipped across the parking lot when he and Julia got out of the car. He yanked his sweatshirt hood over his head, wondering if wearing a heavy coat would have been a better idea. Julia wore a down-filled parka with a scarf, a hat, and giant mittens approximately the size of oven mitts, making herself completely unrecognizable. "Holy cow, it's cold! How can you be in just a sweatshirt?"

"I lack common sense? I don't know...but at least I won't have fifteen pounds of clothing to lug around once I'm inside."

"I'm sensing a little sarcasm. You see how tall I am, correct? I'll sit on my coat so I don't have to sit on your lap in order to see."

"If I knew you needed a high chair, I'd have *offered* my lap."

Julia laughed, yanked off her winter gear and paid for their tickets. This time she had on a loose, fluorescent red Under Armour fleece with light-blue lettering. Her straight-legged blue jeans were highlighted by red Asics gel running shoes. She still hid most of her body, but she looked almost dressy compared to her school attire. Her hair had been straightened and was more wavy than kinky-curly, and she had on a different, stylish pair of glasses. As they chose seats as far from the student cheering section as they could, Blake found himself looking more at Julia than at the teams warming up on the court.

Julia took out a yellow note pad and pencil from inside one of her coat pockets. "Stats," she said, as if that explained everything. "I drop articles anonymously in the school newspaper box, and sometimes I get published. If I take notes, an idea sometimes pops into my head. Plus, I find it interesting when Kevin's 'official statistics' aren't quite reality."

"You mean his dad changes them?"

"Ever since he's been here. They're quite a duo. If daddy didn't change them, people might realize his pudgy son's offense doesn't make up for his total lack of defense."

"How do you know so much about basketball?"

"Because I watch it...and I'm good at it."

"Why aren't you on the girls' team then?"

"I guess you aren't the only one in the world who never got a chance, are you? The difference between us, though, is I don't care. Sports can't define me. I'm who I am, and I'm special. I dress like I want...do what I want...think how I want. I don't bother people, and they don't bother me, and someday when I do something fantastic with my life, it won't matter if I played high school sports or not."

"So why the special interest in me?"

"You looked so lonely and pathetic I decided to reach out." She winked and grinned. "And besides, it's no fun coming to games alone."

Blake beamed. "I *knew* you asked me out."

Julia punched him in the arm, but then she smiled too.

On their way home, Blake stopped off at Tim Horton's, a coffee shop and bakery, to get Julia a coffee and himself a couple of doughnuts. "I watched everything he did," Blake said, talking about Kevin Hahn, "and I swear, barring some sort of lucky shot, I don't think he could score on me."

"He scored twenty-seven points tonight," Julia said, egging him on.

"Right. And they lost. He took thirty-two shots and made ten. Two of eight on three-pointers. Five for eight from the line. He's right-handed, but he goes left almost every time, and he leans left on every shot. When he fakes, he doesn't lean, so it's easy to tell he's not gonna shoot. He only shot two jumpers going right, and he air-balled both of them. When he goes right, he goes all the way to the rim, and he always swings the ball from right to left, back to right again before he shoots a layup. I could knock it out of his hands every time. He never drove left to the rim one single time."

"Here's his shot chart," Julia said. His shots were bunched up near the left elbow and the left baseline. All layups were on the right side. All three pointers were from the top of the circle. All shots he took from anywhere else, he missed. "It's always like this. He only passes when he can't get off a shot. He acts like he was fouled every time he misses, so when you play him, have Mr. Geyer ref because Kevin'll call a foul if he doesn't score."

"What do you mean 'when you play him'? I already turned him down, and I don't have anything to prove."

"He has a huge ego. He thinks he's better than he is, and he thinks he can beat you. Believe me, he'll be back, and he won't let up if you dodge him. You're gonna have to play him, but when you do, you need to crush him. I meant it when I said he needs to be put in his place. And then you can have peace, Blake. *You* need to know who's better as much as Kevin needs to know. The sooner the better so you can move on and release the anger you're holding onto. He's a punk kid, but it's not only about what *he* can or can't do. It's about you too."

"And then I can move on and decorate Christmas trees and spin Hanukkah dreidels with my grandpa for fun. Is that what you're saying?"

"I'm saying there's more to life than high school sports and graduating from Clarkston. It's time to make the best of things, let go of your bitterness, and see what good can come of this year. You're right where you're supposed to be right now."

"Tim Horton's?"

"Frankenmuth...with your mother and grandpa and any stray loner friends you might pick up along the way."

Blake smiled as Julia finished her coffee and stared in misery at the snow flurries outside, blowing sideways through the air.

"All righty then. I'd better get you home, so I can be on the lookout for stray loner friends. Will they be recognizable?"

"They would look like any regular girl...maybe with an empty coffee cup in her hand." She tossed it in the waste receptacle and stuffed herself into her blizzard gear.

"There's something *familiar* about the girl you described, but in the getup she's wearing, she's mostly not distinguishable."

"I love it when you use big words on me." She stretched her hat over her head and yanked on her mittens. "I guess I'm ready to brave the weather." She opened the door, ignoring Blake completely. "Taxi! Taxi!" she called.

Blake shook his head and ran after her. "May I offer a ride, young lady? Cab fare is on me."

"I should hope so," she said laughing. "I spent all my money on basketball tickets. Franklin and Heine Streets, driver! And follow that car!"

CHAPTER 7

Ms. Emily Cook, the fourth hour History teacher, chatted with a man who looked to be in his sixties, his dark, curly hair showing a good measure of graying. "This is an excellent class, so you should feel comfortable talking about whatever you'd like," she said.

Julia entered and sat in her seat behind a table in the third row and began reading from her Kindle. She didn't seem the least bit interested in the guest speaker or anyone else in the room. She wore a Reebok, officially licensed Nicklas Lidstrom Red Wings hockey jersey. It was so big and the sleeves so long, the jersey might have been a straitjacket—the long arms completely covering her hands. She held the Kindle with the arms of the jersey—one finger poking out to manipulate the touchscreen. She had a white turtleneck, black leggings, and UGG boots.

Blake snuck a few glances at her from the back of the room where he pretended to sharpen his pencil. When the bell rang, he sat in his assigned seat. Ms. Cook took charge right away. A well-put-together woman in her mid-forties, she'd worn an attractive dress each of the three school days Blake had attended. Organized and professional described her to a T. "Good afternoon, class. Every year, my seniors are treated with a visit from Mr. Mayer. He's lived in Frankenmuth his entire life and has directed the Frankenmuth Historical Museum for almost thirty years. He's here today to share with you about the history and heritage of our hometown. Please give him your rapt attention."

The polite class applauded, and Mr. Mayer's large, bent nose reddened slightly, but he shook it off almost immediately. Julia flipped open a pad of paper and prepared to take notes on their guest speaker.

Blake conjured up the image of his grandpa threatening Mr. Mayer with his gardening shears and chasing him and his bag of newspapers all the way to the Cass River.

"Good afternoon, class!" said Mr. Mayer with great enthusiasm. "My dear friend, Ms. Cook, has asked me to tell you a little about the history of our great town. I plan to do exactly that, but if you have questions, please raise your hand. I want to talk about whatever *you* want to know."

"Which is nothing," whispered Kevin Hahn to the boy next to him, inducing a short snort...and a stern look from Ms. Cook.

"In 1840, German missionary, Frederick Wyneken, wrote an appeal to the Lutheran church in Germany. He told of the hardships of German pioneers and the lack of pastors, churches, and schools in his missionary region. Pastor Wilhelm Loehe of the country church in Neuendettelsau, Mittelfranken, Kingdom of Bavaria, in Germany, decided to do something about it. He sent fifteen men and women to mid-Michigan with a dual purpose—to encourage the German pioneers and to spread the message of salvation to the native Indians in the area. They approved a settlement location along the Cass River, naming the town Frankenmuth. 'Franken' represents the Franconian Province in the Kingdom of Bavaria, and the German word 'Muth' means courage. Together, the word Frankenmuth means 'courage of the Franconians'."

Mr. Mayer told of their treacherous voyage and subsequent difficulties in getting from New York Harbor to their new home in Michigan. He explained how the settlers were supposed to build a church and build the town around it, but the settlers found the rich, fertile land to be more appealing. He told how Frankenmuth became a farm town, which it maintains "to this day." Eventually, a second group of approximately ninety immigrants arrived to do what the first group hadn't done, and the Bavarian village began to grow. They built the first St. Lorenz Lutheran Church, but the town actually developed about a mile east where a dam and mill were erected on the Cass River. Farms replaced the forests, and friends and families of the settlers continued to arrive from Germany. Frankenmuth established a reputation for flour, saw, and woolen mills, as well as for its production of beer, cheese, and sausage. Hotels and small, self-sustaining businesses flourished, and Frankenmuth became a tourist attraction as well.

Blake's mind wandered. Mr. Mayer was enthusiastic, but Frankenmuth wasn't his hometown, and his interest waned. It was then that Kevin Hahn decided to be his idiotic self. He raised his hand. "I see there is a question," Mr. Mayer said, smiling at Kevin.

"Yes. My dad said your name is Oscar. If so, what is your preference, Oscar...to eat bologna or wieners?"

Some of the kids laughed, but Ms. Cook looked like she might have an aneurism. Blake glared at him like he might rip Kevin's head off. Mr. Mayer, on the other hand, kept smiling. "What's your name, young man?"

"Kevin. Kevin Hahn."

"Are you possibly Leon Hahn's boy?"

"Yeah," he replied. He raised his eyebrows and lowered his chin, making it look like he thought he was something special.

"Kevin, did you know Oscar Mayer, a man who happens to be a great uncle of mine, came from Bavaria in Germany like the original Frankenmuth settlers? He settled in Detroit and moved on to Chicago, but his company has grown to do over two billion dollars a year in sales. It's not bad that I have a billionaire relative, don't you think?"

"Uh, yeah, that's cool, I guess."

"Aren't you interested in your heritage, Kevin? It seems numbers, history, puzzles, and mystery would appeal to people of any age." Blake's attention perked up. Coincidentally, those were the same words his grandpa had said to him. "That's what a genealogy is. I've been giving the genealogy of this town and the relatives of many of your classmates. You have classmates and friends whose relatives started that church...or the mill or brewery. Their folks are owners of those small businesses or work for the founders of our larger businesses in town. Or they're the farmers who provide for our mills. How many of you or your parents have jobs right here in Frankenmuth?" he asked the class.

Hands went up everywhere, including Blake's.

"I'm here because people like to know who they are...where they came from. Sometimes they need to put two and two together to make sense of things." Oscar Mayer was a fantastic speaker. He had everyone's attention, including Kevin's. "Even your dad is curious, Kevin. We've had several conversations over the last couple of years. You *must* know you have a German name. Maybe your family tree could be traced to someone here too. You never know. Life is filled with puzzles like that."

He continued, "Now, we have time for more questions. Does anyone have one?"

Julia's hand shot into the air.

"Yes, young lady. What's your name?"

"I'm Julia Fischer. Ever since I've been a child, I've heard stories about tunnels under the town. Are the rumors true?"

"What a fantastic question!" Oscar's head tilted to the side and his hand reached up and covered his mouth for a few seconds as he considered his answer. "Yes, a fantastic question," he repeated. "There have always been rumors, Julia, of tunnels connecting many of the small businesses in town." His eyes darted away from Julia's. "But to my knowledge, they're purely tales of intrigue with nothing to support them. From what I can ascertain, the stories evolved because of the laagering cellars of our breweries. Excellent question, however. Are there any others?" Julia scribbled away on her notepad.

"What's a laagering cellar?" one student asked, resulting in a glare from Ms. Cook who had a strict policy against "blurting" in class.

"It's where beer is aged after it's brewed," Mr. Mayer responded. "The cellars are quite extensive, and the milling companies have similar basement-like storage. Some people claim when the dam was originally built, tunnels from one business to the others were dug, connecting with the breweries and mills, but I've never seen any real evidence of truth to the stories. Are there any other questions?"

Julia halted her obsessed note taking. Her hand shot up again as Blake worried there might be a test. "Yes, Julia?" Mr. Mayer's memory impressed Blake.

"Has there ever been a famous crime committed in Frankenmuth?"

"As a matter of fact, there has," he said.

Kids sat up straighter, and Mr. Mayer had the class in the palm of his hand. Finally, something besides missionaries, churches, farms, mills, and breweries. Julia poised her pencil for action.

"Way back in 1945, an FBI case made its way to Frankenmuth. Two German spies managed to enter America in 1944 during World War II. No one knows their mission for sure. The FBI had been monitoring some suspicious submarine activity off the Northeast coast of Maine when they were tipped off about the spies. Months later, the two men were identified in Frankenmuth. When they were discovered, they were found deceased in the home of one of our citizens."

Hands shot up everywhere. Mr. Mayer nodded at a girl in the front row. "How were they killed?"

"There was evidence of a struggle, as well as blood traces from someone in addition to the two deceased spies. We now know the blood belonging to the third party was the homeowner who killed the men in self-defense before disappearing and never returning."

Again, hands were raised throughout the room. "Who was the murderer?"

"Well, first of all—even at the initial investigation—it was never considered murder. The spies had sought the man out, and things escalated into violence. However, the man's name was Detlef Hirsch. Once Hirsch disappeared, the FBI, in their investigation, came to believe Hirsch was a German secret service officer—a Nazi who had been strategically positioned in America prior to the World War. There have been rumors he was protecting financial or military resources...some said he was some sort of an informant. At the crime scene, four small diamonds were found of the seventy that one of the victims had claimed they possessed—a claim he'd made to a former college roommate who reported it to the FBI. The diamonds were likely spilled in the struggle. There was also evidence Hirsch was prepared to move at a moment's notice and change identities. A false ID and passport were found. Four months later, his abandoned home burned to the ground."

Ms. Cook called on another student. "Mark?"

"How did it burn?"

"The fire marshal determined it to be arson, so some people claimed Hirsch returned for something he'd left behind and burned down the house when he left for good. Others blamed it on a Halloween prank. When builders tore down the house to build a new home, new claims were made that they found a Spanish gold coin. If Hirsch truly was protecting financial resources, gold would be likely, but no one ever discovered any other treasure, so the coin may have simply been one of Hirsch's possessions he left behind."

Mr. Mayer called upon another student. "Was he ever found?"

"In 1981, the FBI managed to track him down. That's how they connected the blood evidence. While working for Port Erie Plastics in Erie, Pennsylvania, believe it or not, he was found because of a wanted poster in an Erie post office. As an experiment by the FBI, a computerized age progression program printed out a photo of Hirsch and eight other wanted men and distributed them throughout the United States. A local grocery clerk who'd had a recent confrontation with the German spy in her store recognized his picture. When the FBI arrested him, his name was Wilhelm Mueller."

Even Ms. Cook was interested by then—so much so that she broke her own rule and blurted out, "What happened after his arrest?"

"They tried him as a spy and sentenced him to life in prison without parole. He admitted possession of a German war chest. He claimed he'd lost track of his German handlers and was living his life as a productive, law-abiding citizen when the spies attacked him. His new life was simply an attempt to move on safely and start over after he'd killed the two men in self-defense. He claimed no knowledge of where the German assets could be found. When captured, Mueller...Hirsch...was married and had two daughters. He died in prison in 2011 at the age of 91, and nothing else has ever been determined about the German money—whether it be gold, diamonds, bonds, or whatever."

After a few other less exciting questions, the hour wound down and the bell rang. Blake waited for Julia at the door. "That was an awesome class, wasn't it?" she said.

"Better than yesterday." He shrugged, his enthusiasm less than Julia's. "Why were you so interested?"

"It's just Frankenmuth is the picture-perfect town. Top schools, flourishing businesses, low crime, high church attendance, high community pride, yada yada. I hoped Mr. Mayer had some stories. I guess he did."

"I have to admit, he sure took the air out of Kevin—even *he* was interested in that spy story and the treasure. That was impressive. Maybe we should bring the guy along to econ. He can tell us how much money Uncle Oscar Mayer makes, and we won't have to listen to whatshisname."

"I thought we talked about you working on your happiness."

"I'm a work in progress." He winked. She smiled.

CHAPTER 8

"Did you enjoy yourself watching from the bleachers last night, Nolan?" Kevin asked as Blake did squats in the weight room. "Surely, you enjoyed spending time with your geeky girl-friend, at least." Mr. Geyer, who sat in a nearby chair recording circuits for each class member, perked up as soon as Kevin spoke.

"It was super, Kevin...except for the part where you lost the game."

"Hey, it wasn't my fault. I scored twenty-seven points."

"Yeah. Ten for thirty-two. You're amazing. Julia Fischer could do better."

"What's your problem, Nolan? Jealousy? Does it bother you I'm the star and you're stuck being a nobody fan in the stands?"

"First of all, I'm not a fan of yours. Secondly, if you're a star, there must be a definition I'm not familiar with. How about you leave me to my workout while you loaf around here doing nothing."

"You think you can beat me, don't you?"

"Yep."

"Let's do it now. Me and you. I'll kick your..." He looked at Mr. Geyer. "Your butt."

Blake glanced in Mr. Geyer's direction. "Geyer refs so you don't have any excuses."

Mr. Geyer popped right out of his seat, excitement on his face. "Game on. Guys, follow me," he said to the rest of the class. "Everyone take a seat in the gym." When he walked past Blake, he said, "No mercy."

After they agreed to Mr. Geyer's rules—game to seven...each basket counting one point...alternating possession—Kevin took a "make it/take it" shot to see who would start on offense. He missed, so Blake started with possession. Kevin checked it, and the game began. Blake faked a shot, and when Kevin rose up onto his toes, Blake drove right by him for a layup. He was up one-zero. Kevin's ball.

Blake checked it. Kevin also faked a shot, but he didn't lean in the slightest to his left, so Blake never budged. Another fake...no movement. So Kevin leaned left and shot, a shot that Blake blocked as a chorus of "Ohhhh's" sang from the PE class. He recovered it, drove to his left and made another layup. Two-zero.

On Kevin's next possession, he didn't bother with a fake at all. Blake got right up on Kevin's left hand, daring him to go right. When Kevin headed right, Blake used his superior quickness and cut off his obvious intention to go in for a layup. Kevin pulled up awkwardly and shot an off-balanced, contested jump shot that wedged right between the rim and backboard. The gym erupted in laughter. "You gonna get that down?" Blake asked.

"Throw me a ball!" Kevin yelled to his laughing classmates. As he glared and waited for someone to do his bidding, Blake jumped up and dislodged the ball. More laughter erupted. "It's my ball," Kevin growled.

"Why's that?"

"Alternating possession. When a ball gets stuck like that, it's a jump ball. It's my turn to have it."

Mr. Geyer agreed, so Kevin took possession once again.

Blake defended Kevin the same as before except he let him go in for a layup. When Kevin shot it, Blake leaped, and intentionally wedged it once again between the rim and backboard. More laughter erupted. "Goal tending," Kevin said.

"Uh, no, Kevin. The ball never made it over the rim. Look, you can see it's pinned below the iron," said Mr. Geyer.

"By the way, it's my possession. You know...jump ball and all...alternating possession," said Blake. Mr. Geyer laughed.

That time, he dribbled right, crossed over and hit a short jump shot. It was three to zero.

On Kevin's next four possessions, Blake either blocked his jump shot while he dribbled and leaned left—once from the elbow and once from the baseline—or he slapped the ball out of his hands on two attempted right handed layups. After every shot, Kevin called for a foul and each time Mr. Geyer said no. Blake, after gaining possession and taking the ball past the free throw line, simply backed his way close to the rim and either shot over Kevin or faked and shot around him. He won seven to zero, totally humiliating Kevin in front of six of his teammates. Julia watched with the girls from her side of the gym, and all the guys watched from theirs, hooting and hollering while high-fiving each other.

Kevin swore, slammed the ball off the back wall, and walked, humiliated, back to the locker room. Blake recovered the ball and handed it to Mr. Geyer. As soon as he looked at Julia, he knew—though he enjoyed putting Kevin in his place—what he had done was a mistake, and there would be consequences. He could tell she knew it too.

She gave him a proud smile, but her pride turned to concern. He read Julia's lips from all the way across the gym. "Watch your back."

Matthias paced back and forth in the kitchen, one eye on the clock. His hand rattled two items in his pocket. He took them out, shoved them back in, looked at the door, and sighed.

"Dad?" Deborah said. "You've been pacing at the back door since lunch, waiting for Blake to come home. Why don't you come in here and sit down?"

"That's ridiculous," said Matthias. "I've been making eggs."

He'd done no cooking, so Deborah asked, "Are you hungry?"

"I could eat, but I already had eggs."

"We had *grilled cheese* at lunch, but I'll make you something else if you'd like."

"No, honey. What I'd like is to talk to Blake. I've been waiting for him all afternoon. I have some things to give him."

Deborah rubbed her temples and exhaled a deep sigh.

With the day ending so ominously, Blake entered the house hoping to avoid any conversations with an adult. He had an hour before he had to be at work, so he planned to make a couple of peanut butter and jelly sandwiches, grab a huge handful of Pringles and a can of Mountain Dew, and then slip into his room unnoticed, but it was no doing. There stood his grandfather at the garage entrance, awaiting his arrival.

"Well, hello there," Grandpa Bloom said. "What are you doing here?"

"Hi, Grandpa. I just got home from school."

"Oh…I wasn't expecting you."

Deborah sat in the living room and shook her head.

Blake grabbed a loaf of bread from the cupboard and moved to the pantry for peanut butter.

Matthias put his hand in his pocket again and stared as Blake made his sandwich.

"Would you like a sandwich, Grandpa? Is there something I can get you?"

"I had an egg sandwich earlier. No thanks. But I have something for you today. Two gifts, as a matter of fact." First, he handed Blake a stained faux-glass decoration. It dangled from a thin chain intended for use in hanging it from a hook or nail.

Blake set down his knife and reached for the gift. "What is it?"

"It's a light catcher." The object had an oval shape filled with red, colored glass. Inside the red was a set of cream-colored, opaque praying hands. "I saw this and knew it was the perfect gift for you."

"Thank you, but what makes it special for me?"

"You know I'm starting to lose my memory, right?" he asked.

Blake patiently nodded and said, "Yes, sir. I know."

"Well, someday, I'm not going to be able to explain things to you, so I'm giving you gifts to help you know things. These praying hands remind me of my father—your great-grandfather. There was a day when he was a prisoner in Dachau. When he was freed, my grandparents sent him to America alone, to the West. Though it was before World War II, it was still a terrifying time for Jews in Europe. The fighting hadn't begun, but Hitler had already declared war on the Jewish culture. Jews weren't only anxious about their personal well-being; they were fighting for their culture.

"Hitler must have recognized that though he could attempt to destroy a people, they would manage to come back over time, but if he destroyed their achievements...their cultural history...it would be as if they never existed. He decreed Jewish art collections to be illegitimate and began confiscating and hoarding everything he could find. He took things that weren't and could never be his, and he did it to stamp out an entire heritage. My father and grandfather understood our heritage needed to be preserved. These praying hands symbolize the importance of relying and trusting in God to keep the Jewish culture intact."

"Well, thank you. I know your history means a lot to you. I'll keep this to remind me."

"That's nice, Blake, but it's more than a reminder. As you search for answers someday, this light catcher will point you in the right direction. Remember, you're one-eighth Jewish, and my history and culture is yours too. There are things—like your numbers, for instance—that you shouldn't forget, but also things you'll have to learn on your own because I can't *give* you an appreciation or *make* you appreciate something. That's something you'll have to come to on your own. Also, there are mysteries and puzzles needing answers—answers you'll discover you're prepared to find. This light catcher is exactly like a sign, and clues are like windows to look through. When you spot the sign, look to the west like my family once looked to the West. The numbers will lead you to a treasury of answers—some as much as 2000 years old."

"When you say things like 'mystery' and 'puzzle' and 'numbers,' I don't understand what you're saying. What do 'windows' and 'west' and 'signs' and 'treasury of answers' even mean?"

Matthias Bloom smiled and nodded. "Those are the right questions. You were listening. You know I'm a man of games and puzzles. A good sleuth like yourself will figure things out when it's important enough."

"Mr. Schoeffler says you've always been a man of secrets. Little does he know the truth of *that* statement."

"Mr. Schoeffler? Who is he?"

"He's my manager at work. He seemed curious about you."

"Hmmm. I can't say I recall a Mr. Schoeffler."

"That's odd. I'll have to ask him about that if I see him today. I'm sure he said he knew you."

"Dad," Deborah said as she emerged inside the kitchen doorway, "Blake needs to eat so he can get to work on time. Would you like for me to make you something?"

"No, thanks. I already had some eggs. Poached. That's the way I like to make them."

His daughter ignored him. "How about if I make you a Reuben sandwich? It has some good German sauerkraut, which I know you'll appreciate. It's good for your stomach, and it's loaded with vitamin C too."

"Okay. I thought we were having eggs, but I'll eat whatever you make." He looked at Blake as if he noticed him for the first time. "Well, look who's here. I have a gift I planned to give you," he said to Blake. He stuffed his hand in his front right pocket and yanked out a yellow coin, flipping it in the air with his thumb. Blake snagged it and took a close look.

"Is this gold? Wow, thanks, Grandpa." He looked at the oddly shaped coin more closely. "It says 1822. That's almost 200 years old! This must be worth a fortune!"

"It's a Spanish doubloon, which means 'double.' Spanish coins doubled in value as they went from the smallest to largest denomination. They were divided into two, four, or eight pieces so traders could count them on their fingers without using their thumbs. That's where we get the old pirate expression 'pieces of eight.' The smallest denomination was one-eighth of a doubloon, and since one-eighth is an important number for you, I thought it was an appropriate gift. I'll bet you didn't know the New York Stock Exchange used to be based on this Spanish trading system of one-eighth. One-eighth of a dollar was the smallest amount a stock could change in value. And I'll bet you also didn't know that back in the war years, Spain's dictator, General Franco, was a friend of Adolf Hitler's, and quite a bit of Spanish gold ended up in the hands of the German military. There's a lot of interesting history surrounding coins like this one."

"You've had that coin for as long as I can remember," Deborah said. "I think it means a lot for you to give it to Blake."

"Oh, there's more gold where this came from."

"You have more?" Deborah asked.

"Of course. You don't think I'd give my whole coin collection away, do you? I'm losing my memory, but I'm not losing my mind. I didn't hide them *all* away. If I sold that coin, by the way, I could've gotten the whole Barry Manilow collection and maybe a few dozen eggs to boot. I'll bet you'd like that, wouldn't you two?" As he walked out of the kitchen without eating, Blake heard him mumble. "I love pockets."

CHAPTER 9

Blake's shift at Bronner's started at four o'clock and ended at nine. At seven o'clock, he got a short break, so he used the restroom by the west lobby and then crossed the store to the Season's Eatings snack area where he and Julia had agreed to meet via text messages. Hungry as always, Blake bought a bowl of soup and a couple of breadsticks. Julia munched on a few apple slices and some celery sticks she'd brought from home.

"You know, I figure the calories I take in from the apple slices are cancelled by the celery sticks, which are negative calories. It's how I keep my girlish figure."

"If there's a figure beneath those oversized sweatshirts you wear, who would ever notice?" Blake commented so casually one would have thought he was talking about the weather to someone he'd known all his life. Julia wore a huge, green knit sweater with a reindeer crocheted across the front. She had on a Santa cap and a strand of poinsettia and berry Christmas garland looped around her neck.

"I haven't noticed anyone looking, so what does it matter? I don't see any Christmasy garb on you, by the way, Ebenezer. Don't you realize where you're working?"

"I lug around huge packages and set up trees as high as sixteen feet. If I wore what you're wearing, I'd sweat to death. You'd find me in a big puddle of liquid, lying on a tree skirt under a sign saying 'For sale. $499'."

"I don't think too many people would be impressed by a perspiration-soaked high school basketball phenom who's passed out under a tangled string of lights. Maybe $99 tops."

He liked how she flirted and joked with him. "I was talking about the price of the tree, but that reminds me to complain to you. How can a perfectly packaged string of lights unwind in exactly seventy-three knots?"

"Because strings are alive, Blake. Who doesn't know that? They twist into knots in an attempt to see who has genuine Christmas spirit and who's simply a poser under the mistletoe."

"There's mistletoe? No one's kissed me yet."

"Maybe it's because the most interested kisser is working in Customer Service and hasn't happened to notice the opportunity." Her face turned a shade of red equal to her Santa cap.

"Ha! You must be talking about Claudia in shipping. I see how she looks at me, but she's way too old, and I find that hair growing out of the mole on her face kinda gross." He winked, and Julia appeared comfortable again. "Hey, look," Blake said. "I have something I want to show you." He took out the coin his grandpa had given him a few hours earlier. "Plucked this straight from me treasure chest, matey. Shiver me timbers, I have me own pieces of eight."

"You have a gold pirate coin?"

"Well, according to my grandpa, it's a gold Spanish doubloon—minted in 1822. My mom says he's had it his whole life, but he gave it to me today."

"Wow! Is that Spanish gold?" Mr. Schoeffler asked as he showed up unexpectedly.

Blake closed the coin in his fist and immediately felt uncomfortable. "Um, it's a coin from my grandpa's coin collection. He gave it to me today." He returned the coin to his wallet, a little put out that his store manager had appeared.

Mr. Schoeffler took out his wallet and removed a similar gold coin. He handed it to Blake. It was minted in 1822 exactly like the one in Blake's fist. It was shaped a little differently, but other than that, they were the same. "My dad found this coin probably seventy years ago when he worked a summer construction job. His crew was building a new house on a property that had burned to the ground. When they tore it apart to carry away the scraps, he found it in the basement...."

"Detlef Hirsch's house?" Julia asked, interrupting the story.

"Why yes, I believe that's right. He was a supposed German spy. What do you know about him?"

"Only what Mr. Mayer told us in History class. He disappeared leaving some fake ID and diamonds behind. He said the house burned down, but later someone discovered a Spanish gold coin. I figured it might be the one you just showed us."

"That's the story my father told me too, but I've never seen a second coin until today. I wasn't born until my dad was in his mid-forties, but on my sixteenth birthday, he gave it to me and told me the story I assume Oscar Mayer told you. I've carried the coin in my wallet ever since. How did your grandpa get his?"

Once again, Blake's department manager was asking personal questions about his grandfather who claimed he didn't know Mr. Schoeffler. It made Blake suspicious. And with all the mystery and puzzles and such his grandpa had been talking about lately, he couldn't help but wonder if there was something about the coin he needed to keep to himself. "He didn't say. Except that he's getting more forgetful, so he wanted to give it to me as a gift before he forgot about it. He seems worried someday he's going to forget things that are important to him." Though he wasn't close to finishing his food, Blake started cleaning up his eating area.

"They quit minting these in the mid-1800's, so it's quite a coincidence we both have one—especially with the same date. I never knew your grandpa had one too."

"He said he doesn't know you, Mr. Schoeffler, but you said you know him."

Schoeffler seemed somewhat taken aback, but he regained his composure and said, "It's a small town...a community if you will, Blake. People know lots of people around here, both casually and personally. Your grandpa's probably having memory troubles, don't you think?"

"Yeah, of course. That makes sense." He felt the need to escape the interrogation. "Well, I need to get back to work. I'll talk to you later, Julia." He jumped out of his seat, tossed out most of his food, and strode away, leaving Julia wondering what had gotten into him.

———————————●————————————

The Media Center brimmed with activity on the eve of the last day before Christmas vacation. Ms. Cook made her rounds and either approved or disapproved topics for a research essay about World War II.

"Mark, what are you planning to write about?"

"How about Mussolini?"

"What about him?" she asked.

"Uh...like...his life."

"No, Mark. We're writing an essay, not a biography. If you can find an area of his life to research, let me know. Until then, keep looking." She turned toward two girls. "Janie...Shelby? Don't you think you could make more progress on your research if you were looking at your monitors and refraining from conversation?"

They turned back to their work, so Ms. Cook made her way to Blake, who had been thrust into the middle of the unit when he enrolled in the school. He'd already decided to research Dachau because his great-grandfather had been held there. Julia sat beside him, researching Spain's involvement in the war as a neutral nation.

"What makes you curious about Dachau, Blake?" Ms. Cook asked.

"I don't know...I guess it's because it was more of a work camp than a death camp, and there were people interned there even before the war. I've heard of medical experiments too, so I thought there could be a lot of angles to investigate."

"Hmmm...I like it. You're approved." She wrote a note in her gradebook and then turned her attention to Julia. "Why Spain, Julia?"

"Spain was neutral but still clearly friends with Hitler and Mussolini. General Franco even sent troops into Russia to fight at one time. During the Spanish Civil War in 1936, Germany supported Franco with weapons, so during the second World War, Franco was indebted to Germany and provided mineral resources and other raw materials. I'm actually looking into the possibility that Spain sent Spanish gold coins to help finance the war for Germany while purchasing their opportunity to remain neutral."

"Well, that's a fascinating topic. I'm going to approve it. I'm looking forward to what you write about."

Ms. Cook walked away, and Blake and Julia continued to search the Internet.

Blake clicked and scrolled and read. "If my great-grandfather went through the things I'm reading about, it would have been awful," he said. "I'm sure glad he made it here to America." Julia, engrossed in her own research, didn't respond. "What's so riveting that you're disregarding my conversation?"

"You know I love it when you use big words, don't you? No one's going to call you a dumb jock." She grinned at Blake and winked. She seemed cuter each occasion he spent time with her. "Uh, I've been reading about Spanish doubloons," Julia said. "Will you let me see your coin? Do you think I can learn anything about it by comparing it to the pictures?"

Blake shrugged his shoulders, but he took it out and handed it over.

"What was the deal with Mr. Schoeffler and the coins? What was wrong?" she asked.

"I don't know. There's something suspicious about him asking tons of questions. He said he knew my grandpa, but my grandpa says it's not true....Ever since I moved in, my grandpa's been trying to tell me something, but instead of coming right out with it, he's been mysterious."

"Or maybe it's that his mind's slipping."

"No, I don't think so. He has lots of moments of clarity still, and he says things—clues, I think. And he gives me gifts that seem to mean something. This coin is part of the mystery, and I think Mr. Schoeffler is too. Schoeffler's dad found a gold coin in the spy's house, and it's minted the same as the one in your hand. How can that be a coincidence?"

"I don't know, but what do you think your grandpa's trying to tell you? And what does this coin have to do with it?"

Blake felt uncomfortable, and when he looked over his shoulder, several people seemed to be listening. "I don't want to talk about it, Julia," he said. He grabbed the coin from her hand and turned away from her to replace it in his wallet.

"Seriously...what's going on?" she asked again.

"It's nothing. Really. I don't want to talk about it."

He could see the hurt and confusion in Julia's eyes, but his issues with his grandpa seemed personal to him. He needed to be alone to think.

While his back was turned to Julia, the media specialist walked over to Ms. Cook and said, "Do you have a student by the name of Blake Nolan? He's wanted in the main office."

When Blake entered the office, he was instructed to sit in a seat until Mrs. Heussner, the assistant principal, called for him. He'd barely settled into his chair when she stuck her head out her door and said, "Blake? I'll see you now."

Blake wondered what he did wrong, but he simply rose and then took another seat on the opposite side of Mrs. Heussner's perfectly tidy desk.

"So, you're a new student," she said without introducing herself.

He could hear a small, ceramic heater humming under her desk.

"This is my fourth day." Mrs. Heussner had long blonde hair flowing over the shoulders of her business suit. Her nose was slightly crooked, like it had once been broken. Her height and broad shoulders made her seem intimidating.

She handed Blake a pad of paper and a marker along with a photograph. "I'd like you to write something on your paper for me." No explanation. No hint of friendliness. Blake took the marker and did as he was told when she directed him. "Carli is gay. B. Nolan."

Blake wrote the message and handed the notepad to Mrs. Heussner.

"These don't look anything alike," she said. "You didn't even spell Carli right."

She handed him a picture of a wall with the message scrolled across it.

"That makes sense since I didn't write this one in the picture. I don't even know a girl named Carli."

"Carli is Mr. Carli, our principal. You didn't know that?"

"No, I didn't. Did I miss the welcome to Frankenmuth party?" He regretted saying that the moment it slipped out of his mouth, but all he got was raised eyebrows and a crinkly forehead from the daunting AP. "Where was this message written?" he asked.

"In the boys' restroom across from the gym."

"I've never been in there. Do you have video cameras in the hall?"

"We'll check them, and if you entered that restroom this morning, I'll know you're lying. But if you're telling the truth, someone tried to get you in trouble. You having problems with anyone in the school?"

"No," he said a little too quickly.

"Yes," she determined without hesitation. "Who is it?"

"The only person I've had any problem at all with is Kevin Hahn, but how would he be so stupid to think he could get me in trouble for this? Seriously?"

"We'll check the video and take other writing samples if we find some suspects. You're not out of the water yet, but I guess you can go back to class. Oh, and welcome to Frankenmuth."

Blake stood and headed for the door, but he hesitated. "Mrs. Heussner? I'm sorry about the remark about the welcome party. The kids have been nice, and so have the teachers. I'm...I'm just trying to get used to a new school, I guess."

"It's okay, Blake," she said with a smile that made her look almost friendly. "If you ever need anything, don't be afraid to ask."

"Thanks," he said, and then he turned to leave.

After his visit to the office, Blake avoided Julia on the way to Econ and all during class. Then he felt guilty for his insensitivity and didn't want to see her looking at him across the gym in PE. He also had no interest in seeing Kevin sixth hour, so he skipped his last class and drove to Rose Garden Memorial Park where he wandered around, thinking.

The rose garden sat barren with no fragrant, blooming, colorful flowers to give beauty to the park. He stood next to a giant sundial that gave no shadowy indication of the time on such a gloomy day. The fire pit was cold and empty. Trails of blowing snowflakes snaked through a place made for fire and warmth. A monument stood in honor of the Chippewa Indians, a group of people the Germans meant to evangelize, except while they cleared their farmland and built their mills, the Indians migrated to better hunting lands thirty to eighty miles west. He took a seat on a bench behind the sundial where the cold wind was partially blocked. Christmas was coming—his grandpa's Hanukkah had already begun. His dad toiled in Kuwait. His mom fought bad memories, and his grandpa continued to ramble on about some puzzle Blake didn't understand.

There were no dazzling roses to smell—no magnificent colors to behold. It was winter...barren and cold and dead. Depressing. Like the overcast sky, blocking the sundial's function of signifying the time, the gloom of his heart made him feel purposeless. Instead of the fiery intensity of sports and the goal of a scholarship, he felt like the fire pit with no flames—cold and defeated before he'd had a chance to shine brightly. Like the German set-tlers, he thought he knew what he wanted with his life, but then his objective wandered away, and he was left to make a life he never expected. And he felt alone.

As he looked over the empty park grounds—the Cass River abutting to a wooded area with schools, homes, and a church in the distance—the wind picked up and the cold intensified. It was time to leave and head back to the house that had become his home. Blake knew in his heart if things didn't change soon, it would be the worst Christmas and the worst year of his life.

10

CHAPTER 10

Deborah smoothed out the blanket where her father was lying on the couch and dabbed her eyes with a tissue. Finally, Matthias slept. She'd spent the entire day experiencing his nonsensical ramblings and maddening searches for an item he couldn't even name. He didn't remember what it was. He couldn't remember Deborah's name, nor did he know she was his daughter.

She curled up in the chair next to the couch and buried herself under an afghan. "Lord, help him to wake up rested, his mind back to normal—whatever 'normal' is."

Normally, when Blake returned home, his mother would be at work on her computer. His grandfather typically stalked the house, ready to pounce and tell cryptic stories while dispensing additional peculiar gifts. Instead, he saw his grandpa under the blanket, asleep on the living room sofa. His mom had curled herself up in the recliner under the afghan, looking like she'd been crying.

As he snuck his way through the house, her red, puffy eyes opened, and he could see she *had* been crying. Rising from the chair, she put a finger to her lips to silence her son. She gestured for him to head down the hall, so he went to his bedroom and sat on his bed. When Deborah entered, she closed the door and collapsed in a chair in the corner of the room. Her bloodshot eyes began watering up, and tears trailed down her cheeks.

"What's wrong, Mom? Did something happen to Grandpa?"

"It was a horrible day," she said as she sniffed and wiped her face with her sleeve.

Blake's day was bad too, but he put his own discouragement on hold and asked his mother to tell him about it.

"He was so agitated today...talking about his dad...Sammy...you. He kept saying his heritage would be lost. That you were the last hope. He'd forgotten who I am, Blake. He said Sammy used to be important, but once he passed, everything fell on your shoulders now."

"Everything? What is everything?" Blake asked, hopeful his mother would know.

"You have clues, he said. You'll know what to do. You won't let him down."

"But I don't know what you're talking about." Blake wanted to give some comfort to his mother, but anxiety was rising within him once again.

"That's part of what's so sad. I don't think *he* knew either. He'd forgotten his own mystery, and I couldn't help him."

"Mom, is he all right? Should we take him to a doctor?"

"I already did, but when I made the appointment, he got even more agitated. He paced around, sweating and breathing hard. He was looking for some pictures, I think, but he didn't have any idea what they were or where they were. He said his dad would know. He wanted Sammy to help him. He wanted you because he said you ask the right questions and you could figure it out." The tears flowed once again.

Blake rose from his bed and walked to the chair where he knelt before her. "He has forgetful moments and then he snaps right out of it. You've seen that. After he rests, he'll be better." He placed a hand on her arm, hoping she could discern his own anxiety.

"Not today. He never snapped out of it today. The doctor gave me a prescription, but the pharmacy was out, so I have to wait 'til tomorrow. I was so worried he was going to cause himself a heart attack I finally gave him something to help him sleep." She took a deep breath. "I'm not ready to lose him, Blake. I lost my mom and Sammy. I can't lose him. But with your dad gone, I don't have the strength for days like this. That wasn't my dad today. He was a man afraid of something. He couldn't or wouldn't even acknowledge me as his daughter, so I couldn't help him whatsoever. Whatever he's told you, he's counting on you to figure it out for him."

"I can't even figure out my own life. How can I figure out his? This is a one-time thing, Mom. He probably tired himself out or something spooked him." His head pounded, so he closed his eyes and rubbed his temple.

"He was a man who had forgotten his past; that's what bothered him. It might be better when he wakes up, but what if it's not? He stomped around the house all day today, and I was a stranger to him. He didn't know me." Again, her tears streamed.

Blake leaned forward and hugged his mother. "He'll be back to normal tomorrow, and he'll be telling me all about Jewish heroes and how important one-eighth is, and giving me signs for something or other. Maybe more silly gifts to clutter up my dresser." He mustered as much cheerfulness as he could. "And he'll know you too. You'll see."

Another tear rolled to the end of Deborah's nose, so Blake rose and grabbed a tissue for her. She dabbed her eyes, sniffled a couple of times, and wiped her nose. "Thank you. I hope you're right. I should go back and keep an eye on him."

***

The Friday before Christmas break simply meant nobody planned to do anything of value at school. In English 12, they listened to Christmas carols and wrote about the "best Christmas ever" in a journal. In Calculus, they messed around with some story problems like how fast would a snowman melt in a greenhouse, how much ink would be needed to write a Christmas card, and how many trees must be cut down to supply the Christmas wrapping paper for the town of Frankenmuth. It was a total waste of time. In Mr. Hertwig's Physics class, the teacher demonstrated how fast Santa would have to move to deliver Christmas presents around the world on Christmas Eve. Once he factored in the weight of the sleigh and the number of reindeer needed to pull it, he figured out the joules of energy the reindeer would have to absorb and the centrifugal forces Santa would be subjected to. The end result of his figuring was that the reindeer would be vaporized within four thousandths of a second and Santa would be pinned to the back of his sleigh under more than four million pounds of centrifugal force. Mr. Hertwig basically said "bah humbug" to Christmas. Julia had called Blake a Scrooge, but he had to laugh because compared to Mr. Hertwig, he was St. Nick himself.

After an hour of history, learning about the Magi following the star to the baby Jesus's home and the history of the good Bishop Nickolas's evolution from a kindly Christian saint to the roly-poly, red-suited Santa Claus, Blake told Julia at lunch he was considering skipping out on the last two hours of the day. She had on red tights and what looked like a green and red jester's cap with a green elf jacket hanging to her knees and cinched with a belt that had a buckle as big as Blake's hand. The belt actually gave some shape to her body, and for the first time he knew for sure she was thin.

"I can't bear the thought of a fifth hour lesson on the economics of Christmas. And what will Geyer do in PE? Have us drag each other around on sleds? Maybe have a Styrofoam snowball fight? I have to get out of here."

"I don't blame you....Hey, you know I work in the office third hour, right? I was there when Kevin got suspended today. Did you hear about it?" Julia asked.

"Some kids high-fived me when I left Physics. They think I

did something to get him tossed, and they seemed pretty happy about it."

"Three days for defacing school property. They had him on video going into the bathroom. Writing samples matched his handwriting. He's madder at you now than before."

"He really *did* do it? What an idiot. He wrote that Carli was gay and signed my name. Like I would sign my name. Like I even knew who Carli was. I told Heussner even *he* couldn't be that stupid, but I guess I overestimated him."

"The story gets better. Heussner escorted him out of the office to the parking lot to make sure he left campus. About ten minutes later, she brought him back with a bag of marijuana she found on the floor of his car. Heussner asked me to call his parents to the school while she notified the police. When one of his buddies walked through the office, Kevin blamed *you* for all his trouble."

"Leave it to an idiot to try to frame me for something and then blame me when he gets caught."

As he bit into the candy cane he was given at lunch, Mrs. Heussner tapped him on the shoulder. When Blake turned, she said, "Blake, your mother called. You need to go home. Your grandpa's disappeared."

CHAPTER 11

"Mrs. Nolan, tell me what happened." Officer Cristina Bacon sat on the living room sofa with a notepad in her hand.

"I went into Satow Drugs to get my dad's prescription filled. He didn't want to come in, so he stayed in the car. In my opinion, he didn't want to get medicine *or* to be out of the house. He played with a paperclip he'd found on the floor of the car and basically ignored me. I got some milk and a couple of other things, but I was only in the store for maybe five minutes," Deborah said. She wanted to believe it wasn't her fault he disappeared, but the words sounded empty even to her. "When I came out, he was gone. I went back into the store, hoping he'd gone inside, but he wasn't there. I drove up and down Main Street, but I never saw him. I went back to the drugstore, thinking there might have been a restroom or something—that maybe I'd missed him somehow. I searched for nearly two hours before I called the police. There's no sign of him."

"You said he has dementia?"

"Yes, but yesterday is the only day it seemed bad. Until yesterday, he forgot things at times...and maybe acted a little eccentric. *Yesterday*, he was agitated, but he was much better this morning."

"Do you know why he was agitated?"

"Not really. It seemed to me there were things he thought were important, and it bothered him that he couldn't remember them."

As Officer Bacon jotted down a few notes, Blake burst through the door.

Deborah rushed to him and hugged him. "He disappeared, Blake."

"He left the house and wandered off?"

"I was in the drug store, and he left the car."

"Excuse me," the officer interrupted, "did you say if he has a cellphone?"

"No, he doesn't. He only has a house phone." She paused, contemplating. "I should have gotten him a phone. This is my fault."

"Mom, stop. There's no way of predicting something like this. How was he today?"

"Better...but not completely. He remembered me today, and he wasn't as disconcerted, but he didn't know why I was living here, and he kept talking about my mom and brother like he didn't know they were gone. I didn't want to leave him here alone when I went to the store, and he didn't want to go into the store....Why would he wander off?"

"Mrs. Nolan?" Officer Bacon flipped over the pages of her notepad. "Because of his mental state, we'll be able to wave the twenty-four hour rule for missing persons. I'll check with the station in case something's been called in, and you should call the hospital, but you also need to consider other people or places he'd be likely to visit. He's probably safe and sound at some obvious place. In the meantime, maybe you can contact the news station and an alert can be made. You should get them a picture...something I can copy for our department to use also.

And I'll need a physical description, including what he wore today."

It was then that the doorbell rang. Deborah hurried to the door, hope written all over face. What she saw instead created a look of confusion. There on the porch, a cute elf stood shivering in the cold. Her elf cap sat askew on her curly brown hair, and her arms were wrapped around her body as she bounced up and down in an apparent attempt to keep her blood pumping. Disappointed, Deborah regathered her wits and asked. "May I help you?"

Blake peered over his mother's shoulder. "Oh, jeez, Julia. Come in before you freeze to death. You wouldn't do well on the North Pole, would you?" He maneuvered around his mother and pushed the door open. "How did you know where I live?"

"I've been stalking you." Blake wondered if she was serious. "Mrs. Nolan, I'm Julia Fischer. I'm Blake's friend, and I came to see if I can help." She turned to Blake. "Is there any news about your grandpa?"

Deborah had been taken aback somewhat by the outfit, but she seemed to forget her anxiety for a moment out of gratitude that Julia was there. She smiled a tight-lipped smile at the girl. "That's so nice for you to be concerned. Thank you, Julia. Blake, go get your friend a blanket or a sweatshirt or something. And while you're at it, get that picture from your grandpa's desk so we can copy it for Officer Bacon. And you need a jacket too because we need to start looking again."

"I'd like to help, if you don't mind." Julia turned to Blake. "I'll go with you."

"I don't mind...if you don't, Mom. She can ride with me, and you can make those calls and finish here with the missing person's report before you head out again. That way we can start right away." Deborah nodded as Blake dashed down the hall for the picture and one of his sweatshirts.

Officer Bacon stood. "It's best if someone stays here in case he returns. The most likely place he'd head is home. I know you feel like you have to do something, but if you feel you need to search some more, you should find someone to stay here in case he makes his way back to the house."

Tears welled up in Deborah's eyes as she fought the urge to cry. "Staying here would make me feel so helpless."

Blake watched in astonishment as Julia moved forward and grabbed Deborah's hands in her own. "My mom leads the Saginaw County Search and Rescue Team. She's organized searches for other people, so I know your dad can be found. Notify the local news, and I'll contact my mom. She'll have people searching before you know it. And churches. Call the churches. People will come, and people will pray. I know we can find him."

"Ah, you're Janet Fischer's daughter," said Officer Bacon. "Trust her, Mrs. Nolan. If she's available to help, there's no one better."

"Okay," she said, taking a deep breath to calm herself. She wiped away the tears. "Thank you, Julia. Go with Blake, and I'll do whatever I can from here." She turned to Blake. "Please find him, honey. I can't lose him now. Please bring him home."

———————————●————————————

The car came to an abrupt halt in front of Julia's house. She looked completely normal in Blake's oversized Clarkston hooded sweatshirt, but they made the stop so she could change out of her holiday clothes and fill in her mom about the disappearance. While Julia changed out of her Elven get up, Blake gave Janet Fischer a picture and physical description of his grandpa along with both his own phone number and his mom's. When she returned, wearing blue jeans and a form-fitting, long-sleeved T-shirt, Blake couldn't believe his eyes.

"After your jaw dropped, your eyes bugged out," said Julia. She laughed. "You look kinda cute when you're gawking like that."

"You...uh...you look nice," he observed, feeling totally stupid for his reaction. Blake and Julia continued to look at each other in silence.

Mrs. Fischer interrupted the awkwardness. "I'll call your mom and the news station right away, and then I'll get my team together. We'll have to pick a headquarters location near his disappearance, and then we can begin an organized search."

"Thanks, Mom. I knew I could count on you....Blake?...Are you okay?"

He stood there, in a sort of daze but not actually seeing anything. Shaking his head slightly, he turned to Julia's mother. "I'm sorry. I'm worried is all...and thinking about some things my mom said to me. Thank you for helping, Mrs. Fischer. We have to find him. It would kill my mom to lose him."

"I can't make any promises except our team and any volunteers there are will be organized and thorough. We'll do our best."

When the two friends got back into Blake's grandpa's car, Julia asked, "What were you thinking?"

Blake looked at his phone at a text he received from his mom. "We need to go to the St. Lorenz Church. Do you know how to get there?"

"Yes. You're not going to answer my question?" Blake didn't answer as he drove down the street. "Turn here," she said. "It's on Tuscola. I'll direct you there....So tell me."

Blake gathered his thoughts and decided to confide in her. "He's been telling me strange stories and giving me strange gifts ever since we moved in."

"Like the coin?"

"Yeah. But others more odd than that. My mom said the coin is sort of an heirloom, so giving it may have been a sentimental thing, but the others now seem like clues since my mom told me what he said yesterday."

Julia waited when Blake paused. "He was searching for pictures he couldn't find, and he kept saying his heritage would be lost. That I was his last hope. He said everything falls on my shoulders now. When I asked my mom what that meant, she didn't know. My grandpa said I have clues, and I'll know what to do. That I wouldn't let him down."

"What does that have to do with his disappearance? Turn left here. It's on this road...not too far from here."

Blake did as she directed. "Maybe nothing, but maybe he planned to go somewhere, and he left the clues so I could find him."

"Do you think that's what he was doing? Seriously?"

Blake hesitated and breathed in a deep breath, puffing his cheeks out as he released it slowly. "No. I mean, if he planned to go somewhere, he could've just told me where to look. There's no mystery in that. But he's been telling me how important it is to learn our history and remember my numbers and value mysteries. All that stuff he said meant something, and the conversation with my mom confirms it."

"The church is right here on the right. What should we do?"

They passed a brick and mortar sign displaying the church name next to a pair of praying hands. Blake turned into the entrance. He eased to a stop and jumped out of the car. "We'll check if he's here, I guess."

Over the next four hours, until the first signs of darkness began creeping in, Blake and Julia looked inside the church where Matthias attended, wandered the church's graveyard where Blake's great-grandparents, grandma, and Uncle Sammy were buried, and checked out the rose garden where Blake had been only twenty-four hours before. They went to his grandpa's old home, tucked behind Pilgrim Home Accents, which he rented to a friendly couple, and they also took a short walk down the street to the Frankenmuth Brewery where he used to work. They asked at the historical museum if he'd been there. They checked Matthias's bank and numerous restaurants he frequented, including other establishments along Main Street where he might have stopped to get out of the cold. No one had seen him.

"It doesn't make sense," Blake complained. "How could he vanish into thin air? And *why* would he wander off? He wouldn't leave us...his home....I don't get it."

"I've been wondering about something, Blake. Earlier today, when we went into the church, you started to tell me about how your mom said your grandpa was acting."

"Yeah...how he was searching for some pictures. He said he wanted me because I ask the right questions, and I could figure out his puzzle."

Julia hesitated and tilted her head in thought. "So what if the pictures he was looking for are photographs in his room with something hidden behind them or maybe some drawings he made of some maps or something like that? If he was looking for some pictures, maybe you could figure out what they are, and maybe that's where he is."

As they turned into Blake's driveway, he considered what she had said. It was a total shot in the dark, but maybe the answer to what his grandpa was looking for could be found in the clues and gifts he'd given Blake. It was something to ponder.

CHAPTER 12

Sitting at the house made Deborah stir-crazy. All the calls to the hospital, the churches, friends in Matthias's address book, and to her own friends had resulted in nothing but disappointment or tears. Julia's mother had called to let Deborah know a meeting had been scheduled in her home with her search and rescue team, so Deborah left while Blake and Julia settled in as house sitters in case Matthias returned home.

A dozen cars were parked along the street when Deborah knocked on Janet Fischer's front door. A lady answered, and Deborah identified herself.

"Hi, I'm Deborah Nolan."

"Come in...please. I'm Janet Fischer." They shook hands and Deborah entered the house to see approximately twenty people gathered in the living room. Janet had on a thick turtleneck sweater and jeans tucked into fur-lined boots. She looked ready to start searching immediately. Her compassionate brown eyes regarded her guest. "This is almost my entire team. Everyone, this is Deborah Nolan. It's her father we'll be looking for." After some more sympathetic half-grins and words of greeting, Janet turned back to Deborah and gave a friendly smile. "Let me catch you up on what we'll be doing. It's getting dark, but we're planning on doing a search tonight. I'll tell you about that in a minute. Tomorrow, we'll be making our headquarters in Heritage Park at the Harvey Kern Community Pavilion, but for now, this is the headquarters. When community volunteers get involved tomorrow, we'll canvass the businesses and homes along the streets in the area. We'll ask for video tapes at area businesses from anyone willing to check for the first hour or two after his disappearance. We'll show his picture around and hope someone saw him. Until then, we'll do a search here." She walked to a map that had been pinned to a wall.

"He disappeared from Satow Drugs, right here." She pointed. "We've got lots of experience, Deborah, and what we've learned and what we've seen is the most sensible search plan is to draw a one mile circle around the starting point and search the area thoroughly. We have enough people to do that tonight. If we don't find him, tomorrow we'll expand the circle another mile. The two-mile circle will be a much more difficult challenge, but the churches and news will be announcing the need for search volunteers, and we expect a good turnout in the morning. This is a community that cares about its own."

"I see the logic to some extent," said Deborah, "but why limit the search to only two miles?"

Uncomfortable looks filled the room, but Janet answered the question honestly. "You said your father has dementia. It may sound odd to you, but in the vast majority of dementia-related disappearances like your father's, the person is found within two miles of the starting point...usually in areas with lots of trees or near water. That means we'll focus along the Cass River in this one mile circle." She traced her finger around a circle drawn on the map. "We'll make our way down one side of the river and then cross the covered bridge and head back the other way through Heritage Park. There are a lot of trees along the river. We need to focus on Memorial Park because it has one of the larger wooded areas, but we'll also have people comb the smaller wooded areas like Woeizlein Nature Preserve, Eastgate Park, and the wooded area by Jellystone Park. Everyone has been trained to hunt in the trees. We'll cover everything within a mile tonight except the neighborhoods. We'll have to assume if he's hanging out there, someone would have spotted him by now."

"It's getting dark," Deborah observed.

"We have lights," said an intense-looking man standing against the far wall.

"I don't know how to thank all of you, but thank you so much. I'm afraid something's happened to him by now."

Again, uncomfortable silence filled the room, so Deborah looked to Janet for enlightenment.

She took a deep breath and said, "There are only three scenarios to explain a disappearance like this, Deborah. One is he's wandered off...lost because of his memory issues. If that's the case, it's freezing out there, and he'll look for shelter. Why the woods is the logical choice is unclear, but it's what usually happens. He can't survive out there long in this cold, but he can get out of the wind and find ways to shield himself somewhat from the elements amongst the trees. The second scenario is he's been abducted. If that's true, we can look, but we won't find him unless you hear from the abductors. The last is he's wandered off on purpose. If that's true, he's probably safe...somewhere he wants to be. In that situation, all you can do is hope he'll decide to contact you." She paused. "Now, which do you think is the most likely scenario?"

"Well," she hesitated as tears welled up in her eyes once again. "I can't believe he would be abducted from my car in the drugstore parking lot. Why would anyone take him anyway?"

"Maybe he wandered off and someone abducted him from somewhere besides the parking lot?" said the guy against the wall. He looked so closely at Deborah it seemed she was being scrutinized. Deborah, however, nodded in agreement that it was a possibility, but she still saw it as the least likely scenario. "My area of expertise is to look at the possibility of foul play," he said. "I'm Dean Zimmerman."

"Dean used to be a police officer, but now he's a private investigator. He can become consumed at finding the answers to mysteries, and he's good at gathering information that's come in handy in past situations. So you think he's wandered off...either intentionally or...maybe he's lost?" Janet asked.

"I don't know. I can't think straight." Deborah clasped one hand in the other in an attempt to hide her anxiety. "He didn't seem confused enough to get lost." She hesitated. "Yesterday, he was looking for some pictures, but I'm sure they were in the house. He couldn't remember where though."

"Pictures?" Dean asked. "So do you think he might have disappeared in an attempt to find them?"

"*What* pictures?" She paused, knowing she had no answer to his question. "I honestly don't know," she admitted, shaking her head in frustration. Deborah fought her tears, determined to stop feeling so weak. She needed to be strong and to think clearly.

"Okay. We know enough for now. We need to search the vicinity this evening, and the sooner the better. It's cold out there. You all have a physical description and a picture. Cover your area and meet back at Satow Drugs. Everyone, you know your teams and your assignments. Remember to keep in contact if you see or learn anything. Deborah, you're with me. It's time to get a move on."

And that was that. The entire team matched up and headed out, putting on coats, hats, gloves, and scarves. Everyone but Dean Zimmerman. He seemed to have his own agenda. He sat down, opened a laptop computer, and set his phone on the kitchen table where he seated himself. He gave one last visual inspection of Deborah and began typing.

Blake slumped into a chair, wondering what to do next. Worrying didn't sit well with him. Doing something made more sense. His stomach growled, and he realized how hungry and thirsty he was.

"Do you want something to eat?" he asked Julia.

"I guess. I could eat."

"That's what my grandpa would say when we asked if he was hungry. I think sometimes he didn't remember if he'd eaten or not, so he said 'I could eat' no matter what. I also wondered if he knew what he was doing when he gave the gifts and clues or if he was no more than a man losing his mind. It's sad to see."

"I'm so sorry about all of this. I'm sure it's hard. But maybe he knew exactly what he was saying and you and I could figure it out. I think it's worth a try."

Blake paused to consider her words, the fear of failure churning inside his stomach. "How about if I nuke some taquitos and then we give it a shot? We'll be eating in three minutes and sleuthing within five." He forced a smile.

"How can I turn down a gourmet meal like that?" Making herself at home, she opened the refrigerator. "Mountain Dew? Besides a good Monster drink, what could be better?"

"Taste the sunshine, Miss Julia."

"Ha. You don't have to convince me. Dew in a can is the best." She popped the tab and took a big gulp before handing Blake his own drink. "What was the first clue? Or are you too busy slaving over my frozen entrée?"

"It was a poem. He read it to me and then gave it to me as a gift. He said kids nowadays should be interested in numbers and history...puzzles and mystery...."

"That's the same thing our special speaker said in class the other day."

"You have a great memory. I thought it was odd when Mr. Mayer said that, but I figured it was a coincidence. Plus, he used to be a friend of my grandpa's, so maybe it was something they said back in the day. Who knows? Anyway, then my grandpa told me one-eighth was an important number to remember and he read me a poem he wrote." The microwave dinged and Blake removed dinner, forking half of the taquitos onto a plate for Julia.

"Get the poem, and let's look it over while we enjoy the buffet."

She said things so matter-of-factly, Blake couldn't tell if she was offended by the meal, being sarcastic, being witty, or what. "Give me a second to get it," he said.

Julia grabbed two paper towels from a roll on the counter, removed some sour cream from the refrigerator, and carried everything including the plates over to the table where she waited for Blake.

"You like sour cream on your taquitos too?" He settled into a chair with the poem.

"Sour cream's good on Mexican food, so it'll probably be good on faux Mexican as well." She smirked big enough for Blake to realize she was having fun messing with him...and big enough for him to realize she had terrifically white teeth and a sparkle in her eyes.

He smiled back and then took a sour cream slathered bite of his food to get his mind back on the task at hand. "Okay, the title is 'Literally,' which as I recall, has nothing to do with the poem."

"Authors do everything for a purpose. It has to mean *something*."

"You'll see," he replied.

"Rise and ascend the climbing tree;
Come and ponder...thinking free.
Notice the way the puzzle weaves.
Connect the branches up through the leaves—
The crooks and knots of the climbing tree,
Sprouting nails as signs for thee.
So come and think and know your history—
The only way to solve the mystery.
The king's star is what you'll see,
And in the center is the key."

"Clearly, it's a clue for you."

"*What*? How do you know that?"

"Because the title is 'Literally.' That word has nothing to do with the poem."

"See? That's what I said."

Julia rolled her eyes, but smiled in a way that Blake knew she wasn't looking down on him. "What does literally mean?"

"It means exactly or precisely. It sort of means a person should understand the words the way they'd be defined in the dictionary."

"Right. So when a person says something dumb like 'I literally died laughing,' they're misusing the word. They'd be dead. But do you think your grandpa misused the word to mean something it doesn't mean?"

"I don't know why he would....So you're saying we should take the poem literally."

"If we do, what's the poem saying?"

"It says I should ascend the climbing tree....Oh, my gosh. The climbing tree is right there." He pointed out the front picture window. "When I was little, he even *called* it the climbing tree. He wants me to climb that oak tree."

CHAPTER 13

"I'll try, Mike, but I don't *feel* strong. I wish you were here," said Deborah to her husband. "We've been walking for an hour and there hasn't been a single clue."

Janet wandered off to an area between some trees. Leaves filled the low-lying area, so she walked directly through them, shining her powerful light to lead the way. Deborah trailed behind, talking on her cell phone. The bitter wind whistled an eerie sound through the branches, and flecks of snowflakes battered against their faces.

Within a couple of minutes, Janet heard, "Goodbye, Mike. I love you too."

Janet politely didn't ask about the conversation, but Deborah filled her in anyway as they hunched under some low-hanging branches and crunched their way across the wooded landscape.

"It's eight hours ahead in Kuwait, so it's the middle of the night there. He's going to look into returning home in the morning, but considering my dad's only been missing for about eight hours, he'll probably have to wait to see what happens."

"I'm sorry he's not here for you now."

An animal launched itself from its hiding place and bounded away. Both women let out a yelp.

"It's a stupid rabbit," said Deborah, holding her hand over her heart. "Even *it* should be smart enough to stay out of this cold." As her racing heartbeat began to slow, she said, "My husband's a good man, serving our country, but it's hard when he's gone....And right now it's worse. He's a clearer thinker than I am." Deborah thought it didn't make sense walking through the trees. She couldn't see why her dad would be there. "Even if he was confused," she asked, "wouldn't he go to a house or a business? It's hard for me to imagine him hunkering away in the brush in the darkness. Wouldn't he go toward lights? Look at all the lights we can see from here. Wouldn't he try to find someone to call 911 or to take him home? Why would he be out here?"

"I know you're frustrated, and I know this search doesn't make sense to you. That's how it is for everyone who's tired and worried about their loved ones, but you need to trust I know what I'm doing. Maybe he was looking for those pictures you mentioned, and he got lost, or he's hurt. What we're doing makes the most sense, Deborah. Each possibility we eliminate helps us to move on systematically to the next thing. If he wandered away, he was probably heading somewhere. Sometimes through the trees is the most direct path."

"Have you ever found anyone before? Alive? How can you be so sure this is the right way to do it?"

"Again, I know this is hard on you." Janet stopped searching and gave Deborah her attention. "We've been out here an hour or so, and it cold. Super cold," she said as she hunched her shoulders up, hiding her neck from the elements. "It's hard to imagine someone trying to make it out here all night, but we found a man in Birch Run a couple years ago the morning after a hard winter snow. He curled up under some leaves and the snow on top insulated him and kept him warm enough to make it through the night. We've also found two different women that had passed away. I know that's hard to hear, but finding them brought closure to the families. The way we're looking is the best chance of finding him, and the mile perimeter we've searched tonight—all of us on the team—is the most likely area we'll find him if he's wandered off lost or he's hurt."

As Janet spoke, they made their final exit from the patch of trees they were searching. The trees no longer sheltered them from the whipping wind, and leaves tumbled across open spaces. There had been no sign of Matthias Bloom. After another hour of fruitless searching, they met back at the drug store where the rest of the group thawed in idling cars and drank hot cups of coffee. No good news came from anyone. Deborah's father had disappeared without a trace.

Both Blake and Julia donned some gloves and a hat to go with their coats. Armed with a couple of flashlights, they hoisted themselves higher and higher up the climbing tree. The front porch light and the street light helped erase some of the blackness, but it was an adventure climbing their way through the branches in the dark. Blake focused his energy on ascending the tree, but as Julia climbed upon a lower branch, she took a double take at a shadow that moved on the ground beside the garage.

"Okay," said Blake, "I'm as high as I can safely go, and I didn't notice anything unusual. You?"

"Not in the tree," Julia said as she reached a branch opposite Blake's, "but I'm not sure what we're looking for either. Let's stop for a minute and think. If we're looking for something in particular, and the poem is to be taken literally, what's in the poem to look for?"

"Let me throw some mad English skills at you, young lady." He took the poem from his back pocket and shined his light on it. "The obvious nouns—the things we could be looking for—are climbing tree, puzzle, branches, leaves, crooks, knots, tree again, nails, signs, star, and key."

"So we're in the tree, trying to solve the puzzle." Julia peeked at the poem, thinking from her perch on a branch. "'Connect the branches up through the leaves. The crooks and knots of the climbing tree, sprouting nails as signs for thee.'"

"Nails!" they both said together.

"Nails are signs." Blake glanced below. "Did you happen to see any nails on the way up?"

"No, but if we try again, I'll bet you we find some."

They both scrambled back down and dropped to the ground. Julia turned her head toward the garage when she heard something move behind a wall, but there was nothing to see. "Here's a nail," said Blake, diverting her attention again. "Right here on this knot in the center of the trunk, right above these first two branches."

Julia stood on her tiptoes and reached up to touch it as if it were something holy. "We should mark it somehow." She ran inside, and once again making herself at home, she removed a glove and rifled through Deborah's computer desk. When she returned from the house, she carried a pad of sticky notes. She peeled off the first sheet and pushed it overtop the first nail.

"The poem says to connect the branches up through the leaves. Give me some of the stickies, and once we find some nails, maybe we can connect them with string. The poem says the crooks and knots are sprouting nails. Look where two big branches V off or use your flashlight to find knots." Blake crammed the paper into his coat pocket and reached for a branch.

Excitedly, they took the opposite lowest branches on each side of the tree and climbed up. The cold wind stung, but Julia ignored it, mirroring Blake's enthusiasm.

"Look," said Julia. "Right here in the crook of these two large branches is another nail." She impaled another sticky note on it.

There was a crook directly opposite Julia's marker by Blake's right foot. He looked down and saw another nail. "I got one too. Exactly across from yours." Julia watched as Blake took off his gloves, exposing his hands to the cold so he could mark the spot. From there, he shined his light from crook to crook as he stepped higher on the branches. About twelve feet above the last nail he'd found, he reached out and touched a fourth nail pounded into a knot on the tree trunk like the one below.

"Here's another one," he said. "I wish we knew how many we were looking for."

"Check the poem. Maybe it tells you."

"There wasn't a number," said Blake, "but I'll read it again."

As Julie gazed up at him from her perch below, whoever it was hiding beside the garage slipped up onto the porch and entered the house. Blake read silently while the prowler made his way through the living room to the kitchen and unlocked the window over the sink. He then slipped into the garage where he exited from the back door.

"I got it, I think," Blake said. "It says to 'connect the branches up through the leaves.' Later it says 'the King's star is what you'll see.' A star has six points, right? I'll bet there're six nails, making the shape of a star."

"If that's true," said Julia, "then the two nails in the trunk would be the top and bottom, and there should be two more directly above these other two."

Blake lowered himself down below the top nail and eyed the sticky below him on the branch. "There's a crook right here above that other nail," he said. "And here's a nail." He pushed a paper square onto it. "Yours should be right over there." He pointed.

"Got it." Julia marked the spot. "Now we need to connect them. Do you have any string?"

"I don't know, but if my grandpa has some, it's probably in the garage or on the workbench in the basement. I'll check the basement."

They both dropped out of the tree as the intruder peeked back around the corner of the garage. He leaned back into a bush while the two climbers turned and went inside to the comfortable warmth of the living room, having no clue whatsoever the house had been invaded. As soon as the door shut, the figure beside the building zigzagged away among the shadows.

Julia rushed from the living room to the garage, and Blake charged down the stairs. A spool of string hung from a peg on the wall. Grateful for the easy discovery, she hurried over, grabbed the string, and headed back inside. "Found some!" she called out, and Blake bounded back up the stairs.

Julia sat on the couch, rubbing her hands for warmth. Blake plopped down beside her with his mom's afghan in his hands. He wrapped it around them both, sitting so close to her they were touching. She could feel his knee bouncing up and down. He paused momentarily before he said, "Thanks for helping me."

She put her head on his shoulder as he stared at the wall on the opposite side of the room. "I'm sorry about your grandpa. I'm sorry about your dad being gone...you having to change schools...you not playing basketball...your mom being so upset. Something strange is going on, though, and if I can help, I want to be here for you."

"Being here for me is helping." He let out a long sigh and softly set his hand on her head.

Though Julia hoped they'd stay where they were to warm up some and enjoy Blake's gesture of affection, she noticed him tap a knuckle against his lips and teeth for a moment, looking off without focus. Finally, he said, "You ready to go out and make a star?"

She stood up with her back to Blake, hiding her smile as she folded the blanket. Blake had gone out of his way to be respectful and kind and fun, even though he was unhappy and worried. She shed the afghan and stood, eyes glowing. Julia reached for Blake's hands and yanked him from the couch. "Let's go," she said. "There's still something in that tree to figure out." When Blake held open the door for her, she gave him a playful wink and then proceeded to bundle up for the chill again.

"You don't think my grandpa's out here in the cold, do you?" Blake asked.

"Are you kidding? He's forgetful...not crazy. Let's solve his mystery for him and see what happens."

Blake laughed quietly. He stretched his arms over his head and twisted, cracking his back before rolling the kinks from his neck as well, and then he stepped out behind her. Once they stood back under the tree, he wrapped the string around the first nail and then climbed up, over, and down the tree until the shape looked like a hexagon.

"Nice star, ace. Would you like me to draw one on a sticky note so you have a pattern to follow?"

"Oh, jeez. Stop. I forgot. Why did you let me do all that?"

"I couldn't figure out what you were doing until it was too late. How'd you do in Geometry?"

Blake grinned and rolled his eyes, but he dutifully went back around and unwound the string before jumping back to the ground. "I got an A."

"They must be teaching that new math out in Clarkston. We can tell the difference between shapes out here in farm country."

He ignored her sarcasm but smiled nonetheless before taking another look at the poem. "It says 'the King's star is what you'll see.' Capital 'K.' Why the King's star, do you think?" Before Julia could espouse a theory, Blake answered his own question. "The Star of David. That's the King's star."

"Do you know about Jewish culture?" she asked.

"My grandpa is fifty percent Jewish. His father was a Jewish refugee from Germany before World War II. My mom is a quarter and I'm one-eighth."

"Did people know he was Jewish? It seems odd a Jewish refugee would leave Germany and settle in a nearly completely German community."

"He was a German Jew. Maybe it's what he knew best. I don't know."

"You told me earlier today he said one-eighth was an important number to remember. Do you think his clues have something to do with Jewish history too?" She grabbed the poem from Blake's back pocket. "'Come and think and know your history; the only way to solve the mystery.' This poem is about more than just the climbing tree. He's telling you he's sending you on a mystery, and it has something to do with your history."

"But what? I have no idea." He shivered. "Let's get this figured out before we get frostbite, okay? The Star of David has an upside down triangle and a right side up triangle over the top of it." He made the first triangle and broke the string before heading back up and around the tree for the second triangle. Julia still had the poem in her hand, so he asked, "What did the last line say again?"

"It says 'And in the center is the key'."

Blake stood two or three feet up on the large lower branch on the left of the tree when he finished tying off the string for the second triangle. He stepped over to the crook of the branch extending higher up the oak and shined his flashlight on the trunk. "Right here in the center of the trunk is another big knot." He leaned over and touched it. "Wait. It's not a knot. It's a hole with something in it." He tried without success to pluck the item out of the trunk. "My fingers are too big and too numb. I can't get it out, and it's wedged in pretty tightly."

Julia headed for the door, entered the kitchen, and opened drawers until she found two screwdrivers. When she came back out, she climbed up to the branch opposite where Blake rested. She wedged them into the hole and pried out a tiny metal box. Both kids climbed down and went back into the warmth of the house. Julia handed the discovery to Blake who, despite the numbness in his fingers, managed to force the little, cube-shaped container open. Inside rested a small metal key.

"And in the center is the key...literally."

CHAPTER 14

When the search party returned to their temporary headquarters, Janet observed her husband, Ben Fischer, seated in front of the television, watching a report about Matthias Bloom. Dean Zimmerman still sat at the kitchen table, laptop open, talking on his cell phone.

Ben looked at his wife when she entered, but when she simply shook her head no, he didn't bother asking if they'd discovered anything. The short news report told when and where Matthias was last seen. It displayed his picture and gave the information about the organized search meeting in Heritage Park at the Harvey Kern Community Pavilion, starting at 8:00 a.m.

Deborah stood shaking in front of the television. The numbing cold from the evening still existed, but the realization that the search team wouldn't be looking for almost twelve hours was too much to take. Janet reached for her hand, but Deborah shied away and fled the house.

"Deborah, wait." Janet stepped onto her porch and onto the sidewalk, trailing her new friend.

Trying to be strong, Deborah stopped and turned. "I can't stand inside there with two dozen people feeling sorry for me. And I can't go home and sit around for the next twelve hours either. I need to go back out and look."

"Where? Where will you look?"

"I don't know. Mile two? He'll freeze if he's out here. It's too cold for him to live."

"You need to preserve your energy and try to think where he might have gone."

"That's what I've been doing for the past ten hours, Janet. I looked everywhere I know of where he might have gone. Blake and Julia looked too. I called everyone I could think of. It doesn't make sense he's missing."

Before Janet could respond, the house door opened again, and Dean stepped out, carrying his computer bag. Both ladies glanced at him. "I'm sorry about your father, Deborah." He still had the same scrutinizing look as before, his eyes boring into Deborah's as if trying to read her mind.

"Thank you."

"Uh, I'm done in there, Janet. I'll see you tomorrow." He marched past the women and turned down the street, disappearing into the shadows. A car door slammed shut.

"He makes me uncomfortable. I feel guilty enough losing my dad. Being judged by some stranger makes it worse."

"He's an intense man, admittedly lacking in social skills, but if there was foul play, he's the best man for the job. He'll be working all night if he's found a lead. You, on the other hand, should try to get some rest. Maybe look around your house to see if he left any hints as to where he might have headed on his own...if that's what happened."

"I'll text Blake to look around the house. I need to keep looking around town. Thanks for your help, Janet." With that, she lowered her head into the wind and headed directly for her car without looking back. She accelerated her vehicle down the street, glancing at the empty red car she felt certain belonged to Dean. After Deborah maneuvered past, Dean rose from hiding, turned the ignition key, and put his car in drive, pulling out to follow her.

Blake laughed in frustration. "What in the world was I thinking?" he asked. His grandfather had given him a clue that led to a meaningless key. He sat back on the couch, closed his eyes, and laughed because there wasn't anything else to do besides get back in his car and drive around town searching for the nutty man like his mother was doing.

"What?" Julia asked.

"A little, tiny key. This is the key? To what? What could it fit in? A suitcase lock? A padlock? One of those little metal fireproof safety boxes? How will we know what this goes to?"

"You can be so pessimistic. You named several possibilities already. It could be a file cabinet lock or a lock on a desk drawer. Why don't we start looking until we find something?"

Blake shrugged his shoulders and gave a half grin in resignation. "No use sitting around wondering, I guess."

He dragged himself from his seat and headed for the desk in the living room. There weren't even any locks to try. None of the cabinets in the living room, dining room, or kitchen had locks. In his grandpa's bedroom closet sat a file cabinet with a lock, but it wasn't engaged and the key didn't fit anyway. There was no lock box in the closet. There were suitcases in the basement, but the tiny locks were too small for the key. There were no padlocks securing potentially secret contents his grandpa may have hidden.

"I'm running out of ideas," said Blake as he plopped onto a kitchen chair.

"The key *has* to do with something he wants you to find."

Blake took his wallet from his pocket and slid the key inside where it clanged against the gold coin. "We'll figure it out."

"I hate to be a nag, Blake, but you're not giving up are you?"

"We need to think. He gave me the poem as the first gift of five. It led to a key that *has* to be important somehow." He slipped the poem from his back pocket and read it again, but it gave no clue as to what might be locked. "The poem doesn't say what to use the key for."

"You need another clue."

"Holy cow! You say the smartest things. The gifts. They're *all* clues, I bet." He ran to his bedroom and brought out gift number two.

"A record album?" Julia reached out and grabbed it from Blake's hand when he extended it to her. "Neil Sedaka? Who's he?"

"According to my grandpa, he's some Jewish singer who sounds like a girl."

"I don't see a key hole."

"Now look who's pessimistic. Let's play it. Maybe it'll tell us something." Blake went to the turntable that played his grandpa's music. After a minute figuring out how to get the record player started, the needle rose and settled on the vinyl disc at the first song, "Breaking up Is Hard to Do."

In his alto voice, Neil Sedaka sang about being held tight and kissed through the night, and the song stunk from the kids' perspective. "There's got to be a clue here because he certainly didn't expect you to enjoy this, right?" said Julia.

Blake read the album jacket. "How could he? Let's see...side one, song two is 'Happy Birthday, Sweet Sixteen.' Song three is 'Oh, Carol.' Song four is 'King of Clowns.' Anything sounding meaningful to you so far?"

"Well, your grandpa said puzzles, history, numbers, and mystery were important. We're in the process of solving a mystery. The album doesn't seem like a puzzle. That leaves history and numbers that might be important. Do you see anything historical in those song titles you're reading off?"

"Numbers! That's it, Julia. He said if I remember my numbers, it'll give me direction. Side one, song eight. One of eight. My grandpa kept saying..."

"One-eighth is an important number," she finished. "What's the song?"

"It's called, 'The Diary.' Play it."

Julia lifted the stylist up and set it carefully in the groove before the eighth and last song. Sedaka's high-pitched wail started up. They only had to listen for a few seconds. When they heard from the song about the little book that had a lock and key, they both jumped up and headed back to Matthias's bedroom, frustration replaced by excitement. They were looking for a locked diary. Julia went to the closet and rummaged around the floor and shelves. Blake scanned the furniture surfaces before spending some time looking under the bed.

"No luck for me," Julia announced while Blake pushed himself from under the bed, flashlight in hand.

"We're gonna have to look in his drawers," said Blake. "It seems creepy, but there has to be a diary, and honestly, it makes more sense to be there than anywhere we've looked so far."

Blake started with a dresser, and Julia went to an end table. Blake was on his second drawer, feeling among his grandpa's socks when Julia announced, "I got it." She confiscated it from its resting place. "It's locked...and it has a small key hole."

Blake shoved his drawer closed and removed his wallet. He slid his key out and tossed it to Julia who snatched it cleanly from the air. She inserted the key into the hole, and sure enough, it worked. The key unlocked Matthias's diary. The next step of the mystery was solved.

15

CHAPTER 15

Blake rushed to his ringing phone, hoping for some good news. "Hello."

"Hello, Blake? This is Carl Schoeffler."

"Oh, hey...hi, Mr. Schoeffler. I'm glad you called." He cupped his hand over the phone. "Figures he'd call," he whispered to Julia. He put the phone back to his ear. "I meant to tell you I don't think I'll be coming in to work tomorrow. My gr..."

"Of course not. I heard about your grandpa on the news. Is there anything I can do?"

"I don't know...I mean...well, there's a team of volunteers organizing a search tomorrow. I don't know the details though."

"Will *you* be out looking? Would you allow me to tag along? With you, I mean."

"Just a minute, Mr. Schoeffler." Again, he covered the phone. "He wants to tag along with me tomorrow. I don't want that," he whispered as Julia stifled a laugh. He returned his attention to the phone. "That's nice of you to offer, but I'm not sure I'll be out with the team in the morning. Right now I'm at the house in case he comes home...and Julia and I are following up on some other leads."

"Julia's with you? Good...good. You shouldn't be alone. Can I bring you something to eat maybe? A pizza?"

"A pizza's a really nice offer, but..."

"Great. I'll be over as soon as I can get our department closed down. Maybe an hour or an hour and a half at the most. People at the store are concerned. Most have headed out to the chapel during their breaks to pray for you. It's such a coincidence he's disappeared like this, especially after our conversation." Carl blustered on. "And I'm curious about the leads you're following up on. Maybe I could somehow help solve the mystery."

"I don't know if I'd call it a mystery as much as an emergency." Blake tried to get the conversation away from Mr. Schoeffler's curious interests. "And Mr. Schoeffler? We've already eaten, and I can't say for sure we'll even *be* here in an hour or so. I appreciate the offer, but I think if you want to help, it'd be best if you showed up in the morning."

"Uh, okay...if that's what you think is best. If you need anything, please call me, okay? I'd like to help any way I can."

By the time Blake hung up the phone, Julia had read several entries in the diary. He left her and walked out to the living room. The record player had reached the end of the album, but the needle hadn't returned to its starting position. It bounced around making crackling noises instead. Blake lifted the arm and set it in its place before sitting on the couch, once again facing the picture window. Julia followed him out and sat down beside him. She crossed her legs on the sofa, resting her knee against his leg. No one spoke while Julia read and Blake got lost in his thoughts.

Just seven days before, his life had been turned upside down by his move to Frankenmuth, yet it all appeared to be so insignificant now that his grandpa had disappeared. His personal, selfish desires seemed to be swallowed up by the need to help his grandfather. He breathed in deeply and released a long sigh, again rapping his knuckles against his upper lip.

"What are you thinking?" Julia asked.

He took another deep breath to relax himself. "My grandpa told my mom that 'everything' fell on my shoulders now. My mom said he was looking for pictures he couldn't find, but he said I asked the right questions, so *I* could figure it out. My mom said he'd forgotten his past and whatever he'd told me, he expected me to figure it out."

"That's what we're doing, don't you think?"

"It bothers me I didn't take him seriously. I was so wrapped up in myself I probably missed something, and what if somehow the clues were meant for me to find him, and I can't figure everything out? All that Jewish stuff, and one-eighth, and the gifts seemed meaningless at the time. I was trying to humor him is all. I don't think I listened very well."

"Sure you did," Julia said. "So far we're doing great, and you've figured everything out. You're remembering fine if you ask me."

"*We've* figured everything out. We're doing it together. I needed your help."

Julia smiled and then turned onto her back and stretched out on the couch, using Blake's left thigh as a pillow. As Blake's mind wandered, he reached for her hair and played with her curls while she continued to read.

"Want to listen to some music?" he asked.

"Not Neil Sedaka though. Who else is there?"

"There's Barry Manilow."

"The Copacabana guy? You're kidding right?"

"Yeah, I hate that song. How about Linkin' Park?"

"Now you're talkin'." She hesitated. "Blake?"

"Yeah." He'd continued running his fingers through her hair, massaging her head with his fingertips.

"What's the deal with Mr. Schoeffler?"

Blake hesitated, trying to sort his thoughts. "It's hard to put a finger on it. First impression was great, except when he said he knew my grandpa and my grandpa said he didn't know Schoeffler. That seemed odd. And then one of my gifts was that coin. It's doubly strange Schoeffler has one too, especially since he asked all sorts of questions about my grandpa's mysteries. He could be a great guy trying to make conversation, or he could be someone to be careful of. I don't know which, but I don't want him hanging out with us while we figure it out."

"We could've had a free pizza though."

"You're hilarious." He liked talking to her. He couldn't remember another girl he could talk to so easily...who made him feel so comfortable. In the middle of something bad, maybe he'd discovered something good. "What's in that book?" he asked, attempting to get back on track.

"Nothing. Seriously. It's dated all official diarylike, but it's nothing like any diary or journal I'd expect to read. He tells about work, car repairs, and a day at the lake. I've read an entry about cooking some German dish, about a special message at church, about a home furnace repair. It almost seems like the diary entries are fake—meaningless life accounts. Like the diary is supposed to look used and purposeful when the reality is it doesn't say anything about him. If you were trying to learn your grandpa's deepest personal thoughts, you wouldn't find them here."

"But the diary *is* part of the mystery. The poem led to the key. The album led to the diary, and then the key fit the diary's lock. The trail can't go cold here. The diary has to say something. A passage about history? A puzzle in one of the entries? Is there a page one-eighth?" He laughed.

"One-eighth?" Something dawned on her. "There's no one-eighth, but there *are* dates, and January 8 is one eight. What if there's an entry dated January 8?" She flipped through the pages. Page after page was dated and filled with boring drivel. Anyone reading the diary would have given up long before reaching the end. However, Julia didn't give up, and about twenty percent from the last page, she discovered a passage written on January 8. It had the heading "To Blake."

CHAPTER 16

Deborah drove straight back to Satow Drugs on Main Street and parked one place to the left of where she had parked in the morning. Inside the drug store, she purchased a flashlight and two D batteries and observed there were no security cameras aimed at the parking lot. Before leaving the store, she stood in the entryway between the two sets of doors and called Blake.

Blake answered on the second ring. "Any news?"

"I'm sorry, but no. It's so frustrating. A team of about twenty people searched the mile closest to the drug store, and no one came up with so much as a hint of his whereabouts. I'm back at the store, starting over. Did you get my text to look around the house?" Deborah glanced casually across the lot at a red car as she talked.

"Yes, we've been looking around quite a bit tonight. Are you okay?" Blake asked.

"I'm confused and irritated. I'm scared something has happened to him. Maybe I'm even a little angry at God for letting this happen. It doesn't make sense he'd wander off for no reason. He wasn't that confused this morning. It doesn't make sense someone would abduct a sixty-five-year-old man sitting peacefully in a car in a public parking lot either. And it especially doesn't make sense he left on purpose. Where would he go that you and I haven't already looked?"

She looked out the glass doors of the store at the traffic flowing along, cars driven by people living out their daily existence. People were heading home to loved ones or leaving to meet people they cared about. They weren't giving a single thought to Matthias Bloom and where he might be. "The search team says dementia sufferers head to water and woods more often than not, but why would my dad do that in this weather? Plus, we searched and didn't find a single clue." Anxiety built up in her stomach as she considered her father lost and alone. "I'm going to keep looking. Maybe there's something out here that I'll find."

"We'll stay here while you keep looking. We're following up on some clues Grandpa may have left me."

Deborah stood in the doorway of the drug store as she ended her conversation with her son. She unscrewed the flashlight she'd purchased, dropping the two batteries inside before screwing the cap back on. Stepping out into the cold darkness, she shined her flashlight onto the passenger door of her car, examining the window, the door handle, and the door itself.

Deborah climbed through the front driver's side door and examined the floor of the car's passenger side before returning outside to the right-hand side of the car and aiming the light on the next parking space over. A few seconds later, she bent down and picked up a large, blue paperclip. She shined the light on it, examining it before she put it into her wallet inside her purse. She scanned the entire parking lot, trying to determine the most likely direction her father might have walked, but neither seemed logical for him that morning. Finally, she clambered back into the driver's seat, started the car, and backed out of her space. As she exited the parking lot, her headlights illuminated Dean's red vehicle while he once again ducked below the window. When she drove past, he crept out behind her.

Blake read the handwritten journal entry out loud.

To Blake,

I don't know the circumstances leading you to this entry, but I knew there'd be a day in your future when you'd take up the mystery and find the key to this diary (though I'd prefer to call it a journal). On May 29, 1939, my father entered the United States, a Jewish refugee from Germany. In an attempt to escape Hitler and the hateful Nazi party, he brought his father's two most valuable possessions—as well as a significant portion of the Jewish culture and sailed to Cuba from Berlin, Germany. He had boarded the S.S. St. Louis as Jewish Yosef Bloomberg but sailed in a commercial freighter from Havana to St. Petersburg, Florida, as Joseph Bloom, German immigrant to America. After a spell on the ship, he arrived in the states with his hand-made furniture—a wardrobe, two nightstands, and an ate-drawer dresser—hideing remnants of his beloved Jewish culture. I find it humorous to admit, my father was a smuggler, sent by his own father, who carefully designed and built-inn the protection of a valuable share of their heritage, a heritage dating to Jesus himself.

Blake, the protection of the culture was passed on to me and now to you to determine for yourself what should be done with it. No matter how you've been raised, you have Jewish blood and a responsibility to the people who sent your great-grandfather Yosef Bloomberg on a solitary journey to this country of ours.

I have more to tell you, Blake. Even on the ship, my father observed the reach of Hitler's party, but he was completely shocked to discover a German spy in the town he chose to live in. As you continue to decipher the clues I've left you, be aware there are people you cannot trust. In my father's own workplace was a man named Detlef Hirsch, a Nazi hiding his own secrets. He discovered my father was Jewish and hated him, but my father also ascertained

Hirsch was a Nazi spy long before the FBI made the same discovery. When Hirsch fled Frankenmuth, he left behind a secret of his own, something men would be willing to kill for—something that would turn the most trustworthy of men into the devil's own handymen.

Blake, you must discern the passage I lead you to for the one mystery and unbury the answer to the other. To do so, you must use the gifts I once gave you, and the clues I spoke to you...and you must have the courage to trust someone to whom I'll point you—someone who may seem untrustworthy. You'll need the wisdom to know what to do. Because trust is a fragile thing, you may have to choose a different direction. Know that what you find could easily be lost, and who you trust could easily be found untrustworthy or lead you astray. But I'll tell you this as you read my journal; I have complete faith in you. Yes, I trust you, Blake. You ask the right questions. You're able to take this puzzle and solve any mystery. When you have doubts or feel like you've reached a dead end, remember your numbers. They'll prove valuable again and again. I know this message is somewhat cryptic, but I couldn't risk the secrets falling into the wrong hands. You, however, have been equipped to find the answers.

If you're doing this search because I've passed away, please know I love you, and tell your mother I'm proud of her and love her with my whole heart. She's the best little girl a father could ever have.

Grandpa Bloom

"Okay, that was the most interesting entry in the diary, but what did it tell you?" Julia asked.

"I'll figure it out," Blake replied. He tore out the page as he spoke.

"Why are you doing that?"

"I need it with me, and I don't want anyone else who finds the book to discover the message. It's written directly to me, hidden amongst a journal full of meaningless entries. This one means something."

"But do you have any idea what it is?"

"No...not yet, but my grandpa said I'll figure things out when it's important enough. It's important enough right now, so let's figure it out."

The private investigator followed Deborah all around Frankenmuth. At regular intervals, she parked her car long enough to traverse up and down the city streets, showing her father's picture and asking questions to store employees or pedestrians bundled up but walking around sightseeing and shopping. Through the town, horse-drawn carriages were rented to entertain shivering tourists amazed by the decorations and sparkling lights. Wine tasting events, Santa Claus at Bronner's, and outdoor walks to shopping venues occupied the busy people, but Deborah appeared focused and determined to not give up her search.

Dean had seen enough, so he made a phone call. "Crispy, I need a coffee, and we need to talk. Meet me at Tim Horton's café."

He was seated in a booth, facing the doors, when Officer Cristina Paulette Bacon entered. He nodded but stayed seated, so she ordered a hot chocolate, carried it over to Dean's booth, and sat opposite him at the table.

"You called?" Cristina sipped her drink. "You know, I had some Christmas shopping to do." She winked as she crossed her legs under the table.

"You know how I operate. All work and no play."

"Except occasionally with me."

"There's that." He smiled back—something he didn't do often.

"It's good to see you're not always a sourpuss. That smile of yours can warm the heart on a cold day."

"That's the hot chocolate."

"Probably. What's the emergency?"

"I want to know what you know about the Matthias Bloom case," Dean said.

"He wandered off. Dementia. He's lost or hurt—out there with hypothermia probably. Dead or dying as we speak would be my best guess."

"What's the news about his daughter?"

"No news, Dean. Uh...she's upset? Why are you asking about her?"

"I'm thinking there's more to her than simply a worried daughter." He took a sip of his coffee and a bite from a donut. They sat in silence.

"Um...you're the great gumshoe, Dean. Is that what you're looking for? A pat on the back? Or must I act all interested and beg you to expound? I have Christmas shopping to do."

"Matthias Bloom is the son of Joseph Bloom. In 1939, Bloom senior was a German immigrant from Berlin, Germany."

"That's *super* suspicious. Shall I get a bagel and plan on an extensive stay as you explain how one particular German immigrant to Frankenmuth is so extraordinary? The whole town *exists* because of German immigrants."

"I have connections. There was no Joseph Bloom who emigrated out of Berlin in 1939. I suspect he changed his name."

"And this would be especially unusual? A German man moving from Germany right before World War II might have felt conspicuous. I'm getting bored quickly. Here I thought you wanted to see me, but instead I find you with some half-formed theory percolating in your suspicious mind."

"Crispy, wait. What if Bloom is hiding something? There're people in town that think he was." He looked away with a thoughtful expression. "Maybe he left that drug store on purpose...or maybe someone abducted him because of some secrets he's hiding. You assume he's dead. I say maybe not...and if he's alive, there's some hope of uncovering whatever it is he might've been hiding over the years."

"Secrets? Oooh...the man may have skeletons in his closet? Or maybe he chose to be a private person. You'd better have more than rumors of secrets and a father's name change."

Dean ignored Cristina's comment as he tended to do. He inhaled slowly and continued. "If there's one thing in common about what people say about the old dude, it's that no one knew much about him at all. And his daddy was more secretive yet. The word *mystery* seems to be the number one description of the men. When I hear 'mystery,' I get interested in what it is."

"Well, Deano, I'm sure you'll keep plugging away while the

rest of your team tries to find his frozen body in the woods somewhere. If truth be told, I feel bad for the family. Why don't you leave them alone...because the odds are he's gone for good."

"There's about the same chance I'll drop this as for you to stop being a smart-aleck."

"True. Well, it's been a pleasure discussing rumors and innuendo, but I have a life to live when I'm off duty. By the way...thanks for going Dutch once again. You can use the money you haven't spent on me and get me something sparkly for Christmas. Or a gun. I'd take that too."

"Maybe I'll get you a sparkly gun."

As she turned and departed without looking back, Dean got an eyeful, and then went back to his surmising. There was more to learn about Joseph Bloom and the secrets he and his son were hiding.

CHAPTER 17

The copier whirred as Blake stood in silence, considering his grandpa's message. Julia gazed at him, looking intrigued by his serious, locked-in appearance of intensity.

"You have the same look you had when you annihilated Kevin in that basketball game."

"That game seems kind of petty now, doesn't it? Funny how important playing basketball seemed only a couple days ago, but losing a grandfather and discovering his mystery puts a dumb competition to shame. I'm kind of embarrassed about the whole thing now."

"Life *does* take its little turns, doesn't it? You'll figure this out. Your grandpa seemed pretty confident of that."

"*We'll* figure it out...together. Here's your copy of the note. Look it over and tell me what you think."

Blake headed to the refrigerator where he removed two more Mountain Dews. The same feeling of butterflies in his stomach he had before a basketball game presented itself, and with it came the same determination. He had no intention of failing his grandpa, but with the winning resolve he felt, there was apprehension too. Pushing the insecurity from his mind, he handed Julia a drink and asked, "Well...any thoughts?"

"My first thought is about Detlef Hirsch. When Mr. Mayer mentioned him in class, he said Hirsch was a Nazi spy. Mayer spoke about a gold coin and unsubstantiated rumors of financial resources, but he didn't say anything about Hirsch leaving behind a secret when he left Frankenmuth. So either he didn't know about the secret or he's keeping his knowledge of it to himself. Your grandpa said the secret was something people would kill for and something that would turn trustworthy men into the devil's handymen. Gold could do that, don't you think? What if there were a *lot* of gold coins? Your grandpa gave you a doubloon as one of his clues, right? Maybe the coin has something to do with the secret, and he's hoping you can figure it out."

"I don't know. Maybe. My grandpa mentioned there was some interesting history about gold coins when he gave it to me, and he mentioned Hitler and the Spanish leader dude."

"Franco."

"Yeah, Franco. Your memory is incredible. Remind me not to play Trivia Crack with you. You'll destroy my pride."

"Everyone could use a little humbling once in a while."

"But no one would seek it out. Anyway, I think we're getting ahead of ourselves. The coin was the *fifth* gift, and we're only on the second one, so it seems like we're getting off track. The only thing I'm sure of from the Hirsch part is that I'm convinced even more I can't trust Schoeffler. He has a coin too." Blake paused and rubbed his eyes before squeezing the bridge of his nose. He took a deep breath like he'd take when shooting a pressure free throw in an attempt to calm his overactive mind.

"What are you thinking?" Julia let the hand with the note drop to her side and instead focused her attention on Blake as he struggled to put the pieces together.

"I'm thinking the gold coin was the last gift he gave me. Talk about Hirsch is in the third paragraph. I can't help but think something in the first two paragraphs is more important to us right now." He walked over to Julia. "Look again at your paper. Do you see the word that's underlined?"

She glanced at the journal before saying, "Spell?"

"Before my grandpa gave me the third gift, he said that sometimes poor spelling can be a clue. He said it would be a clear clue to me one day. So I'm thinking he reminded me by underlining *spell*. I saw some misspellings in the note."

Both teens read through the entry again. "*Eight, hiding,* and *in* are misspelled," said Julia. "Does that mean anything to you?"

"Eight does, sort of. I mean, he told me several times one-eighth was important."

"How about eight-drawer? When you use a hyphen, it makes two words into one. That would make *eight-drawer, hiding,* and *built-in* as the misspelled words. What does that mean?"

Blake closed his eyes and ran his fingers through his hair before looking at the journal entry again. "A wardrobe, two nightstands, and an eight-drawer dresser...hiding remnants of his beloved Jewish culture...carefully designed and built-in the protection of a valuable share of their heritage...."

"Blake?" Julia grabbed his hand and practically towed him back to Matthias's bedroom. "Look at your grandpa's furniture." She pointed. "A wardrobe, two nightstands, and an eight-drawer dresser. Is this the furniture your great-grandpa brought over on the ship?"

"I don't know. I didn't know much at all about how my great-grandpa came to Frankenmuth until this week. I didn't know *anything* about him bringing furniture until I read this note." Julia gave him a moment to think, and finally, it dawned on Blake. "Holy, wooden furniture, Batgirl. He's telling us there's something in that eight-drawer dresser—something that's built-in to hide remnants of the culture he was protecting."

Blake went directly to the dresser, examining it before dragging it away from the wall. There were some papers and a couple of picture frames to remove, which he sat on the floor before rubbing his hand over the smooth finish.

"I have this vision of a secret compartment, like if I push a specific knot or if I run my fingertips under the trim, I'll find a button to push and the whole dresser will open up to some sort of treasure."

Both teenagers tried to find a button or latch or key hole or anything that would turn a piece of furniture into the solution to a puzzle, but on outward appearance, there was nothing.

Eventually, they removed the drawers, stacking them beside the dresser, and looked for anything hidden under the clothes. "It's kind of creepy feeling under the drawers in his drawers," Julia said with a giggle.

"Boxer briefs. That's what these are, right?" Blake said as he pinched a tiny corner of one pair and held it up for Julia to see before tossing it at her.

"Oh, yuck!" Julia grabbed a throw pillow from the bed and whipped it at Blake with such force it practically knocked him over as he squatted on the balls of his feet. When he scrambled up to fire it back, Julia jumped on the bed, bumping the drawer full of socks, which slid from the top of the pile and tipped sideways.

Blake jumped to his feet and steadied the antique drawer before it could tumble to the floor.

Some items spilled, ending the near pillow fight, so Blake knelt and began putting the fallen socks back into their place. Julia, however, noticed something unusual. "Blake, look at this. Isn't it odd how short these drawers are? I mean, they're stacked right beside the dresser, but they must be a good five or six inches short of reaching the back."

Blake looked and then peered inside the dresser only to see the back panel looking absolutely ordinary. "Do you think there's some sort of hidden panel in the back?"

"Maybe. Let's imagine there is. How do we get to it?" Julia asked.

Emptied of its drawers, Blake moved the lightweight dresser to the middle of the room, where he circled it like an animal stalking its prey. "I don't see any cracks or grooves or anyplace where the wood fits together. The whole cabinet, with the exception of the drawers and some trim, seems like it was built as one piece." He continued to study and inspect the workmanship while Julia made her own investigation. "Everything's always a puzzle with my grandpa," Blake said. "Puzzle pieces always fit together, but I don't see anything visible suggesting a compartment."

"Then what *can't* you see? Maybe think the exact opposite for a minute."

"I can't see much inside where the drawers sit. I can't examine that back panel too closely. I can't see underneath....Wait a minute!" Careful to not damage the dresser, he laid it face down and then tipped it again so it rested on its top, its short legs sticking in the air.

"Look!" Julia exclaimed. "It fits as snug as can be, but there it is. It looks like it could be a compartment to me."

A thin rectangular outline about five inches in width and nearly the entire length of the dresser was discernable. It fit perfectly, and though he had no clue how to remove it, it comforted Blake to see it and know the note had led him to the discovery. He flipped the dresser back over onto its legs and felt inside the drawer openings along the back inside panel.

"Do you feel anything?"

"Here's something. And here's another one. It's like two tiny pieces of metal at the top, but I can't move them at all." He stepped away from the dresser. "I'll be right back." He went into the kitchen and opened a junk drawer. It took him a minute to locate some needle-nose pliers, but once he did, he hustled back into the bedroom. "I remember once my dad said if it can't be fixed with duct tape, then you're not using enough duct tape, but look at all the actual tools we've actually used tonight. This whole night is strange." He winked.

"*My* dad said you can't fix stupid with duct tape...you can only muffle the sound," Julia added with a playful grin.

"I can see where you get your sense of humor." Blake reached the pliers inside the dresser and used the tool to grab hold of the metal piece. He couldn't get it to slide right or left, but when he pulled on it, out slipped a sturdy metal strip about six inches long. He moved directly to the other piece and slid it all the way out as well. When he did, there was a thump on the bedroom floor.

Julia's eyes lit up as Blake tipped the dresser over onto its back. He grabbed the hidden drawer and tugged, but he couldn't remove it. It fit so snugly Julia had to help slide the hidden compartment all the way out. The top piece was hinged, so he flipped it open and there inside were two canvas paintings. Once removed, they could read the name Chagall on one, and on the other was Lieberman.

CHAPTER 18

"Your great-grandpa's two most valuable possessions?" Julia pointed to the diary entry.

"That would be my guess....Which means what he smuggled was probably paintings. My grandpa said I needed to know numbers and history, puzzles and mystery. He said I'd figure things out for myself when it became important enough to me. He told me Hitler must have recognized that though he couldn't destroy a whole people, if he destroyed their achievements...their history...it would be as if they never existed. So he confiscated and hoarded important Jewish culture. My grandpa might have been talking about art—paintings like these. Hitler was taking things that weren't his, and he did it to stamp out an entire heritage. My great-grandpa understood our heritage needed to be preserved, so maybe he smuggled a huge art collection here to preserve our culture."

"Did you say 'our'?" Julia asked.

"I did, didn't I? Maybe I did because it's important now. I *am* one-eighth Jewish after all....So where's the rest of the treasure? He said *some* things dated back to Jesus. Do you think we'll find it in the other furniture?"

"I'll tell you what. You search the furniture while I search the Internet." She left and returned with Deborah's laptop.

Blake raised his eyebrows. "You sure know how to make yourself at home, don't you?"

"Yep. Can't use this dinosaur iPhone of mine. No Siri. But with a keyboard, I'm a whiz. So what's your mom's password? Let me guess. B-l-a-k-e. Nope. What's your dad's name?"

"Mike."

"M-i-k-e. Nope. M-i-c-h-a-e-l. Bingo. I'm in."

Blake stared at her in astonishment.

"It's a Windows log in, silly. I'm in Windows is all. I'll stay out of her private stuff."

Blake stared at her with his eyebrows raised.

"Hey, it's better to use the password than to hack into it other ways."

"Or you could have used *my* laptop."

"There's that. But what's the fun? Shouldn't you be absconding treasure from your grandpa's smuggling apparatuses? Leave me alone while I prowl the World Wide Web."

Shaking his head, Blake diverted his attention to a nightstand. The outside wind whipped sleet-like pieces of precipitation against the bedroom window, creating little tapping noises. He yanked out the three drawers from the nightstand to the right of the bed and stacked them on the floor. "He won't survive the night in this cold if he's really out there. I hope what we're doing leads us to him. Otherwise, I'm gonna feel pretty guilty if I'm in here and he's out there and I wasn't looking for him."

"Don't you get the feeling you're doing exactly what your grandpa would want you to do? Let's solve this puzzle and see where it leads us."

Again, the drawers were shorter than they should have been, and a precise outline was cut into the wooden bottom. When standing back on its short legs, the nightstand had a small, metal piece at the top, but when Blake extracted the sturdy, iron strip, there was nothing in the hidden compartment. The wardrobe, which stood nearly empty of his grandfather's possessions, also had nothing in its hiding place. The second nightstand had been designed exactly as the first. Losing enthusiasm, Blake reached the conclusion that the diary only mentioned the dresser, which meant the last piece of furniture was probably empty like the others. If a stash of art had been preserved by his great-grandpa, it almost certainly was hidden somewhere else. He stacked the drawers on the floor and flipped the article over like he had before, mostly out of habit.

"Holy cow, Blake! Do you know anything about art?"

"Only that I'm not good at it."

"I found an article saying nearly 1,500 priceless paintings, stolen by Nazis, were found in a Munich apartment in 2011." She had scribbled notes on a notepad she began to read from. "Their estimated worth was 1.3 *billion* dollars. The *average* value of each painting is almost nine hundred thousand dollars. There were paintings by both Marc Chagall and Max Lieberman in the find. So I tried to find these two paintings on line to see what they're worth. Chagall has a painting called *Bestiare et Musique* that sold at an auction in Hong Kong for 4.18 million dollars."

"You're kidding! What are *these* paintings worth?"

"The four million dollar painting was painted in 1969. Your grandpa's painting is called *Calvary*, and it was painted in 1912. I can't find an estimated value, but it *has* to be worth a lot. The Lieberman painting is called *The Twelve-Year-Old Jesus in the Temple with the Scholars*. It was painted in 1879. One site I found said only a sketch of the original painting remains. There aren't even *prints*, Blake. That one must be priceless."

"I wonder why neither grandparent ever framed them and hung them up. They're both pretty cool looking."

"Who knows? But considering how much they're probably worth, you'd better put 'em back in the dresser. I'm guessing the other clues are meant to lead you to other paintings your great-grandpa saved when he came to America."

"And the clues might lead us to my grandpa too."

The bedroom was a mess with every piece of furniture lying

face down except the one nightstand. Drawers were stacked in three piles and the few things from the wardrobe were piled on the bed. With reluctance, Blake slipped the canvas paintings back into the compartment and slid it back in behind the dresser. He had to flip it over so he could slide the metal strips back in place from the front. He did the same with the wardrobe and nightstand and replaced the clothes and drawers.

"I still have to check the compartment in this nightstand," Blake said after the other furniture had been put back in place. He reached to flip it back right-side up so he could unhook the compartment when his eye caught something white on the underside of the plywood bottom panel on which the top drawer would rest. "What's this?" he said. "Some paper or something is taped to the wood."

The tape broke away easily, and Blake removed a yellowed, brittle-looking, sealed envelope. The excitement level in the room returned. On the front of the envelope was written—"Deliver to Detlef Hirsch."

"Hello." Oscar Mayer marked the page he'd been reading in Dan Brown's *The Da Vinci Code*, with a bookmark while he held the phone to his ear with his shoulder. He sat in his easy chair beneath a reading lamp.

"Oscar? This is Carl Schoeffler. I hope I'm not disturbing you." Carl sat at his dining room table with a pen, a notepad, and a bottle of water. After making several phone calls, several people had directed him to the town historian.

"No...of course not. I was just catching up on some reading. It's a lost art these days, reading is, what with computers and smartphones and video games and such."

"It is. Nothin' like a good book to get the imagination working. Anyway, I don't mean to keep you long, Oscar. Why I'm calling is one of my employees at work lost his grandfather today. The whole situation got me thinking, and I think you're someone who can help." On his notepad, Schoeffler scribbled *gold coin* below *Detlef Hirsch, German spy,* and *secrets and puzzles.*

"It's not unusual for grandfathers to pass, but it's kind of strange for me to get called about it. What is it you think I can do?"

"No one passed away, Oscar." Carl hesitated. "Well, at least not that I'm aware of. I'm talking about Matthias Bloom."

Why is Schoeffler concerned about Matthias Bloom? Oscar wondered. "You've lost me, Carl. You said someone lost his grandfather today. What's that got to do with Matt?"

"Haven't you been watching the news? Matthias wandered off and disappeared. His grandson works for me at Bronner's."

"No...books are television for me. I read instead. Why the concern about Matt wandering off? He's a grown man—probably in search of the answer to some puzzling question he discovered. And I don't know who his grandson is. I must be missing something."

"Matthias has dementia, Carl. I thought..."

"Dementia?" Oscar interrupted. "That's horrible. What if he's forgotten things?" The town historian rose from his lounging chair and paced across his living room. He rubbed the bridge of his nose, thinking about his old friend and their old friendship.

"Dementia is horrible for everyone involved, and, uh, forgetting is a primary symptom. I think it's inevitable he's forgotten things. Anyway, I learned something from his grandson recently that made me extra curious about the recent disappearance. I've been told you knew Matthias well, and since you know the town's history better than anyone else, I'm hoping you're the one to talk to."

"I don't know much at all about Matt if that's what you're inferring. He always kept secrets...and from what I know, so did his father before him. They're two of the most mysterious men this town has known. But I've lost track of him over the years. Haven't heard from him in ages."

"More mysterious than Detlef Hirsch? He was a Nazi spy who killed two other spies and fled the town, disappearing for decades."

"Well, you may have me there, but what does one have to do with the other?" Oscar's nervous pacing picked up in intensity.

Oscar kept quiet, hoping his silence would motivate Carl to keep talking. "As a young man, my father discovered a gold coin in Hirsch's basement when he worked on a construction crew," said Carl. "He gave the coin to me—an 1822 Spanish doubloon. I'm wondering what you might know about it."

Gold? Why is he *asking about gold?* Oscar wondered. "I don't know anything about gold coins," he lied. "What does that have to do with Matt?"

"This week, Matthias gave his grandson a Spanish doubloon. I saw it myself at work only two days ago, and I overheard the date get mentioned—1822. His friend, Julia Fischer, told me you spoke about Hirsch in their class earlier this week. She said you mentioned the very coin I have in my possession."

"Oh...yes..." Oscar stumbled for words. "I talked about it in the Fischer girl's class. As a matter of fact, she asked me if there were any famous crimes in Frankenmuth. That's why I told the story, but it was only a rumor I'd heard about the gold. I like to embellish my tales for the kids' sake. I never knew if the story was true or not." He hoped he'd sounded convincing. "Who is this boy, Carl?"

"His name is Blake Nolan. He and his mom moved here about a week ago to help take care of his grandpa. Blake's a senior at the high school now."

"Deborah's back? Hmmm."

"Oscar? What do you know that you're not telling me? What about Hirsch and the gold?"

"All I know for sure is Hirsch lived in this town for years and never let on he was more than a normal citizen. That Nazi spy stuff surprised everyone. Apparently the men who were killed in his home came for *him*—were hunting him down. I heard the diamonds found in the house were from the other spies who died—not from Hirsch. The gold coin was found months later after the house burned down. I didn't know your father possessed the coin until now. All I've ever learned is there were rumors *someone* found a coin in Hirsch's basement, and more than a few rumors were thrown out that he had to leave gold behind when he fled. It's a popular theory he returned for his treasure and then burned down his house. How Matt ended up with a coin would only be speculation. I have no idea personally."

"So my big question to you is, if Matthias knew something about there being more gold, and maybe he got worried his mind was going and he needed to locate the treasure before he forgot about it, where would he be looking?"

"I'm sorry, but there's no way to answer that question, Carl. Seriously. But I can tell you this. If Matthias knew something about hidden gold, he'd make it a puzzle to find it. Never met anyone who loved mystery and intrigue more than him."

"I see. Well, I thank you for your time, Oscar. I'm grasping at straws here. Trying to be optimistic, actually. The notion of the man dying out in this cold weather and Blake and his mother losing him is a grim thought. I hoped there'd be reason to be optimistic, and that gold coin was my only idea."

"I'm sorry I couldn't tell you more. Maybe I'll turn the news on for a change and see what happens to old Matt. Goodnight, Carl."

"Goodbye, Oscar."

Carl, who had learned practically nothing new, slammed his fist on the table out of frustration. His only idea had met a dead end.

The phone rang five times before Emily Cook could reach it. Sounding out of breath from her scamper from the bathroom into her bedroom where her cell phone sat recharging, she answered, "Hello."

"Emily, it's Oscar. I had an interesting conversation with Carl Schoeffler a few minutes ago. He asked questions about Detlef Hirsch."

"The spy? The man you talked about on Wednesday? That's interesting...and a strange coincidence too." She walked back into the bathroom, leaned over her bathtub, and turned her water on for a hot bath.

"He asked about gold coins, and he said one of your students had one. Uh...Blake Nolan was his name...I think." Oscar went for the nonchalant approach as opposed to acting overly excited.

"Blake's a new kid. Seems nice. What's the big deal if he has a gold coin?"

"I guess it's because I always wondered if more existed...if Hirsch somehow had more than one coin. Schoeffler mentioned Nolan and the Fischer girl were talking about the gold coin at Bronner's a couple days ago where he overheard them and saw it. Schoeffler claims his own dad found the coin in Hirsch's basement. I guess Carl now possesses it. But he also claimed the Nolan kid had one like the one his father found—given to him by his grandfather, Matthias Bloom."

"The man who disappeared today is Blake's grandpa? Oh, my, that's so sad. The news said the man had dementia and he's probably wandering around lost somewhere."

"That could be...or he could be on a treasure hunt. That's what Schoeffler seemed to have in mind."

"Well, I sure hope so! If he's outside, he'll freeze. I feel terrible. Blake seems like a nice young man. What a terrible way for someone to lose his grandfather."

"What can you tell me about Nolan and the Fischer girl?"

"Not much. She's super smart and about as anti-social as one can get. Kind of cute, but doesn't seem to care a lick what other people think of her. She and Blake seemed to be friendly, but I know almost nothing about *him*. Polite and quiet and responsible so far."

"Tell me," he continued. "The Nolan boy was there in your classroom when Julia Fischer asked me about tunnels and Frankenmuth criminals and such, I assume?"

"Of course. He was present all week. He's doing his World War II project on Dachau. And Julia's doing hers on Spain during the war—she mentioned the possibility of Spain using gold to help finance the war for Germany."

"She was researching Spanish gold?"

"Well, now that I think of it, yes. She had a discussion about a coin with Blake, and Blake seemed to be especially self-conscious when some of the other kids were eavesdropping. I'll bet that coin was the gold you just mentioned."

"Hmmm. Don't you think it's odd Matthias disappeared right when all this talk about Spanish gold, Detlef Hirsch, and German spies came up? The Fischer girl seemed mighty interested. Even took notes, as I recall."

"She takes notes on everything, Oscar. Listen, friend, I've got a date with some bathwater and *The Book Thief*. You're a good friend and a curious person, but right now, instead of losing your head over two gold coins, maybe you could help the family somehow. Matthias is an old friend. Maybe your connection could be of use in finding him. I heard they're looking for volunteers in the morning to search. I've got a knee that's bothering me, and I can't be stomping around out in the cold, so I think I'll bring over some hot soup for the volunteers in the afternoon. That poor boy must be worried sick. I have to run, Oscar. I have some bathing, some reading, and some cooking to do."

"I'm not much of a hand with cooking, but if you need any help with the bathing, you let me know," he said, smiling.

"You're a dirty, old man....I'll be fine all by my lonesome. Goodnight."

"Goodnight, Emily. I'll message you my dirty thoughts."

"Now don't you be interrupting my quiet time. Talk to you soon."

Oscar ended the call and sat back in his chair. *Gold*, he thought. *More than one coin existed, and if Matthias Bloom knew about more coins, it would have been a mystery to be solved; that's for sure. I think I need to catch up to that grandson of his.*

CHAPTER 19

Blake held the envelope up to the light as if maybe he could see through it and not be forced to open it. The sealed envelope had no indication it had ever been opened. Julia's eyes followed Blake's hand as he attempted to peer through the brittle, yellow paper.

"Are you going to open it?" Instead of answering, Blake flipped the envelope over and examined the other side as carefully as the first. "Aren't you curious about what's inside?"

Blake inhaled a long breath of air through his nose before puffing out his cheeks and exhaling through his mouth. "It's never been opened," he finally said. "I don't believe my grandpa or great-grandpa, for that matter, ever knew this existed....I mean, look. It was on the underside of the wood over the second drawer. Since they knew how to open the compartment, they'd only ever have to take out the top drawer. They'd've never seen this."

"Open it, Blake. You've just become a part of history...maybe."

"I need a knife or a letter opener or something. I don't want to tear it in case it's something valuable."

"Just a minute." Julia disappeared out the bedroom door. When she came back, she handed Blake a metal nail file.

"Where'd you get this?"

"In your mom's room."

"Seriously?...I hope I haven't left anything personal lying around. Have you checked the medicine cabinets yet?"

"We haven't needed anything from the medicine cabinets yet. Let me know when you do though. I'm curious."

"You're kidding, right?"

She smiled. "Open it, Blake. What's in the envelope?"

He carefully slid the file under the sealed flap, and it popped right open. After seventy-five years, the envelope begged to have someone discover the secrets it hid. Blake slid a note from inside, unfolded it, and began to read the typed message.

Operation Samland has had change of plans. Funding needed for final solution of the Jewish question. Gold must be shipped to Himmler in Germany for Einsatzgruppen death squads. Abort original orders and notify Duquesne in New York. Depart Erie immediately. Obtain passage from St. Lawrence River to Gulf of St. Lawrence. Be at rendezvous point at Meat Cove on Cape Breton Island by June 29. Sailors from U-43 will commandeer treasure and deliver to the Schutzstaffel. Once your delivery is made, leave from Douglas McCurdy Airport in Sydney. Return home to await your next orders.

Admiral Canaris

"Wow," said Julia.

"Wow? Pretty much the only thing I understand of the whole note is that gold was to be shipped to Germany. It might as well be written in code." Blake plopped down on his grandpa's bed and looked to Julia for answers.

She stood and moved to the bed to sit next to him, laptop across her thighs. "Let's do some fact-finding. We'll figure it out. I know Himmler was a big shot during World War II, but I don't remember his role. And I know where the St. Lawrence River is...so we practically have it all figured out." She grinned at Blake and shoved her glasses higher on her freckled nose. Their knees and elbows were touching. The girl had no concept of her "own space," but Blake didn't mind how she made herself so at home.

"Well, type away then. I'll sit back and watch the magic unfold."

She took out her ever-present notepad and then began her search with "Operation Samland." She had a hit on a Russian operation in the Baltic in 1945 but nothing about any German initiative in the United States. "Samland," however, was a word associated with Uncle Sam in America, so the best they could figure was the note named an operation that didn't make the Wikipedia newsfeed.

They moved on to the "final solution of the Jewish question," discovering it referred to Nazi Germany's plan during World War II to systematically rid the world of its Jewish population through genocide.

Himmler, they learned, was the military commander of the Schutzstaffel (SS) and a leading member of the Nazi Party. Adolf Hitler appointed him Commander of the Replacement Army and Supreme General for the administration of the entire Third Reich. Himmler was one of the most powerful men in Nazi Germany and one of the persons most directly responsible for the Holocaust.

"I see 'Schutzstaffel'," said Blake. "What's that?"

Julia searched and then orally read that the SS was Himmler's powerful paramilitary group responsible for many of the crimes against humanity during World War II.

The Einsatzgruppen death squads, they discovered, were Nazi paramilitary death squads—led by Himmler, of course—who were responsible for mass killings, predominantly by shooting, during World War II.

"This is horrible," remarked Julia. "I feel dirty just reading this."

"I hear that. So who are Duquesne and Admiral Canaris?" The note had begun to make sense, but there was more.

Julia did another search and some reading before she explained that Fritz Joubert Duquesne led the Duquesne Spy Ring, which was the largest espionage case in US history. Thirty-three members were convicted in 1941 of espionage after an investigation by the FBI. He worked out of New York where he was arrested.

Julia had incredible note-taking speed. After another search, she explained that Admiral Wilhelm Canaris headed the Abwehr, Germany's division of military intelligence.

"This is crazy," said Blake. "My guess is somehow my great-grandpa gained possession of this note while on the S.S. *St. Louis*." Blake began re-reading the diary page his grandpa had written him. "Look at this," he said to Julia. "It says 'even on the ship, my father observed the reach of Hitler's party.' I'm assuming there were Nazi spies or officers or something like that on the ship who my great-grandpa knew about. I wish we could know somehow. Maybe he intercepted this note and smuggled it off the ship with the art."

"But why was it never opened? Maybe someone on the ship hid it in the end table, expecting to retrieve it later. His diary also mentions the German spy in the town. Maybe it wasn't a coincidence. Maybe the spy had tracked down your great-grandpa."

"But why would anyone try to track down a note in the furniture long after the missed rendezvous in June?" Blake asked. "And Hirsch lived in Erie, Pennsylvania, right? Not Frankenmuth."

"Who knows? Maybe someone didn't want the names to fall into the wrong hands. Maybe Duquesne or someone on the ship tried to keep an identity safe. Maybe it was all some weird coincidence," Julia said as she typed in a Google maps search. "I'm curious about the shipping route too," she said, changing the subject.

She quickly located a Google maps view of the St. Lawrence River and the Gulf of St. Lawrence. She clicked on several views. "I don't know what I'm looking for, but maybe I'll get lucky."

When she began her search for Meat Cove on Cape Breton Island, that's when the pieces clicked. Meat Cove was a harbor at the northernmost tip of Nova Scotia on Cape Breton Island where the Gulf of St. Lawrence ended and the North Atlantic Ocean began—and it was an ideal place for a German submarine to hide for drop off and retrieval of German sailors. Julia traced a possible sailing route from the Gulf to the St. Lawrence River, through several locks, to Lake Ontario, through several more locks, and then to Lake Erie to the city of Erie, Pennsylvania. On Cape Breton Island, there was a town called Sydney with an airport for Hirsch to fly back to Pennsylvania and his home town of Erie.

"Do you get what this means?" Blake asked. "Hirsch had a load of gold that was intended to be used for Duquesne's spy ring. But Admiral Canaris, who headed up German intelligence, sent a note on the S.S. *St. Louis* to be delivered to Hirsch, telling him the gold was going to be sent to Germany to be used by Himmler to fund extermination of the Jews instead. I don't know how Hirsch ended up in Frankenmuth, but it sounds to me like he never got the message because it got lost in my great-grandpa's furniture. Because this note never made it to Hirsch, the gold never made it to Germany, and possibly lots of lives were saved. That's awesome."

"Hirsch would have had a bunch of gold intended for a spy ring, so maybe he stole it and moved to Frankenmuth where those two spies tracked him down and were killed." She took her notepad and flipped to the Oscar Mayer lecture. "Remember this?" she asked. "When Hirsch got captured, his name was Wilhelm Mueller...and he was in Erie, Pennsylvania. When he left Frankenmuth, he eventually went back home."

Blake pondered things for a moment. "By 1944, when Hirsch killed the men and ran, Duquesne and the spy ring had already been captured."

"I'm sure that would've been newsworthy too. Hirsch *had* to have known about it."

"True. And the war was coming to a close," Blake noted. "Whatever the circumstances, Hirsch changed his name and eventually went back home—*without* the gold."

"According to the diary, when Hirsch fled Frankenmuth, he left behind a secret of his own—something men would be willing to kill for."

"And something that would turn trustworthy men untrustworthy. Gold would do that. Do you think my grandpa knows where the gold is?"

"Holy cow, Blake! There's probably a treasure of art out there somewhere that's more than likely worth millions, and now there's possibly a treasure of gold too."

"My grandpa was losing his memory, and he wanted me to find the treasures—to determine for myself what to do with them. So that's what we're going to do. It's time to get out gift number three."

CHAPTER 20

"He gave you a what?" Julia asked. "I've never seen anything like that before. It looks like a wooden top."

"It's a dreidel. Basically, it's a game piece, but these letters you see have meaning."

"What do they mean?"

"Uh...would you mind looking it up? I don't remember exactly." Julia did a search for *dreidel* while Blake explained. "My mom wasn't much into the Jewish traditions, and well, her brother died while they were playing this game, so for my mom, it brought up bad memories. Anyway, it's a game played at Hanukkah for candy. The symbols on the sides represent stuff."

"Here it is," said Julia. She copied down four Hebrew symbols from the web site onto her note pad—ש ,ה ,ג ,נ. "They're pronounced nun, gimel, hei, and shin."

"My grandpa said the letters correspond to some words. 'Great miracle happened there,' I think it was."

"That's right. It says right here it's a mnemonic. The four letters are the first letters in each of the words."

"Yep, and my grandpa told me about a miracle in the temple in Jerusalem when some priests were doing a purifying ritual. The priests had to light a menorah for eight days, but they only had enough oil for one. The great miracle was the oil lasted all eight days."

"I never knew that. But what about the top? They spun it for candy?"

"Yeah, the letters didn't only remind Jews of the miracle, though; they also told the players what to do."

"You're right. It's explained here. It says in English the nun symbol stands for 'nothing,' the gimel is for 'get all,' the hei for 'half,' and the shin for 'to share.'"

"I remember now. We'd spin the dreidel, and depending on the letter, we'd do nothing, or we'd take half or all of the pot, or we'd put a piece back in. I remember playing my grandpa until someone had all the candy. And then if I didn't win it, he'd give it all to me anyway."

"He sounds like a good guy. I'm looking forward to meeting him someday. So what does it mean to you...this dreidel...as far as this mystery is concerned?"

"I don't know. Wanna play it and see what comes to me?" He smiled at Julia. "Like all the candy, for instance."

"Oh, game on, hotshot. Don't be surprised when I win."

Blake got butterscotch candies from the kitchen cupboard. He counted out eight pieces for each person, but Julia reached over and grabbed an extra, which she unwrapped and popped into her mouth. "I love these," she said a second before Blake could tell her they were his favorite candy.

"You like Mountain Dew, sour cream, butterscotch candy...I think I've found my long-lost twin. Put a piece in the center to start," he said.

Before long, Julia was giggling, pouting, talking smack, celebrating, and pouting all over again, depending on the dreidel roll. It turned out to be a nice stress relief for both of them. Out of curiosity, Blake asked a question that he'd wondered about.

"You're awfully competitive. Why did you stop playing basketball?"

"And softball too," she said. "It's a long, sad story."

"Well...I'm listening."

"Don't take this the wrong way, but I was better than everyone else."

Blake shrugged his shoulders. It made sense to him.

"The downfall came during basketball in ninth grade. I made the varsity team, and I was the best player even as a freshman. But the other girls never liked having me."

"Why do you think they felt that way?"

"Girls are petty. Guys make better friends. Maybe they didn't like me being only a freshman. Maybe they didn't like how hard I played. Maybe they didn't like that I stayed away from all the drama and never said anything. It could have been something else. I never asked. But they set me up."

"How?"

"The first time, someone stole a teacher's answer key and put it in my locker. Some anonymous tip led Mrs. Heussner to find it. She suspended me for two days, and I missed a game. When I came back, somehow I ended up with a teammate's iPod in my bag. Two strikes. Another suspension. Missed another game. Heussner, I think, believed me, but witnesses said they saw me steal it. When I returned, everyone treated me even worse. The last straw was when I got pushed into the wall in a practice scrimmage and sprained my wrist. When the doctor said I would miss a couple of weeks and the season was nearly over, I quit. And I never went out for another sport."

"That's a horrible story. I'm sorry." Again, it made his concerns about not being added to the team seem petty. While considering what to say, Blake spun the top. It stopped on the upside down G shape, so he threw a butterscotch back in the middle.

"There's no reason to be sorry. Basketball's just a game. Something to do. I don't miss it at all. Do you realize I'm good at lots of things? I moved on. Retreated a little more into the shadows than before, but I'm happy as ever. When I stopped playing on the school team, it opened up all sorts of time. I write. I read good books. I tried Judo. I play the piano. I get good grades. I have a job and my own spending money. I'll bet you wouldn't have guessed I can cook. I don't usually eat Taquitos, you know? The teams weren't as good without me, and I was better without them."

"You're totally serious too. I can tell," Blake said. "It's a pretty darn good attitude, even if it doesn't make complete sense to me." Blake spun again and got the same upside down G. "I hate that side. What was G for? Give?"

"Wait a minute," Julia said. "I copied down the symbols, and there's no upside down G. Remember when we were going over the rules? We figured out the other three symbols were for do nothing, take half the candy in the middle, or take all the candy in the middle. That left the one you said meant sharing a piece. According to my notes, it's a shin...for share. But this website says P, or Pei, is for share too. It looks like this." She showed Blake the symbol— פ—and then scrawled the image in her notes. "The shin looks kinda like the top of a pitchfork," she said. "That's not what this is."

Julia returned her gaze to the internet and tried to figure out the difference. "Hmmm, it says here when Israel established itself as a nation again in the Promised Land in 1948, they changed the symbols on the dreidel to mean 'great miracle happened *here*.' The dreidel you have doesn't say 'there.' It says 'here'."

"Well, that's strange because my grandpa said the word 'there.' I'm sure of it. But he also said that one day the letters on the game piece would help me to know what to do. He said when I remembered my numbers, the dreidel would help me."

"Your number is..."

"One-eighth," Blake interrupted. "We play dreidel because one day's worth of oil lasted eight days. One and eight. And the burning menorah represented that." Blake's eyes widened. "Oh, my gosh. Do you know what a menorah looks like?"

"Not really. Bunch of candle sticks, I think."

"Look up a picture."

Julia typed in the search word and numerous images appeared.

"Look," Blake said. "One candle sitting above eight. One over eight. He wants me to get the menorah he told me he stored in the attic. The numbers are guiding me to the candle holder. He's letting me know when I have the menorah, the letters on the dreidel will tell me what to do."

It took Blake a while to find the attic, but he discovered a door in the mud room with a recessed handle. When he stood on a chair and pulled the handle, the door opened downward, and there were stairs folded on top of it. He unfolded the stairs and climbed into the attic. Blake yanked a string to illuminate a light bulb. A box with "menorah" scribbled on the side sat directly in front of him. He carried it down and set it on the kitchen counter. Julia handed him an ice cream sandwich from the freezer.

"Still making yourself at home I see. Thank you."

"You're welcome." She beamed the amazing smile that so constantly graced her face.

He took the menorah from the box. The base was exposed, but the rest of the candelabra was wrapped in paper, held semi-securely with a rubber band. Blake easily removed the elastic band and took off the paper. Setting the covering aside, he stared at the candle holder. "Great miracle happened here," he said quietly to himself. "I don't see anything obvious that helps me."

"Nothing?...Get all?...Half?...Share? I don't see how those words mean anything either. Do you?" Julia asked.

"Not off hand. What's that new letter for the upside down G?" Blake asked.

Julia checked her notes. "It was pei, I believe. Yep, it stands for here. I can't believe I didn't notice this before, but the S is for there and the P is for here."

Stepping back to think, Blake noticed the paper, which had been wrapped around the menorah, sprawled on the counter top. It was a map of downtown Frankenmuth with a star and a message. The message said, "You are here." Blake pointed at it. "Here. What's here, Julia?"

She looked at the map. "It's the Frankenmuth Historical Museum. It's where Oscar Mayer works."

It all clicked together for Blake at that exact moment. "I get it now. My grandpa told me a story about Mr. Mayer a few days ago. He said as I learn my history, it's good to know his friend was the town historian. He told me not to forget it. I'm sure he told me the sides of the dreidel were for the words 'great miracle happened there,' but that's not what the dreidel actually says, and my grandpa would have known that. It uses 'here' instead. And he said the game piece would help me know what to do as soon as I remembered my numbers. Well, the numbers led me to the menorah and this map, and the map points out the museum where the word 'here' *has* to be a clue. We're supposed to go *here* to find Oscar Mayer."

***

Blake grabbed Julia's ice cream wrapper and headed for the kitchen waste basket as Deborah walked in the garage door. She looked disheveled and exhausted. She arrived alone, speaking on the phone with her husband. It was 10 o'clock—6 a.m. in Kuwait.

"Like I said, Mike, there's not a sign of him. No one's seen him or heard from him all day. Even the search by the rescue team didn't turn up any clues whatsoever."

She listened for a moment and then said, "There'll be an organized search in the morning. I hate to say it, honey, but if he's out in the elements, I can't imagine him making it until tomorrow. Our best hope is he's someplace inside...but where? I've called and checked every logical place, and Blake checked earlier today too."

Again she paused as Blake and Julia eavesdropped on the conversation. "Thank you for saying that," she said. "I *know* it's possible he's safe somewhere. I'm praying it's true. This might not be so hard if you were here, honey." Blake noticed that suddenly her demeanor took on a different look. "Wait...there *is* something that has me worried....In the parking lot where he disappeared...I found a paperclip on the ground where I'd parked. Let me put you on speaker phone. Say hi to Blake. He's standing right here." She put the phone on speaker and dug into her purse.

"Hey, Blake, how're you doing?" asked his dad.

"Hi, Dad. I wish you were here too. I'm okay. Grandpa left me a bunch of clues, and Julia and I made some progress tonight toward solving a mystery I think he put together for me."

"Julia?"

"Hi, Mr. Nolan. I'm Blake's friend from school." Julia made herself right at home per usual, and she kept right on talking. "Your father-in-law left Blake a slew of clues. I think they're going to lead us to him."

"Really? That's a nice, positive thing to hear. I wouldn't put it past the old guy to be playing some game. Maybe that's what he's doing."

"I'm not so sure." Deborah interrupted the conversation. She'd taken out her wallet and removed a folded, blue wire from a pocket. "When I took Dad to the pharmacy with me this morning, he didn't want to go. I'm sure he didn't have plans to leave the house. As a matter of fact, he wasn't happy I made him come with me. He was playing with a paperclip in the car and totally ignoring me. He knew we were there to get medicine, and he didn't think he needed it. Anyway, what's memorable is that the paperclip was blue. He was bending and refolding it and bending it again. Well, I found a blue paperclip on the parking lot beside where we parked."

"Why is that so odd?" Mike asked. "Maybe he dropped it when he got out of the car."

"I highly doubt that," Deborah replied. "My father would sooner lose a limb than litter. If he dropped it on the parking lot, he would've picked it up."

"So what're you saying, honey?"

"I'm saying if he left the car and the pharmacy on purpose, that paper clip would've been either inside the vehicle somewhere or in his pocket. The only way he dropped it on the pavement is if he dropped it in a struggle or if he dropped it on purpose as a clue. What I'm worried about is he may have been abducted."

"That's crazy," Mike said, but Blake and Julia looked at each other as if to say, *That kind of makes sense.*

"Dad?" Blake had his elbows on the counter while he rubbed his eyes and face. "We think there's more going on than a simple scatterbrained man wandering off and forgetting where he is. We think there's a large collection of paintings Great-Grandpa brought over from Germany...and we think there's a treasure of gold too. Grandpa left me a note about the reach of Hitler's party on the S.S. *St. Louis*. It got me wondering who was on the ship. Do you think you can find a ship manifest naming the passengers and crew? There might be something there that's another clue."

"It's possible. I know someone here at the base who might know how to get a copy. You said S.S. *St Louis*? When did it sail?"

"It was May of 1939." Julia had her notebook opened before he'd even asked the question. "It sailed from Berlin to Havana, Cuba, where only a handful of passengers, including Blake's great-grandpa got off, and then it sailed back to Europe." The girl was a treasure trove of knowledge.

"So you think there might be some funny business going on there relating to some treasures? The manifest could be helpful?" asked Michael.

"I don't know. It's just a piece of information I'm curious about. What we know is Grandpa's dad smuggled a treasure of Jewish artifacts here in some furniture he brought, and he's hidden it somewhere. I think a spy for the Nazi party was on the ship and put a note in one of the end tables Great-Grandpa took from the *St. Louis*. The note suggests there's a treasure of gold, and we think *it's* here in Frankenmuth too."

"Are you serious, Blake?" Deborah asked. "That's what all those stories and gifts for you were? Clues to a treasure?"

"Maybe two treasures. And maybe the manifest won't help at all, but I'm curious."

"I'll do my best, Son. If it can be gotten, I'll get it and email it to you. Now let me talk to your mom again. And Blake? If there's some shady business going on, you be careful, you hear?"

"I will, Dad," he said.

"Love you, Blake."

"Love you too."

Deborah picked up the phone, turned off the speaker, and walked into another room to tell her husband about the plans for the morning search. Julia reached for Blake's hand.

"You're not planning on being careful, are you?" she asked.

"I plan on figuring this out—*whatever* it takes. You in?"

"You'd better believe it. If you didn't ask me to come with you, I planned on attaching myself to you like a leech and not letting go."

"Hmmm. I might've liked that." Semi-embarrassed, they both blushed a light shade of red before Blake broke the awkwardness by saying, "Let's make plans for tomorrow. We have some sleuthing to do."

CHAPTER 21

Deborah found it difficult to show up at the search headquarters on Saturday morning where she had to deal with apologetic looks and strained words, mostly from people she didn't know—like Carl Schoeffler. Blake's boss showed up with the earliest volunteers and came right up to her, giving his condolences and promises of prayers and asking how Blake was doing. He seemed disconcerted that Blake wasn't there and came right out and asked when he might show up.

Luckily for Deborah, Janet Fischer was well-organized. At only a few minutes past 9:00, she rounded up the dozens of people who were already in attendance at the Community Pavilion in Heritage Park, including Carl Schoeffler. The park happened to be across the Cass River from Satow Drugs, which would inconvenience the searchers looking north and to some degree west of the drugstore, but a covered bridge and a road crossed the river for the volunteers who needed to get to the other side.

Janet explained that searches had been done in the first mile, so it would be the second mile they would focus on with the new volunteers. Everyone received a photograph and physical description that included Matthias's clothing. They were also given a phone number to call at the headquarters with any news or any questions. People who weren't able or willing to walk outside were bringing in food and drinks for the volunteers. Maps were hung and teams of people were assigned locations in parks, wooded areas, and business areas and were given instructions about what to do.

After Janet gave the first batch of early attenders their search zones, Deborah slipped away privately so the volunteers wouldn't have to run into her on their way out, but then more and more people arrived with the same sad faces and words of encouragement. By 10:30, literally hundreds of volunteers were out searching. At 11:00, a different search team member took over the duties for Janet, giving search assignments to groups who were returning, frozen and without any good news.

Most of the Saginaw County Search and Rescue team worked along Main, Tuscola, and Genesee Streets—the main business streets nearest the drug store—asking owners along the way to check video footage between the time Matthias disappeared and a couple of hours later.

Dean Zimmerman isolated himself at a nearby table where an electrical outlet kept his computer powered. He seemed to be eyeing everyone with equal suspicion, including Deborah when Janet sat with her after refilling a cup with hot chocolate. "Where are Julia and your son? I'm surprised they aren't helping with the search," commented Janet. "I've been so busy I didn't have a chance to ask before now."

"Blake has a theory of his own he's following up." She hesitated when she realized Dean was eavesdropping. "Uh, Julia is with him. She seems like an amazing girl, by the way." Deborah tried to act casual while Dean made her feel like she'd stupidly disclosed something she shouldn't have spoken about.

"Thanks. We love her. It seems she's found a friend in your son. We met him Tuesday night before the basketball game...and then I spoke with him again yesterday, of course. He seems very responsible and respectful."

"Thank you. He's determined to both find his grandpa and keep your daughter close by." Deborah conveyed a weak smile and concluded she wouldn't mention the mystery Blake was working to solve. Her mind still reeled from all the pieces of the puzzle Blake and Julia had uncovered the night before while she spent futile hours looking for her father. The art, the gold, the clues he'd left—those were all things she needed to keep to herself for the time being.

Dean rose from his seat and came to their table. "Hello, ladies. Crispy said there's no news from the Police Department."

"Crispy?" asked Deborah.

"Crispy's the town's cutest but grumpiest law enforcement officer whose real name is Cristina Paulette Bacon....Cris P. Bacon. I call her Crispy."

"She came to my house yesterday," said Deborah.

"She seems convinced your father's story is he wandered off and forgot where he was."

"But you aren't?" Deborah asked.

"Well, my job for the team is to investigate *other* possibilities. Did you know your grandfather well, Deborah?" Dean asked the question as he took a drink of coffee. His blue eyes again seemed to bore into Deborah's. He was the most emotionless person she'd ever seen. There was no way to read him. His wavy blond hair accented a nice-enough looking face, square-jawed and showing a couple days' growth of beard. His eyes were the most disconcerting, though, because they seemed analytical and suspicious. He made her feel like he didn't trust her.

"Yes, I knew him....Well, no not very well. I mean, he was my grandpa, and I loved him, but he was extremely reserved. I knew my grandmother much better."

"Do you know when he emigrated from Germany?"

"Um...before the war?"

"How did he get here?"

"A ship?" She wasn't being specific at all.

"Why did he come here?"

"To live. To start a new life away from the concentration camp where he was tortured." She found his questions irritating.

Interest flashed in his eyes. "Concentration camp? Does that mean he wasn't German?"

"Yes. Why are you asking me this? What could my grandpa, who passed away probably twenty-five years ago, have to do with this search?"

"People around here seem to think he was hiding something. Always secretive. Maybe your dad's been protecting your grandpa's secrets. What could he have been hiding?"

"Scars from beatings? Sadness from watching his sister be raped and killed by the Secret Police? Sadness from being forced to leave his parents to the Holocaust?" Deborah said, emotion rising. "He was Jewish. From what I know, Hitler's monsters were hunting down Jews. They let my grandpa out of the concentration camp only after he agreed to leave the country. Maybe he didn't want people to know his nationality."

Zimmerman didn't back down. "How'd he end up here then?"

"No idea. He came from Germany. This was a highly Germanized population. Maybe he felt he'd fit in here."

"What camp was he in?" He leaned forward, a little too close, being a little too aggressive for Deborah's liking.

"Dachau. Do you think this will help you find my dad? Or are you wasting my time with offensive questions? My grandfather, seventy or eighty years ago was in a German concentration camp, and I'm supposed to believe that has something to do with my father's disappearance in a different country three quarters of a century later? How'd you make that leap, Dean? Was it sometime during the time you were following me around last night?"

"Hey." The accusation surprised him, and he leaned back out of her space. "If someone disappears because of foul play, family members are the most likely suspects."

"So I'm a suspect? Am I?" Intensity shot through her eyes. Dean leaned back even farther from her, actually a little flustered.

"No. No, you're not. But I had to check you out to know. How'd you know I was following you?"

"Because you're a moron. I saw you. I saw you get in your car at Janet's and never drive away. I saw you from the doorway of the drugstore, and I saw you two or three other times while looking for my father. Maybe you could've gotten out of your heated car and given me a hand."

Dean seemed to have regained his composure. "You're not a suspect. I apologize. But if he's not lost and he's still alive, there's a reason he's gone, and maybe clues from his past could help solve the mystery. If I find answers, maybe you'll find the old dude back home safe and sound."

"Your people skills suck."

"I've been told that on occasion."

Janet laughed. "Well, now that the truth has been established, I should get back to work. Deborah, we'll keep looking until it doesn't make sense to look anymore. Dean? Maybe you should head on back to your loner table. Maybe spend some research time looking up surveillance techniques." And with that, she laughed again and headed back to her duties at the main table. Deborah stood and headed out for some air, and Dean grinned because he'd learned two things. One, Joseph Bloom had been interned in Dachau, so he might be able to find the man's real name. And two, Blake Nolan wasn't searching the woods for his grandpa because he was following up on a theory of his own. Maybe Dean was tailing the wrong person.

Blake had copies of both the diary letter and the spy letter tucked into his pocket. He had his key, his coin, and gift number four, the light catcher, stuffed into an inner pocket of his coat. The Frankenmuth Historical Museum didn't open until ten o'clock, so Blake arrived at Julia's house a few minutes before the hour, and he drove her to meet Oscar Mayer at his workplace.

"You seem nervous," Julia said as they turned into a parking space behind the museum.

"My grandpa's note said I needed to have the courage to trust someone he would point me to. I'm sure Oscar Mayer is that someone. But he also said I needed the wisdom to know that trust is fragile. So to begin with, I'm nervous I don't have the wisdom he expects me to have."

"Your grandpa said he had complete faith in you, and so do I."

Blake looked at Julia as he removed his keys from the car ignition. Her hair hung in a frazzled ponytail. She wore a red winter coat so thick she could barely put her arms down. It reminded him of Ralphie's brother, Randy, in *A Christmas Story*, but the more he looked at her face, the more attracted he was to her. Her eyes sparkled with joy and enthusiasm. Self-confidence and encouragement emanated from her personality. "He also said what I find could easily be lost and who I trust could easily be found untrustworthy. I'm nervous that if we tell Mr. Mayer too much, he may let us down."

"Already, I see the wisdom. Ask your questions, be careful what you say, and solve your mystery, Blake. I'll help if I can."

"Okay. I've had my pep talk. Let's go." Julia yanked on a heavy knit cap with a dangly ball and walked around the car to stand beside him. Blake reached over and tried to grab her hand in his. She wore her giant oven mittens again, but the gesture must not have gone unnoticed. Julia grabbed his arm instead.

The sun shone brilliantly and the wind had calmed, but it was still below freezing as the teenagers made their way around the building to the front entrance. The main entry room was a gift shop where a sign told about the cost to tour the museum. As soon as they were through the door, the lady behind a counter asked if she could help them.

"We're here to see Mr. Mayer. I'm Blake Nolan, and this is Julia Fischer."

"Is he expecting you?"

"No." That's all Blake said, but he flashed his pearly whites and gave direct eye-contact. The lady looked him over and appeared to like what she saw, so she didn't ask any more questions before calling the office.

"He said he'll see you," she said sweetly as she hung up her phone. "Go through that door and take the elevator to the second floor." She gestured to the back of the gift shop.

"Thank you." Blake flashed another manipulative smile at the lady.

"You're welcome, sweetie."

When they entered the elevator, Blake had a grin on his face. "She was nice."

Julia bopped him on the back of the head. "Focus, Blake. She was pretty, and she could be your mother. At least your flirting got us through the door."

Blake shrugged and smiled again. He liked that she seemed jealous.

When the elevator opened, they turned right, and there was Mr. Mayer with the same energy he exhibited at the high school. "Hello, Blake! Hello, Julia! It's so nice to see you again so soon." He shook both of their hands with great enthusiasm. "Blake, I'm sorry about your grandfather. He was a friend of mine a long, long time ago. I rather enjoyed his company. Come. Come sit down. I'm curious why you're here."

Immediately, Blake's Spidey senses were askew. He never said a word in class the day Mayer visited. He didn't say a word to the lady in the gift shop about who he was either. His last name wasn't Bloom, and to his knowledge, he'd never been mentioned on the news regarding his lost grandpa. He was a teenager who'd been in town one week. Mayer shouldn't have known his name.

There were two chairs in front of his desk. Oscar stepped around to his own seat where a bagel, slathered with strawberry cream cheese, and a cup of coffee sat to the right of his keyboard. Blake glanced at his computer monitor where he saw a headline—"German Spy Captured after Thirty-Six Years." The historian quickly minimized the screen and then closed an open book on his desk—but not before he noticed the picture of a Spanish doubloon.

"Have a seat...please. Make yourself comfortable. May I get you something to drink? Coffee? Water?"

"No...no thank you," Blake said while Julia simply sat in her seat, content to observe the others.

"What can I do for you this morning?" The charming man seemed genuinely pleased Blake and Julia were there.

After seeing the computer screen and realizing Mr. Mayer

somehow knew who he was, Blake decided to avoid the mystery of the treasures and simply talk about his grandfather. "My grandpa disappeared yesterday. He once told me you were his friend..."

"Really? That's nice, but we haven't been in contact for years. I wasn't even aware of his dementia. That's so sad. I'm sorry, Blake."

Again, Mayer had information that made him leery. "It's okay, Mr. Mayer, but he told me I should know my history...that it would help if there was a mystery to solve, and since you two were friends, and you're the town historian, I hoped you might know something that would help me find him."

"So you don't think he just wandered off and forgot where he was?"

"I don't know, but I'd rather have hope he's still alive. So do you think you might know where he could be?"

"Honestly? No, I don't." His head did a tilt to the right, and his eyes focused above Blake's head. "Maybe if I put some thought into it, I could come up with some ideas, but I assumed he'd wandered off like the news said and got lost. Dementia can be an evil thing. Honestly, I can't think of anywhere off hand."

"You're lying," Julia said.

Mr. Mayer's cheerful demeanor disappeared. "Why would you say such a thing, young lady?" His face drooped in an obvious attempt to appear hurt by the accusation.

"Well, one thing," Blake interjected, "is you know who I am. I never told you. I never spoke in class. I'm new to the town. So how do you know Matthias Bloom is my grandpa? Seems suspicious to me."

Oscar's hand rose, and he paused to massage his throat while he appeared to formulate a response. "Word travels quickly in a small town like this. People talk, and I listen."

"What book were you reading?" Julia asked without hesitation.

Oscar's head tipped again to the side. "Oh, this? It's a random history book. I'm a historian, so I read history books."

"And the website you were on?" Blake asked. He found he

rather enjoyed helping Julia double-team Oscar. "German Spy Captured after Thirty-Six Years?"

Again, his fingers massaged his throat. "*Ahem*," he coughed. "Your grandpa's disappearance brought back memories of the spy. He worked with Matt's dad. Did you know that? I mentioned the spy story in school a few days ago, but Matt's disappearance got my curiosity up."

"Why did you lie about the tunnels under the town?" Julia asked, again shocking both Oscar and Blake with her pointed accusations.

His greedy-looking eyes shot up, avoiding eye contact. "I didn't lie."

"You just lied again. I'd love to play poker with Mr. Mayer, Blake. He's easy to read. You lied about the tunnels in class. The telltale signs of your dishonesty were obvious. You're doing the same things here. Averted eyes to avoid eye contact, hand protecting a vulnerable area—your throat. Repeating yourself to try to convince us. Quick change of head position right before the lie."

Mr. Mayer was speechless, so Blake piled on. "Tell me how you knew who I am."

Oscar breathed out. Deflated. His shoulders sank, and he slouched in his chair. "Carl Schoeffler called me."

Blake looked at Julia, anger in his eyes, but he refrained from saying anything. He had Mayer talking, and wisdom said to let him continue.

"He told me about the gold coin your grandpa gave you. He has one too...if you didn't know that. He claimed your grandpa liked to solve mysteries, so he thought he might be looking for lost gold. Julia, that's why I was looking up the coins. I got his call last night, and I've been researching the gold since the first thing this morning. After Carl's father discovered a gold coin in Hirsch's basement, it had always been speculated our infamous spy left gold when he escaped town. I was looking up the articles after his arrest, and I was curious about the coins, so I found a book to peruse."

"So tell us about the tunnels. Did my grandpa know about

them? How do I find them? He disappeared, so maybe that's where he is."

Oscar dropped his head into his hands and rubbed his eyes and his temples. Finally, he scratched the back of his neck and looked back up. "The tunnels exist. They connect some of the important factories. Entrances have been sealed under most of the smaller businesses, but the tunnels still span all over under the town."

"Who knows about them?" Julia asked. "Would Blake's grandpa know about them?"

"Hitler once said, 'Tell a lie loud enough and long enough and people will believe it.' The lie is there are no tunnels. What would happen down there if people knew? Crime? Invasion by homeless people? Possible damage to the tunnels and maybe the businesses above them? Break-ins? Possible harm to individuals? The church became the voice of reason, and key members of our town agreed. The tunnels exist, but they aren't used, and as years and years have passed, the lie has been propagated that the tunnels are 'tales of intrigue with nothing to support them.'"

"So again I ask...Who knows about them?"

"Leaders of the church. A few members...owners...from our oldest families—the mills and breweries and our large businesses like Zhenders and The Bavarian Inn."

"Bronner's?" Blake asked.

"Yes."

"Carl Schoeffler?"

"I doubt he'd be privy to knowledge about the tunnels because of his position at Bronner's. But the pastors and elders at St. Lorenz know and Carl's an elder, like me. Carl oversees all issues pertaining to the cemetery, while I oversee issues pertaining to our private school."

"Would my grandpa know?"

"Probably. The existence of the tunnels is a mystery. He loved his mysteries. Plus his father worked for the mill, and *he* worked for the brewery. Who knows what either of them may have discovered. Plus..." He hesitated. "Plus, my father was an elder before me. I knew of the tunnels as a boy. I may have mentioned them to your grandpa." Again, eye contact broke and his hand massaged his throat.

"May have?" Julia asked.

"Okay. I did. But he didn't seem surprised. Just smirked in that mysterious way of his."

"Tell me the way in, Mr. Mayer."

"The only sure way for you to get in is through the St. Lorenz church." He stood and stared down at Blake. His voice and eyes betrayed his confident glare, however. "The church is open to tourists, so you can get inside and get to the basement. You wouldn't be able to do that through other businesses...not get to the tunnels, anyway. It's through the church you need to go. I'll go with you," he volunteered.

"I don't think so. I think you've been enough help already." Blake stood and returned Mr. Mayer's gaze, only with much more intensity.

"I see. Well, if he's down there, I hope you find him. I always thought of him as a brother. I hope I've been of help to you."

Blake continued to stare down the man who finally plopped back down in his seat, beaten. "There's a boiler room another level down in the basement. Take the stairs to the boiler, and then there's a built-in bookshelf stacked with lots of tools and such. You'll have to locate a lock under the bottom shelf. Unlock it, and the door can be swung open. Blake? Don't let anyone know I sent you there. Please? I want to find your grandpa too. If searching there will ease your mind, you need to look."

"You're still hiding something," Julia said, "but thanks for your time anyway. We'll find our own way out."

The historian looked defeated as Blake continued to glare at him, but once they disappeared into the elevator, Oscar grinned and said to himself, "The easiest way into the tunnels is from the basement of this museum."

CHAPTER 22

Dean Zimmerman made a call to a female friend at the FBI. He thought he might be able to convince her to track Blake Nolan's phone, but she refused to cooperate. Said something about the fact he was an idiot and should learn how to treat people. Apparently, he'd burned a few too many bridges over the years. So instead of locating him simply, he sat in his car doing surveillance on the empty Bloom home.

Blake had left. Deborah seemed content to do whatever Janet asked of her and remained committed to the search for her father as Janet directed. Dean had other ideas in mind. Being a private investigator was boring work at times, so Dean learned to have plenty of patience. Besides, being alone was the only time he wasn't irritating people. His alone times were his least awkward and tense moments.

His newest stakeout, however, didn't even give him time to settle in and think dirty thoughts of Crispy. Before he could bring up a picture of her on his cell phone, a figure caught his eye. A person who looked to be a teen-aged boy wove his way from tree to tree to stay out of sight before disappearing behind Matthias Bloom's house.

Dean slid out of his car and along the opposite side of the house, covertly making his own path to the back yard. He didn't see anyone, however. The figure should have been somewhere Dean could see if he was taking a shortcut through the Bloom yard, but since he'd completely vanished, it most likely meant the boy was in the house. He'd broken in somehow.

Dean slid close to the outer wall and peered through a side window. Seeing no movement, the private eye stepped over to another window at the back of the house. From there he caught a glimpse of the intruder moving down a hallway to the opposite side of the residence—probably the bedrooms. He slid over to a bedroom window at the back of the house, but the room was unoccupied. The window to the side was for the bathroom, so Dean completed his circuit to a front bedroom, where a shade covered any view he might have. With his investigation complete, that left one thing to do. He called Crispy.

"Hello, Dean," she said. "I'm on duty, so though I'm sure you'd love to chit chat, you need to cut to the chase."

"At least you said hello. And since chit chatting is one of my least favorite activities, I guess I'll cut right to the chase and let you know I'm standing outside the Bloom residence while an intruder is prowling around inside. You might want to charge on over here and make an arrest. I'm curious what he's looking for."

"And if he tries to leave?"

"I figure I'll impede his progress."

"Just don't do anything illegal, and I'll be there in three minutes."

"I can't wait. Love a woman in uniform."

Click. Dean had an amazing capacity to annoy women.

He leaned on the corner of the house under a window, listening to the intruder bang drawers in the bedroom when Cristina eased to a stop and climbed out of her police car.

"It would be best to catch him inside the house," Dean whispered as Cristina met him under the bedroom window. "I've checked, and it appears he went in through a window over the kitchen sink. How about I pick the lock, and then you can walk right in without breaking the door down?" He smiled at the prospect of Cristina's entry.

"This is legit, right? You're not just trying to get inside to have a look around, are you?"

A *bang* sounded as the intruder shoved what sounded like a drawer back into place. With raised eyebrows, Dean smirked. "Would I ever think to do such a thing?"

Cristina cocked her head slightly to the side and raised her eyebrows skeptically. The look said yes without the words escaping her frowning lips. "Unlock the door and then stay out of the way. I'd hate to shoot you by mistake."

Dean picked the lock within a few seconds. Cristina scowled and shook her head. She motioned for him to step aside, but when she entered the house, he walked in right behind her and took his own revolver from its holster. With her gun drawn, Cristina crept down the hallway toward the bedroom. A closet door screeched open as she paused at the bedroom entrance, Dean at her back. When she peered around the corner, the intruder stood with his back to her as he reached up to the top closet shelf.

"Don't move!" Cristina shouted. "Keep your hands in the air. You're under arrest."

Dean moved inside the room as well, his gun also drawn, and his body blocking the route to the window in case the boy was stupid enough to try to make a run for it. He wasn't. He turned, facing the police officer.

"Crap," the boy said. "I wasn't doin' nothin'. I didn't take nothin'."

"Oh, good. The chubby fellow confessed. I guess we can haul him in to jail and throw away the key," said Dean.

"What?"

"Well, if you did *not* take nothing...never mind. You're not likely to understand." Cristina lowered and holstered her gun. "Face the wall and keep your hands above your head."

The kid did as he was told, but when she reached for a wrist to lock in her handcuffs, he tried to run. Without hesitation, she whirled and elbowed him so hard in the kidney he yelped and collapsed on the floor in a heap. She landed on him with a knee in his back and yanked his right arm back so aggressively he screamed out in pain a second time. She cuffed the second arm within seconds.

"You assaulted me," he cried out...well, *wheezed* out would be a better description.

"No, I saved your life because my friend there is trigger happy."

"Seriously?" Dean said. "I wouldn't have killed him. I'd have shot him in the nuts and saved the world from his reproduction. I'm all about looking after the betterment of mankind."

The boy groaned. Cristina helped him up and sat him on Blake's bed. She read him his rights and then asked, "Do you understand your rights as I've explained them to you?" He groaned again and nodded his head yes. "Are you willing to answer our questions without an attorney present?"

"No...I mean yes. What would be better for me?"

"Up to you," she said as she called in her arrest to the department.

Dean spoke up. "What's your name kid?"

"Kevin Hahn. I didn't take nothin'. I already told you."

"But you were clearly looking for something. Look at what you did to the room. You mind telling us what you were looking for?"

"Gold. I was lookin' for gold, but I didn't find none."

"I guess you should search his pockets, Crispy. The way he butchers the language, who knows what he's really saying."

"I need to call my parents. I need a lawyer."

"Yeah, you'll get your chance," Cristina said. "Stand up and let me search you." She patted him down and found only his wallet and keys and something in his right front pocket. She reached in and tossed what she found on Blake's bed. A Spanish doubloon bounced on the comforter.

As Blake and Julia drove down Main Street and turned onto

Tuscola to head to St. Lorenz Lutheran Church, the streets, landscape, and trees were scattered with volunteers searching for Matthias Bloom.

"My mom's working her magic again." Julia pointed out several groups of people searching the landscape.

"They're *everywhere*. If my grandpa's out there, someone'll find him....But I don't think he's out there."

"Me either....The church is coming right up," Julia said.

To the right, the beautiful church emerged. A brick and mortar sign announcing worship times highlighted a pair of praying hands and the words "The Evangelical Lutheran Church of St. Lorenz." Blake took a double take as his cell phone began ringing. He turned into the parking entrance and answered a call from his mother. "Hello?"

"Blake, our house was broken into. You need to come home."

"Be right there." He ended the call, turned the car around, and headed for his house. "Someone broke into our house." Blake gritted his teeth. "One bad thing after another. I'm getting tired of this."

He could see the compassion in Julia's eyes, but she didn't say anything while Blake steamed in the driver's seat.

In the few silent minutes it took to get home, Blake's mind reeled from a mixture of what he'd already learned in the morning and what he was about to see. Parked in the street in front of his house was a patrol car. Another idled in his driveway, so Blake parked in the street. As he hurried to the house, Julia at his heels, he looked into the back seat of the police car in the driveway and noticed the thorn in his side, Kevin, cuffed and looking terrified. A policeman sat in the front seat, talking on his radio.

Blake and Julia climbed the porch steps and entered the house. Deborah sat on the couch. Officer Cristina Bacon, who he'd met on Friday, was there once again, her notebook open. Dean Zimmerman, a man he didn't recognize, stood alone in the corner of the room. A slight grin turned up on his lips as Blake entered. Then Dean's eyes refocused on Cristina's breasts.

"What's going on?" Blake asked. "Did Kevin Hahn break into our house?"

Before anyone could answer, a commotion occurred outside where Leon Hahn arrived and began shouting at the police officer in the car. "He's handcuffed! Uncuff my son. He ain't a criminal. He may be a moron, but you can't arrest someone for being a moron!"

The police officer stepped out of his car. "Sir, step away from the car. You can talk to him once the arrest is processed and he's booked at the station."

Leon raised his hands and stepped back, but he still seethed. "He's a minor...just seventeen years old. It was probably a prank." He looked into the car window. "It was a prank, right?" he shouted. "Officer, we can clear this up right here. You don't have to take him in."

By then, everyone stood on the porch watching the scene while Cristina made her way down the steps toward the patrol car. "We have him for breaking and entering, robbery, and resisting arrest." Leon bent down and looked at his son, fury in his eyes. Kevin looked mortified. "You should probably call an attorney. We'll be booking him and locking him up."

"What did you steal?" he yelled through the closed car window.

"This," Cristina said. She displayed an evidence bag holding the gold coin. "Found it in his pocket, and when we asked how it got there, he shut right up. All he's said since is he needed to call you. So here you are. You can follow the car to the station."

Blake pawed his chest where his interior coat pocket was located. Satisfied the coin his grandpa had given him was still there, he noticed the stranger smiling at him and nodding his head, like he'd learned something important.

Fuming, Leon yelled again, "You're an idiot, Kevin! A freaking idiot!" He stomped to his car, slammed his door, and made a phone call. When the patrol car backed out of the driveway, Leon followed it away.

As Officer Bacon herded everyone back into the house, another car drove up, and out stepped Carl Schoeffler. "Blake!" he called out as he trotted to the porch. "Is everything okay?"

"I can't talk right now, Mr. Schoeffler. I'm sorry." He turned and re-entered the house, Julia at his heels. Carl was about the *last* person Blake had any interest in talking to, but his boss managed to slip into the house with the rest of the group where he stood beside Deborah's desk, concern written all over his face.

Inside, the first question asked by Officer Bacon was directed to Blake. "He claimed he didn't steal anything, and this is the only item we found on him. Once we found it, he never said another word. So the question is...did he steal this?" She held the coin up again. Schoeffler peered at it with ardent interest.

In a split second, Blake's mind was flooded with thoughts. If he said yes, two more people would become aware of the fact his grandpa had ancient Spanish doubloons and maybe Schoeffler, who he noticed had barged into the house, would put two and two together and realize there were more coins to be found. A yes would also assure Kevin would stay in jail and out of his hair for a while, but yes might not be the truth. Kevin may have found the coin in a search through the house, but neither Blake nor his mother had ever seen another coin. When his grandpa had given Blake the doubloon as gift number five, he'd said there were more where that one came from, but it didn't mean they were in the house. And if Kevin found it in the house and stole it, why did he only have one coin? "More" implies more than one. A no on the other hand could possibly throw off three people who smelled gold, but it would mean Kevin wouldn't be punished for possibly stealing something valuable of his grandfather's, and he'd even get to keep it. And if saying he didn't steal it happened to be the truth, it opened up the possibility Kevin actually had a gold coin too, and that seemed inconceivable. So he said the only thing that made sense.

"I don't know. It's not mine, but it could be my grandpa's. He has coins, but I've never seen that before. You'll have to ask him when we find him."

"*If* you find him," said Dean from the station he'd resumed in the corner of the room. Deborah gave him a foul look that couldn't have said any clearer. *You're an idiot!*

"Obviously, you know Kevin. Any reason why he'd be rummaging through your things in your bedroom?"

"No," Blake answered. "All I know is we don't get along very well. He tried to set me up for some vandalism at school, but he didn't get away with it."

"When he got suspended, I heard him blame Blake," Julia added. "He seemed pretty upset with him, considering Blake had nothing to do with the suspension."

"So he happened to be rummaging around your room to what...get back at you somehow?"

"He's not the sharpest tool in the shed, that kid," Blake said.

"No kidding," added Dean.

"Who are you?" Blake asked.

"Private investigator. Looking for your grandpa." That's all he said, which was good because anything else would have probably ticked someone off.

Officer Bacon asked a few other trivial questions before excusing herself, followed by Dean, who first nodded at Blake and then resumed his staring at Cristina's backside.

Schoeffler managed to stay in the house, still looking like a concerned parent.

Deborah went to Blake and hugged him as soon as the others had left. "How are you doing, Blake? Have you found out anything new?" She looked over her shoulder, wondering why Blake's boss remained in the house.

"No, but I think I discovered a lead." He also looked at Schoeffler and thought *Keep your friends close and your enemies closer.* "I need some help at the St. Lorenz church though."

Julia gave him a stupefied look as Carl volunteered. "I'm an elder there, Blake. I'd love to help any way I can."

"Then meet us at the church in a half hour. I've got a clue to figure out, and I could use your help." After a little more small talk, he ushered Carl out the front door and turned to his mother. "I don't trust him, but he might be able to help us, and it's better to keep him where we can watch him than to wonder what he's doing behind our backs."

"Is this the 'wisdom' your grandpa spoke about, Blake? I'm not sure it's a good idea," said Julia.

"I'm not sure either, but when the clues led us to Oscar Mayer, he didn't prove to be trustworthy, so maybe this is the different direction the diary said we might need to pursue. Finding my grandpa is the number one priority, and I'm thinking Schoeffler can help."

Blake grabbed the light catcher from his inside coat pocket before removing his coat and knitted beanie and throwing them on a living room chair. He went into the kitchen and grabbed a can of Pringles from the pantry and two Mountain Dews from the refrigerator, handing one to Julia who had removed her own coat and followed him into the kitchen, the ball of her stocking cap swaying behind her on a string. She wore UGGs, blue jeans, and a blue sweatshirt with black polka dots and the word *Batgirl!* imprinted over a logo of the crime-fighter.

She pushed her glasses higher on her nose. "Thanks for the Dew. What's on your mind?"

Still carrying the light catcher, he walked past his mother who sat at her desk, logging into her computer. He plopped down on the couch and Julia nestled in right next to him, their shoulders, arms, hips, and legs touching. Blake set gift number four in his lap while he grabbed a handful of chips, offering the can to Julia also. She shook her head no, so Blake put the can on an end table before holding up the light catcher.

"Do these praying hands look familiar to you?" he asked.

"Sort of. Why?"

"Because they're on the sign in front of the church too. My grandpa said this light catcher is exactly like a sign...and he said something about how clues are like windows to look through. He said when I spot the sign, I should look to the west. He also reminded me again to remember my numbers and said they'll lead me to answers—some as much as 2000 years old."

Understanding dawned on Julia's face. "The stained-glass windows on the west side of the church are clues, aren't they?"

"These same praying hands are on the sign, and I think the clues are in the windows at the church. The tunnels are also at the church. Maybe my grandpa is down there protecting or seeking or hiding the treasure. Schoeffler knows his way around. Maybe he can help us understand how the windows are clues too. Maybe he wants the treasure. I say let him have it if it'll help us find my grandpa."

Just then Blake's phone vibrated. A text arrived from his dad.

Manifest sent. Check your email. Yosef Bloomberg was one of only 29 who made it off the ship. Any news?

Blake texted back. *Thanks. Grandpa still missing. Working on the mystery still.*

He accessed his email from his phone as soon as he sent his text and saw a note from his dad.

Officers first, then 231 crewmen and 900 passengers. Alpha list. Hope it helps.

There were well over eleven hundred names, but Blake didn't have to read past the very first one. He saw it as plain as day—Reinhold Schoeffler, Captain. "Oh, wow! The captain of the S.S. *St. Louis* was Reinhold Schoeffler." He scrolled through the names of the crew members, looking for other Schoefflers or Mayers, but there were none. He found Yosef Bloomberg, but no Joseph Bloom, so that verified his great-grandpa had changed his name after he disembarked the ship. At the bottom of the manifest, it listed two members who didn't survive the voyage—Solly Wernher committed suicide and Otto Rechtsteiner was lost at sea.

While Blake skimmed the names, Deborah lifted a piece of paper from her desk and gasped.

"What is it, Mom?"

"A note. Someone put a note on the desk. It says, 'Find the gold and maybe your grandpa will live.'"

168

CHAPTER 23

After finding the threatening note, Deborah called her husband and then told Blake she would be going with him, no matter what. She sat in the front seat of the car, relegating Julia to the back, as Blake headed for the church and his meeting with Carl Schoeffler. Blake hoped if Carl could help them locate the treasures, maybe they'd get his grandfather back. Dean, who had moved his car down the street to wait for Blake to leave, once again followed behind.

"So what will we find at the church, Blake?" Deborah asked.

"I'm not sure, to be honest. I hope more answers to this mystery."

Carl was on his phone when they turned into the church parking lot, but upon recognizing Blake, he wrapped up his conversation and climbed from vehicle. The sun continued to shine, and all evidence of snow flurries from the night before had disappeared. The temperature had risen into the forties, so it was pleasant enough to congregate outside in front of the church—except Julia still bundled herself up like an Eskimo.

Blake vaguely outlined his "theory" that using a few clues his grandfather had given him, he might be able to find him alive. He didn't mention anything about Captain Schoeffler of the S.S. *St. Louis* or that they'd discovered the note that happened to be found on the desk where Carl stood in their house. Instead, he got right to the mystery.

"Mr. Schoeffler, my grandpa gave me this light catcher and told me it was exactly like a sign, and the clues were like windows. It didn't make sense when he said it, but it does now. The hands on the light catcher are exactly like the ones on the sign in front of the church. And one of the things most distinguishable about this church..."

"...Are the windows." Carl turned and pointed toward the church.

Blake nodded in agreement. "So I think the windows are clues. My grandpa said to look to the west. Where are the windows on the west side?"

"These windows are the ones facing west—the ones we're looking at right now. Follow me inside, and I'll show you something fascinating."

The noontime sun hung over the top of the church, and light flooded the sanctuary through stained-glass windows displayed on both the east and west sides of the auditorium as well as from the rear. What didn't look quite so impressive from the outside was incredible from the inside. Light shined gloriously through the colored glass.

"The windows all tell stories. Some are of the Lutheran church; some are of Biblical stories; some are of the history of this town...like this one showing the story of how the town was settled." He directed their attention to a tall panel of glass. "The name St. Lorenz was brought to Frankenmuth by its earliest settlers. Pastor Wilhelm Loehe, who you see represented in the glass, brought a team of missionaries from German Bavaria who first settled in Frankenmuth. Lorenz Loesel—he's over there—was the first missionary volunteer. Other windows tell other stories."

He continued his discourse to Deborah while Blake sat stoically in one of the pews. Julia settled in next to him. She unzipped her pillowy coat, exposing a form-fitting cable-knit sweater ending all speculation in Blake's mind that she was perfect. "What's on your mind?"

He refocused, unwilling to share what had flitted through his mind when she'd exposed her outfit. "How am I supposed to figure out what part of these windows is a clue? I mean, there's a picture of the church." He pointed to a pane of colored glass on the auditorium's west wall. "Right under it is the original community house Schoeffler is droning on about to my mom right now. I heard him mention it was the original church and parsonage. Below that is what looks like a representation of a Bible story. Maybe that's Jesus teaching the little children. Or maybe I'm supposed to pick a different set of windows to focus on. How am I to know?"

"What did your grandpa tell you to do in the diary when you have doubts or you reach a dead end?" Julia asked.

"He said to remember my numbers. One-eighth. What does one-eighth have to do with all these windows?"

Deborah sat down in the pew in front of Blake and Julia. "I haven't been in here since I was probably a young teenager. I remember staring at these windows...especially those round ones at the top." She pointed at a pane of glass with four circles inside a larger circle. "I could never see those highest ones well enough to figure them out. I used to try to count all the windows when I was young and bored during church services. Being in here brings back so many memories."

Carl sat in the pew in front of Deborah, but he handed back a brochure the church provided to tourists who visited the attraction. "The brochure tells about the stories in the glass. You can keep it if you'd like."

"Thanks." Blake intended to look at the brochure, but he noticed Julia counting the windows.

"The tallest set in the middle has nineteen windows. The two sets to the right and left of it have fifteen windows. The two even farther right and left have nine windows. Obviously, I'm not coming up with one-eighth anywhere."

"Sure you are. Look." Carl pointed to the set of nine windows to his left. "The round one at the top is sitting above eight windows below it. One over eight is one-eighth. Same on the other side," he said, pointing again. "What's the significance of one-eighth?" he asked.

"It's a number my grandpa told me to remember every time I got stuck. So far it's helped me several times....Mr. Schoeffler? Would this pamphlet you gave me tell me about the stories those windows represent?"

"Not a lot of details, but there are general descriptions."

Blake opened the brochure. Each of the different pictures were numbered with a footnote, and on the last few pages, the stories were described. He skimmed though the stained-glass images until he found the number for the round image on his left. It was the story of Ruth and Boaz. The window to his right, which rested above the other eight rectangular windows, was the story of creation.

"So we have the story of Ruth and the story of how God created the world. Does that mean anything to anyone?" Deborah asked.

Blake began thinking out loud. "The world was created in six days...seven if we count the day of rest, so there's no 'eight' there."

"Genesis is the first book of the Bible and Ruth is the eighth," said Julia, who seemed to have a limitless knowledge of trivia.

"That could be something, but what do the two stories have in common that would make this another one-eighth thingy?" asked Blake.

Everyone sat in silence.

After a moment, Blake turned to Carl and said, "We're not getting anywhere. I need to think on this last clue some. There's another reason I asked you to meet us here. You said you wanted to help."

"I do, Blake. What's happened to your grandpa is horrible. I'll do anything in my power to help you find him."

"Do you mean that?"

"Of course I do."

"Then I want you to lead the three of us through the tunnels.

I know they start here in this church, so I need you to help us through them."

Speechless for a few seconds, Carl wavered on whether he should do what Blake requested or not. Finally, though, he agreed. "The tunnels are secrets this town isn't supposed to know about, but I assume your grandpa must've known about them and told you. As an elder of the church, I know about them, but I was also asked to not share my knowledge. It's best that others aren't aware they exist. If you think your grandpa might be down there, though, I think we *have* to look. This could cost me my seat on the board, but I think it's worth the risk."

Blake bit his tongue. *Yeah, a fortune in gold is definitely worth the risk.*

"Well, come on. Follow me before I change my mind."

* * *

Since being discovered by Deborah harmed his huge ego, Dean focused more intently on demonstrating his clandestine skills. The group not only hadn't noticed him, but he'd overheard Carl Schoeffler agree to take Blake, his mom, and his girlfriend "through the tunnels." He'd heard rumors for years and years that they existed, but he'd been convinced they were no more than a myth. Somehow a teenaged boy, one week after moving into town, had figured out the truth.

He slinked through the church on the heels of Blake Nolan, super sleuth—that was what he'd decided to call Blake. His great-grandfather, Yosef Bloomberg, a prisoner at Dachau from November 10, 1938, to May 1, 1939, boarded the S.S. *St. Louis* on May 13, 1939. Dean had discovered he was one of only 29 passengers to disembark in Cuba, and there had been no record of him since. Yosef Bloomberg, he believed, became Joseph Bloom, resident of Frankenmuth, Michigan, and Dean assumed he'd spent his life hiding some secret Matthias Bloom knew about and his grandson was well on his way to discovering as well. If Blake continued to pursue his theory, as Deborah had said, Dean could find the secret. At least that's what he believed, so he worked his way stealthily through the church, following the super sleuth, expecting to be guided to the secret tunnels and answers to questions that had been nagging at him.

The group went down some stairs into a lower level that included some storage areas, offices, and what appeared to be classrooms. Dean had to hold up at the top of the stairs until Blake and his entourage were out of sight before he slipped down onto the lower floor. From there, he followed the voices.

Carl chattered away about the floor plan of the lower level of the church, but Blake lost patience. "Where's the boiler room, Mr. Schoeffler? I don't mean to be in such a hurry, but I know that's where we're heading, and my grandpa's been missing for over twenty-four hours now. I know there's a bookshelf. I know how to open it to get inside the tunnel. What I don't know is if he's down there, so I want to start looking."

"How do you know these things?" Carl's face displayed absolute bewilderment.

Blake never promised Mr. Mayer he wouldn't tell, but he decided to keep his name out of it anyway. He was practicing being wise. "I just do." He stared at Carl and said nothing else.

Carl shrugged in confusion. He led the way to the boiler and down a set of metal steps about eight feet further below into the maintenance area. The floor descended lower than the rest of the basement space they had walked through, but the walls extended the full eighteen feet to the ceiling. Noise echoed in the room as the huge apparatus chugged and spit heat through-out the church facility. Dean, sneaking along behind, squatted above the steps leading to the boiler, but he could no longer hear the group's conversation.

Carl wasted no time, heading directly to the built-in book-shelf. The dusty shelves were a storage location for parts and tools. It looked inconspicuous, like it was positioned there pur-posefully to house junk exactly as it did. Tight against the wall, Blake gave it a tug, it didn't budge.

"No one would suspect it hid anything from the looks of it."

"That's the purpose." Carl dropped to a knee and reached to the back underside of the bottom shelf where he did something resulting in a clicking sound. Blake tugged on the bookshelf again, and that time it swung easily open.

"There are two extremely long passages..."

Julia gasped.

"What?" Blake asked.

"Uh...nothing...I saw a mouse. It surprised me."

"Mice?" Deborah and Blake glanced at Julia who didn't seem to be the scared-of-mice type. Julia put a finger to her lips and shrugged her shoulders, so Blake assumed she gasped at something else. "I don't want to go in there if mice're running around," Deborah said.

"I wouldn't think there are many mice, Mrs. Nolan." Carl tried to reassure her. "I've never seen one and most would be in town, I would think, where there are lots more tunnels. As I was saying, from here and from Bronner's are two lengthy, straight passages. Once we're in town, mice have a lot more places to enter and hide if need be. There's nothing to worry about here."

"Where are the passages in town?" Deborah asked.

"Well, one passage starts behind Lager Mill at the dam. From the mill, there are passages connecting to the Frankenmuth Brewery, the Brew Haus and Grill, Star of the North, Zehnder's, The Bavarian Inn, the historical museum..."

"The historical museum? Really?" Once again, Blake felt tightness behind his eyes. He breathed a deep breath to calm the rising anger. "Do you think we've been sent on a wild goose chase, Julia?"

"Definitely trust is a fragile thing," she replied. "I could tell he was lying though."

"Who we trust could easily be found untrustworthy....We were warned."

"Blake, I think we're getting ahead of ourselves." Julia pulled on a loose strand of hair before continuing. "In the letter, your grandpa said we had to discern the passage. That could mean more than one thing, but I think either one suggests we've missed a clue."

Dean could still hear voices, but he couldn't determine the words, so he stayed put.

"What are you getting at?" Blake asked.

"What are some ways one-eighth or one over eight or one of eight come to mind."

"Dates," he said. "Measurements."

"The windows in the church," added Carl.

"Side one, song eight," Blake continued. "The menorah with one candle over eight."

"The stock market share prices used to go up or down by eighths," said Carl again. "The Spanish doubloons we both have are referred to as pieces of eight. Eight coins together would add up to the Spanish dollar. Our stock market based its pricing on the Spanish system."

"I remember reading that," said Julia.

"The clock could read 1:08," said Deborah.

"And Bible verses," said Carl. "Chapter one, verse eight."

Blake reacted to Carl's comment like an electrical current woke him from a slumber. "Oh, my gosh! I think I know where the next answer lies." Blake turned to Carl. "I'm sorry I made you bring us here. Julia's right, though. We're getting ahead of ourselves. We may need you again, but for now, we have something else to do." He grabbed Julia's hand and headed back for the steps. "Mom, we need to go."

As Dean began to head down the steps to the boiler, he heard Blake say they needed to go. He straightened up and quickly found a room to hide in. When the threesome exited the boiler area, they passed by Dean's hiding spot and made a beeline for the stairs up to the main level.

Confused by the turn of events, Carl lagged behind to close and relock the door to the tunnel. A minute later, he climbed the metal steps from the boiler room and headed down the hall where he saw the private investigator who he noticed at Blake's house, sneaking up the stairs behind Blake, Julia, and Deborah.

CHAPTER 24

As Blake led the girls out of the building, he grabbed a pew Bible and tucked it under his arm. Julia looked up at him in mock curiosity. "I'll put it back," he said, "but we need to get out of the church—away somewhere I can think."

Blake's phone rang while the trio loaded into the car. The number was familiar, but it wasn't in his contacts. "Hello," he answered.

"Blake, it's Carl Schoeffler. I don't know why you stormed out of here, but I wanted you to know the detective who was in your house this afternoon is following you."

"Is that so? Thanks, Mr. Schoeffler." He ended the call and looked to the building entrance. He could see someone peeking around the edge of the entry door. "You recognize that dude, Mom?"

Deborah glanced up as Dean took another peek and then scanned the parking lot for the car he drove, which would confirm his identity. "Dean Zimmerman...the private eye who works with Julia's mom. It's not the first time he's followed me. What's his deal, Julia?"

"I don't know him except he investigates possible sources of foul play during my mom's searches. She's never said anything bad about him that I recall."

"And Julia recalls everything," Blake added. "Let's get out of here. Maybe I can lose him." Blake squealed out of the parking lot and took a quick left, despite his mother's worried glance. At Mayer Drive, he turned left again and then veered right on Mission Ridge, his mother holding onto the handle above her head, complaining about his crazy driving. From there, he took three more quick turns before settling into a parking spot behind Frankenmuth Insurance. Julia watched out the back window the entire time and was satisfied they hadn't been followed.

"I think he thinks I've done something wrong." Deborah was clearly relieved the car was no longer barreling down public streets. "He acts like he suspects me of harming my dad...and that's unnerving. I don't like him at all."

"I'd be more worried he has other intentions, Mom. Grandpa warned me that Detlef Hirsch's secrets were something people would be willing to kill for, turning trustworthy men into the devil's handymen. But I only care about finding Grandpa."

During the lengthy pause in the car, Julia zipped her heavy coat up to her chin. Deborah nervously continued her search for Dean Zimmerman's car. Blake rubbed his temples. A buzz indicating a text message on Deborah's phone broke the silence.

She gave out a long sigh. "Your mom says I need to come back to the pavilion. A news team is on site to interview me, and she says it's important I'm there."

Blake didn't even hesitate. He backed out of his parking spot and headed to the pavilion. Deep in thought—and keeping an eye out for Zimmerman—Blake dropped his mother off without incident and then, instead of driving home where he kept picking up undesirable followers, he drove to Julia's house to think. The teens shed their winter coats, and Julia made some hot chocolate. "You've got that intense look on your face again. What's up?"

"Well, besides wondering why you hide your amazing looks under a sea of material, I think I've thought of something to do with this mystery."

Julia looked pleased. "Me too. When Schoeffler called the tunnel a passage, something occurred to me." She took out the copied diary page. "It says 'you must discern the passage I lead you to for the one mystery and unbury the answer to the other.' I thought leaving the tunnels was the right thing to do since we haven't discerned the right passage yet. *Or*," she stressed, "passage might be something written, and we haven't found anything new that's written."

"But *I* think we have. Schoeffler gave me the idea. One of the possible one-eighths would be Bible passages. One of the windows told a Genesis story, and one came from Ruth." He opened the Bible he'd borrowed. He flipped a couple of pages to locate the first verse and began reading. "Genesis 1:8 says 'God called the vault "sky." And there was evening, and there was morning—the second day.'"

"What could *that* mean?" Julia asked. "A clue's in the sky? We'll find what we're looking for on the second day? Your grandpa does a good job disguising his clues."

"For some reason, he thinks I can figure them out."

"You can. What does Ruth 1:8 say?" Julia took a sip of her cocoa.

He flipped ahead, looking for the verse. When he found it, he read, "Then Naomi said to her two daughters-in-law, 'Go back, each of you, to your mother's home. May the Lord show you kindness, as you have shown kindness to your dead husbands and to me'...Crap. I thought it might be easy. Now I'm unsure if I'm right about the Bible verses."

The friends sat down on the Fischers' living room couch. Julia grabbed Blake's hand as she peered at him over her mug. Blake gave her a squeeze, but he flopped back against the couch and closed his eyes.

"The stress and the uncertainty are tiring me out," he said, wishing Julia would snuggle up into his arms.

Instead she did a more practical thing. She said, "Let's analyze the verses. We've done this before with your grandpa's poem.

Something in them has to be meaningful, so let's pick out the possibilities. The Ruth passage seems easier. Key words are *daughters-in-law, go back to your mother's home*, and maybe *dead husbands*. So what do you think?"

"Well, my grandpa doesn't have daughters-in-law. My great-grandpa did, though. But if he meant *his* daughter-in-law, he would be referring to my grandma, and that doesn't make sense to me."

"What about the dead husbands?"

"None of us has a dead husband, though I'm pretty sure the clues are written specifically for me, so that one's not too likely either. That means *go back to your mother's home* is most likely. But she has two homes—one in Clarkston and one here. Do you think something's in one of the houses?"

"Remember," said Julia, "the note said to discern the passage he leads us to for the one mystery and to unbury the answer to the other. We found the tunnels. If he wants us to find a particular passage, there wouldn't be a tunnel in Clarkston, so could there be a tunnel from your grandpa's house?"

"It isn't likely. I mean my mom or I would know about it, I'd think."

"So that's a dead end too."

"Schoeffler didn't mention anything about tunnels going into residential areas anyway, so a house would have to be right in town....Wait a minute! The *old* house where my mom *used* to live. Remember my grandpa's rental we visited when we were searching yesterday? It's..."

"Right across a parking lot from the mill!" Julia finished. "Your great-grandpa worked for the mill, and a tunnel goes there for sure."

"Maybe there's a tunnel from the house. We'll have to check that out for sure. It's the best possibility so far." Blake was no longer exhausted.

"That leaves the other verse. What are the key words in the Genesis passage?"

Excited, Blake turned the pages back. "*Vault, sky, evening and morning*, and *second day* stand out."

"Well, there's already been an evening and morning, and this is the second day, but that doesn't help us find anything....Plus, when the clues were left, how would he know the circumstances that would make you start looking? He couldn't know you'd be to this point on the second day, so logically, vault and sky are the key words to consider."

"How could the sky be a clue? It's so general. Does vault mean anything to you?" Blake asked.

Julia's took out her phone and typed in the word *vault* for a definition. "I'm not even sure what it is. All that comes to mind is a bank vault. Maybe your grandpa has a safe deposit box or something....It says here it's an arched structure...an underground chamber...a room for storage or safekeeping—like a bank vault. It could also be a strong, fireproof, burglarproof storage cabinet...and a burial chamber."

"So possibly we've discerned the passage for the first mystery, and now we have to unbury the answer to the other."

"Burial vault, Blake! Do you know where your great-grandpa is buried?"

"At the St. Lorenz Cemetery. And guess whose duty it is to oversee the cemetery?"

"Mr. Schoeffler's."

"Let's go to the rental and see what we find. If we don't find gold at the house, we'll have to contact Schoeffler for his help with the vault. If we find the gold, maybe he'll let my grandpa go."

"You think Schoeffler has him somewhere?" Julia asked.

"Don't you?"

When Blake dropped Deborah off, she immediately became nervous—nervous that she'd left her son alone again and he and Julia could be in danger, nervous about the reality of her father being a kidnapping victim who could be hurt, nervous about the TV interview, and mostly nervous about what she was going to say.

Janet came right to her to prepare her about what to say.

"Make sure you thank everyone who's helping. Explain how we're systematically checking off areas he might be found. Tell them you're hopeful and desirous of prayers. This is a wonderful community, and they'll continue to rally around you. I wouldn't mention we've been investigating foul play since there isn't any evidence of any."

"Did you know someone broke into our house?"

"Oh, dear no. When it rains, it pours. I wouldn't mention that either, Deborah. Keep the interview about the search. That's why they're here."

A camera sporting the logo WNEM Channel 5 rested on the right shoulder of a guy with a Nordic patterned trapper hat, tassels dangling from ear flaps. Matching fingerless mittens completed the ensemble. The female reporter wore an attractive grey knit cap over beautiful, long blonde hair. Her stylish black leather boots had three inch heels, helping her to tower over Deborah and making her somewhat intimidating.

"My name's Lacy Valentine," she said.

Deborah raised her brows as if to say *Really?* She bit her tongue, however.

Lacy explained a few basics to Deborah, including the fact they had another story to cover, so the interview would be short and sweet. Finally, the camera rolled.

"This is Lacy Valentine here at Heritage Park in the Harvey Kern Community Pavilion in Frankenmuth where volunteers are actively searching for local resident, Matthias Bloom, who is suffering from early stage dementia. I have with me today Mr. Bloom's daughter, Deborah Nolan." The camera zoomed in on Deborah's face. "Deborah, we understand your father has been missing for over twenty-four hours."

"Yes, that's true," Deborah said. It would have been easier and less uncomfortable, she assumed, if the reporter had asked a question.

"How are you going about searching for him?"

"Janet Fischer and her Saginaw County Search and Rescue Team have organized a systematic search of the two-square-mile area from where he disappeared at Satow Drugs yesterday.

I'd like to thank her and her team as well as the hundreds of volunteers who showed up today to help locate my father."

Janet, attempting to be encouraging, nodded at her response.

"Do you have any theories as to why your father may have wandered off?"

Deborah hesitated. She considered her options...her son's safety...her father's well-being, and then she said it. "I don't believe he's lost...at least not in areas we've been searching. I feel strongly we need to call off the search. My son and I can't express our gratitude enough for all the physical help and all the moral support and prayers we've received, but circumstances have led me to believe that a lot of people are wandering around this town unnecessarily. It's time to end the search."

"Mrs. Nolan? Why do you feel that way?" Lacy asked.

"I'm not able to answer that question right now, but I'm convinced he's not lost or injured or hiding outside, and it isn't right to accept help from the community when the help's futile. People simply need to go home and be with their families. I'd be grateful for their continued prayers, but if my father's found, it won't be where the search and rescue team is looking. That's all I have to say." Deborah walked away.

The camera refocused on Lacy. "Well, that was unexpected. It seems Matthias Bloom's daughter has reached the conclusion the search for his body is pointless. As more details for this story develop, WNEM Action News 5 will be reporting. This is Lacy Valentine."

Janet rushed to Deborah's side. "Deborah, what are you saying?"

"Thank you for your help, but call off the search. Someone left a note on my computer desk. It said, 'Find the gold, and your grandpa won't be hurt.' Blake and Julia are going to find it, and I'll get my father back."

"This is a kidnapping? Is my daughter in danger? Who would do such a thing?"

"I'll contact the police, Janet. As for who? Well, I'm thinking your friend Dean is about the best possibility."

CHAPTER 25

Blake and Julia stood with flashlights on the porch of Matthias Bloom's rental house on a plot of property behind Pilgrim Home Accents and across from the Star of the North Milling Company. The doorbell didn't work, so Blake resorted to pounding on the window of the outside screen door. After three tries, Sandy Meager opened the front door, her two-year-old grandson on her hip.

"Well, it's you again," Sandy said with a half-smile. "Sure am gettin' a lotta activity 'round here lately. Between you, your mother, the police, a lady from some search team, and a sweet older fella—said he was a friend of the family—and now you again, there's no peace and quiet."

"We're looking for Mr. Bloom, Ma'am. Your landlord," said Julia. "This is a likely place he might have come since he lived here most of his life. Plus it's only a short way down the street from where he disappeared."

"You can call me Sandy, young lady. Mr. Bloom is a sweet man, he is. But he still hasn't showed up here. I'm so sorry."

"We came here for a different reason, Mrs. Meager. In order to solve a mystery related to my grandpa's disappearance, we need to get into your basement. Would you let us do that?" Blake asked.

"Oh, Lordy, it's a mess down there. I'd be so embarrassed. Your grandpa's such a sweet man, but he'd be mortified by what we done in the cellar. Junk everywhere. Could you come back after we pick some things up?"

"Let 'em in, Sandy!" a voice—probably Mr. Meager's—yelled from somewhere in the house. "First of all, it's winter out there. Show some hospitality. Second of all, his grandpa owns the place. It ain't ours to keep from the boy. Let 'em in. And third of all, while I'm at it, that grandbaby of yours is gonna catch his death of cold if you don't shut the door!"

"How'm I gonna take care of this child and clean the cellar at the same time, old man? You and yer dagnabbed notions!"

By then Mr. Meager came to the door, bumping his wife aside and ushering the kids into the house. "I'm sorry about your granddaddy, son. If goin' down in our junky basement might help you find 'im somehow, then make yourself at home. Just watch your footing down there because though Sandy here may have forgotten her manners, one thing's dead certain. She didn't lie about the mess."

"Thank you, sir, and thank you Mrs. Meager."

"I'm Sandy, young man, and I apologize for my manners I forgot." She frowned and glared at her husband.

"And I'm Lazarus. Yeah, named after a man raised from the dead. *I* don't want to be raised from the dead though. My back's hurtin' all the time. If I came back healed, that'd be diff'rent. But to come back with an achin' back...and a trick knee..."

"And a pot belly," Sandy chimed in. "Think you'd come back with a six-pack for your old lady?"

"Stop it! That's just silliness. Besides, if I came back all fit and trim, I'd drink myself another beer belly." He laughed a hearty laugh along with Julia, and he gave her a flirty wink. "The basement steps are over here."

He flipped a light switch and the first thing Blake noticed was the blood-stained cement at the bottom of the stairs. It was impossible to miss. No wonder his mom needed to move. But regardless, they were 'back to his mother's home,' and they needed to find a passage.

The teens filed down the steps. "Find the south side. That's where the mill's at." Julia did a half turn and pointed to the wall behind them.

As soon as she pointed, they both noticed a cabinet leaning against the cemented blocks. Stepping over mounds of junk—the Meager's weren't exaggerating—they made it to a shelving unit that fit snuggly against the cement. "It's screwed into the wall," Blake said after giving it a once-over. "I need a Phillips-head screwdriver...a big one."

Julia bounded over the junk back to the steps and dashed up the stairs. "Lazarus? We need the biggest Phillips-head screwdriver you have!" The girl certainly wasn't shy.

A clamoring sounded upstairs...the baby cried temporarily...and then Lazarus said, "Here you go, little lady. You sure are a sparklin' breath of fresh air. Haven't seen someone to make me smile like you in a long while."

His description was perfect, Blake thought. *That's exactly what she is.* Julia pounded back down the stairs with a grin on her face. "Are you happy I didn't just run up there and take it?"

She was beautiful any way Blake thought about it. "Your ethical standards have taken a turn to the virtuous."

"I love it when you use big words on me. Unscrew the cabinet, brainiac. I'm curious."

The thick screws were each about four inches long. Exhausting as it was, Blake didn't give up until all four were in his hands. Together they prepared to move the sturdy piece of furniture to the side.

"It's kind of unnerving, isn't it?" Blake said. "I'm hoping we'll move this, and there he'll be. But I'm also kind of afraid he'll be there...just not alive."

"Or hurt," Julia added. "But let's not think negative thoughts. If he's there, we did it! If not...there still might be a treasure." Her words were spoken with eyebrows raised and a smirk on her face. Blake had to laugh. She made him feel better. Together, they moved the cabinet aside, but instead of a tunnel, they found another door. A locked door. Blake rattled it a couple of times before feeling around to find a button or latch of some sort. What he found was a small keyhole in a metal door lock.

"It's such a small hole...kind of odd for a door this size." Julia knelt and examined it. "You'd think if it needed a key, your grandpa would've prepared us." They both stood in silence for a moment. "Have you ever picked a lock? I mean, this one seems pickable; I'm sure I could do it."

"Seriously?" Blake shook his head. "You're a woman of endless surprises."

Before any lock picking could occur, however, a *clang* of metal on metal sounded on the other side of the door. Both teens froze. Another *clang* preceded a *ting, ting*. Someone was inside!

"The door's locked, Blake. Whoever's in there can't get out."

"He should have given us a key." Blake's eyes displayed the rising panic he was feeling.

But one look at Julia's expression said it all. "He *did* give us a key, didn't he? Do you have it?"

"The one for the journal? Believe it or not, I do." Blake reached into his inside coat pocket and took out the small diary key. "It would be crazy if this worked," he said, but when he fit it into the hole and turned, it rotated easily, and a click followed.

Again, clanging and tinging sounded, not precisely behind the door but rather from somewhere beyond the other side of it. Blake looked again, but there was no handle or knob to turn as the clinking and clanking continued. A voice roared in frustration and out of panic Blake pushed. The heavy door groaned and swung inward, banging off the wall and bouncing back into Blake's left shoulder. The tunnel was dark except for the light filtering in from the half-closed doorway and a faint glow from the other end of the passage. Blake could make out something—possibly crouching— maybe twenty feet away. "Grandpa!" he called, fumbling with his flashlight. "Grandpa, we're here!" The tight hinge strained to pull the hefty door closed again, so Blake pushed it open once more, and Julia slipped inside.

"Mr. Bloom!" she called. The clanging stopped, and the feeble light disappeared. She and Blake both shined their flashlights into the tunnel. The entryway was only about six feet high, but the ceiling gradually sloped, like Great-Grandpa Bloom had tired of the difficult labor, until approximately fifteen feet ahead, it couldn't have been more than four feet high. They saw a stack of wooden containers—probably the thing Blake had imagined crouching—but there was no sign of Matthias Bloom. Just dirt and some wooden beams wedged into the clay ceiling for braces.

Blake stepped away from the door, stooping to move forward. "There's no one in here unless he's behind those containers. Grandpa! Are you back there? It's Blake."

The only response was the creaking of the complaining door hinges behind him. The teens turned as the entryway banged shut. The sickening *click* it made could have only meant one thing. The door locked behind them. They were trapped.

Blake spun back to the door, but not in time. There was no knob on the solid, heavy oak door. He slid his fingers partway under the wood, but not far enough to grab and tug it back open, but it didn't matter. They were locked in with no key hole on the inside.

He rolled from his knees onto the seat of his pants and shined his light on Julia. "We're not getting out this way." Again, Blake resorted to his deep breathing to calm himself. The anger that had risen so many times during the week threatened to boil over.

But Julia eased the anxiety. Blake shined his light onto her face, and she grinned. "I've been *trying* to get alone with you." In the midst of the tension of the moment, she sat on the floor next to him, put her head on his shoulder, and giggled.

"Why didn't you just say so?" He puffed out his cheeks and released another lungful of air. His heartbeat settled some.

After sitting still for only a few seconds, they heard a *clack* and a *scrape* coming from the opposite wall. Blake moved away from Julia and crawled toward the containers, using his flashlight to guide the way. He got on his knees and moved each wooden box out of the way until he could see a metal grate. The noise sounded like cement bricks or rocks being stacked or slid into place.

"Is someone out there?" No one responded. "My name is Blake Nolan. Julia Fischer and I are trapped in this tunnel. Could you help us?" The wall building on the other side stopped. Blake placed his ear to the grate, and he heard someone breathe hard and eventually talk to himself in a whisper. "There's someone out there. I can hear you. This is an emergency."

"Give me the gold first!"

"Mr. Mayer?" Julia asked. "You should be ashamed of yourself. You're nothing but a liar and a thief. We're trapped in here. What are you gonna do? Walk away and leave us to die...and go back to the man who you probably kidnapped?" She looked at her cell-phone. There was no service, so she couldn't call Deborah or her mother for help. "Are you a murderer and a kidnapper too? And besides, Mr. Mayer, there's no gold here, but *we're* the ones you need to find it."

After a pause, a light from Oscar's tunnel lit, and the rocks on the other side of the grate began tumbling down. Whatever was going on in his head, he didn't say.

Without speaking, Blake checked *his* phone too before shining his light on the metal grate. Like with Julia's, the lack of bars indicated no service, but the barricade he observed was a mechanical masterpiece of *real* bars. There were levers and springs and latches and hooks. Metal rods had been sprung and set deeply into the clay sides, floor, and crown. Hidden behind a rock wall, it seemed unnecessary, especially considering a person could dig his way around the grate if he had the time and desire to, but at the moment, it seemed impassable.

Once Oscar cleared enough stones away to peer through the opening, he rattled the grate with both hands and said, "Barring digging a new tunnel, I don't know how to help you. Do you have a suggestion?"

Blake told him the only idea that made sense. "I have a key.

You'll have to go to my mom's old house by the mill and convince Lazarus Meager that Julia and I need help. He's taken a liking to her, and he seems to respect my grandpa too. Hopefully, he doesn't know what kind of man you are."

"There's really no gold? What's in those containers?"

"I'm pretty sure you'll find out when you get here, Mr. Mayer," Julia said. "And if Blake's suggestions don't work with Mr. Meager, lie to him. You're well-practiced at that. Tell him you're a God-fearing church elder."

"I deserve that, Miss Fischer. I'll be there as soon as possible. He'll know who I am."

Blake slid the key to Oscar through the metal barricade, and once again, the man replaced the stones to rebuild the tunnel wall, hiding evidence as best as possible of the passage Blake's great-grandpa had almost certainly dug. "What shall we do while we wait?" Blake asked. Alone, in a dark tunnel, beautiful girl—his male hormones were speaking to him.

"Find out what's in those crates, I would think," said Julia. "You can kiss me later."

"Ha! I was thinking we should dig our way out so Oscar doesn't get his hands on the goods."

"You must have a shovel in that pocket where you stored the key."

"Let's go take a look before I die laughing." He hesitated a moment. "You know smuggling is a crime too." The thought of being caught with what he assumed would be priceless art pieces smuggled from Europe through Cuba worried him some.

"Well, yeah, but the authorities should look the other way to save a culture and to flip Hitler the bird."

"Possibly. Here...you hold the flashlights so I can use both hands." The tunnel was so low where the containers were leaning that Blake slid them all back to the entry door where he barely needed to hunch over and where Julia could stand without stooping. The containers were similar to the ones Blake had found in the old furniture in his grandpa's bedroom. They were hinged and flipped open easily. Just as he expected, the first container was filled with canvas paintings. With care, Blake lifted them partway from the box—enough to realize there were at least thirty of them. The second box was packed to the same capacity. The first small, wooden case was filled to bursting with smaller paintings. With more confidence, Blake lifted them completely out before slipping them back into the container. There had to be a hundred or more paintings to that point.

Finally, he opened the last wooden box. Again, he lifted the paintings, but that time, he heard a muffled metallic *ting* as something fell back to the bottom of the container. Not wanting to let the paintings touch the tunnel dirt, Blake dropped to his knees and tilted the container upside down, holding the paintings inside while shaking the lightweight wooden box. With a *clink*, out fell a small, heavy, wrapped paper bundle. Tied in a bow with string, the package was of the consistency and look of a paper grocery bag. Blake made sure the paintings were settled back undisturbed before focusing his attention on the item on the ground.

"Open it, Blake." Something indescribable hung in the air. A tension, an electricity that was indefinably powerful, or for lack of a better word, fear could be felt. Blake stared at it like it might be holy, and he didn't want to defile it. "Do you feel that, Blake? That's not more art."

"I don't know what to do."

"Open it. It's what your grandpa meant for you to do. It's yours to decide what to do with it, but how can you decide if you don't know what it is?"

Blake tugged on the bow to untie the package. He unwound the string and then, after setting the item on the ground, opened the multi-folded paper. Julia shined both lights on the objects that appeared.

On the thick, course, brown paper were maybe forty to fifty long, sharp thorns bundled together; five large, wooden slivers; and three long, thick metal nails. Two were approximately five inches long, while the third measured about an inch longer. No one spoke. They stared. They pondered. They felt awed. With nothing else to do or say, Blake rewrapped the items with care, tied the package as before, and stuffed it inside his coat in the pocket with the letters, the coin, and the light catcher. He closed the small container with the pictures and sat on the ground.

Julia snuggled right next to him, turned off the flashlights, and held his hand. She rested her head on his shoulder once again and Blake listened to her breathe while he listened to his own heart beat in his ears. He closed his eyes, knowing the incredible journey they were on still had to play out, but what in the world was he going to do with three relics the diary said dated back to the time of Jesus—three relics that appeared to tie to Jesus's crucifixion?

CHAPTER 26

Blake dozed in the darkness, relaxed temporarily, his mind at ease in the comfort of Julia's presence. When the adventure ended, he'd determined to give her flowers, take her someplace extra nice, and treat her like his girlfriend. Those pleasant thoughts were on his mind as he drifted off into a badly needed rest.

Julia nudged him awake when she heard the sounds in the basement.

"Well, I'll be darned, Oscar. Had no idea there was a door behind the cabinet. Is it some sort of a hidin' place? And you say the kids're stuck back there, but you have the key?"

"That's the truth, Lazarus. We all appreciate your help."

Julia turned her flashlight on to give Blake light to move the containers away from the door. It took Oscar some time to find the small keyhole, but when he did, they heard the familiar *click*.

"There's no handle," Oscar said. "How do I open it?" But before Blake could respond, he pushed and the door opened.

"There's my beautiful, little lady," Lazarus said to Julia. "Hope you weren't scared in there."

"I wasn't, Lazarus," Julia said, smiling. "I had Blake with me, but you saved us." She exaggerated, but Mr. Meager liked the sound of it, and his face beamed in satisfaction. "There you go makin' my day better once again. She has a smile to light up the world, Oscar. I envy your friendship."

Oscar's head drooped. "Blake's grandpa and great-grandparents were good people. Matt was my friend. I lost my head, Blake. I apologize." He turned to Lazarus who still stood there with his goofy grin. "Lazarus, would you excuse us? I need to talk to the kids...privately."

"Sure, sure. You just yell if ya need somethin'."

While he stepped over the clutter and headed up the stairs, Blake held out his hand for the key. Mr. Mayer handed it over without hesitation. Blake slipped it back into his interior coat pocket. He slid out the four containers, closed the hidden door, slid the cabinet over all by himself, and set to putting the screws back into place.

"I'm sorry. I lost my head," Oscar said. "Gold. Gold fever's a real thing, isn't it?" He chuckled, but Julia glared at him. Blake said nothing as he continued his work. "I have a confession to make."

Julia raised her brows as if to silently say *and why should we believe you?* But she let him continue purging his soul.

"Your great-grandpa was Jewish. There were things about him that anyone Jewish could see. I noticed them because...well...my father was Jewish too."

As soon as he said it, Blake knew it to be true. "Did you change your name too?" he asked.

Julia added, "What about Oscar Mayer, the bologna dude? He wasn't Jewish was he?"

"Mayer is as much a Jewish name as a German one. No, we never changed our name—there was never any reason to. When my parents named me Oscar, Julia, I was destined to be teased, but as soon as I said I was the nephew of the great Oscar Mayer, millionaire wiener tycoon, the teasing mostly stopped. I've been telling that story ever since. As far as my family hiding our heritage, Blake, we didn't have anything to hide like I assume your great-grandpa did. We weren't practicing Jews, though, because my mother was Lutheran, and my father loved her so much, he had no problem changing his religion to please her. When your grandpa and I became friends, I learned he loved mysteries. He grew up with a father who had a past he didn't share and a story he always concealed, but Matt befriended me. He once told me there would likely be a day when I'd understand the great puzzle his family hid. He said someday someone would be asked to trust me, and I needed to be trustworthy. Well, when Carl Schoeffler called me and told me about the gold, I figured the big mystery was a stash of gold, and I lost my head. You were the one, I believe now, who needed to trust me, but I proved myself untrustworthy, didn't I?" Again, silence filled the basement. The answer to the rhetorical question was obvious. "There's a tunnel entrance from the museum, so when I sent you all the way to the church to find your way in, I wandered through the passages I hadn't been in for years. I'd told your grandpa about the tunnels when we were kids, though I'm certain now he knew about them already. Anyway, I knew his father worked at the mill, and it occurred to me they lived barely yards away. If he'd discovered the Star of the North entrance, he wasn't far from home. Maybe he'd made a connecting passage."

Blake finished with the screws. "And once you got gold in your head, you thought you might find it and steal it?"

"I'm embarrassed to say it, but yes. The tunnels under the town have stone walls. Rocks are fitted and cemented together like on a retaining wall from floor to ceiling. Both the floors and ceiling are cement. The tunnels are sturdy and strong and built to last. I found the entrance to your grandpa's tunnel because the lowest stones weren't cemented together securely. When I removed the wall section, I discovered the metal grate. You heard me trying to disassemble the thing. Your grandpa—or his dad—was a mechanical genius."

"Mr. Mayer, I believe my grandpa pointed me to you. He said to trust you even if you seemed untrustworthy. He said you could easily be found untrustworthy and lead me astray—which you did—but that I needed to have the wisdom to know what to do. I've decided I'm going to trust you. Are we on the same page at the moment? Because if you try something else dishonest again, I might just beat the crap out of you. *Kapish*?"

"That word's Italian, smarty pants," Julia said.

"*Atah Mevin Ivrit.* That's 'do you understand' in Hebrew," said Oscar. "I do. Matt told me this day would come. I almost let him down. I won't anymore."

Julia moved to open a container. She removed the thirty or so canvas paintings and began to display them. "Blake's great-grandfather smuggled these here from Germany to keep them from Hitler. He wanted to preserve the Jewish culture before the Nazis could destroy it. All four of these wooden cartons are filled with paintings like these." She laid the first on a blanket on the floor and continued to lay the others, one after the other, on top of the prior one. Lieberman, Oppenheim, Freundlich, Nussbaum, Weber, Chagall, Soutine, Pascin, Modigliani, Schatz, Gutman, Goldberg—all priceless paintings thought to be lost forever.

As Julia laid them down, Blake snapped pictures. "I'm going to do this for all hundred plus paintings, Mr. Mayer, and so help me if one of them disappears, I'll keep my promise."

"We'll store the pictures in the Cloud, Blake."

"The what?" Oscar asked.

"Cyberspace," answered Blake. "It's your heritage too, though, so I'm going to trust you to catalog them and begin work to send them back to the families that gave them up and the museums that sent them with my grandfather to be preserved. My grandpa said I'd know what to do with them, and that's what I've decided. Are you on board?"

"This is the most exciting thing I've ever seen. The value of these must be incredible, but the true value lies in the history that's been safeguarded. I'm a historian—a Jewish historian—and you're giving me a chance to help prevent something terrible and make it right...to restore a decimated culture. I won't let you down."

"Then let's photograph the rest of these and get them some-place safe. I assume the museum has such a place?"

"Indeed it does," Oscar said. "Indeed it does. I brought my truck. We can unload the containers behind the museum, and store them away safely as soon as you finish photographing them."

"And then I can get back on my way to finding my grandpa."

———————————●———————————

As soon as they exited the basement, both Blake's and Julia's phones blew up. Voice mails and text messages from Deborah and Michael Nolan, Janet and Ben Fischer, and Carl Schoeffler lit up the phone screens, and all of them were about the fact that Deborah had informed the media she had cancelled the search. Though the only person Deborah had told about the note was Janet, rampant speculation about foul play and a ransom demand emerged.

The Nolans and Fischers knew the truth. Matthias Bloom had been abducted and the way to get him back was to find gold. The ones searching for gold would be Blake and Julia, putting them in imminent danger. And what became apparent to Blake was if gold actually existed, Carl Schoeffler was the person needed to get to it. If Schoeffler wanted gold in exchange for Matthias, Blake wouldn't think twice about the swap, and Schoeffler could run off to whatever exotic locale he wanted, as long he didn't hurt anyone.

They decided to not answer the calls until they delivered the art safely to the museum, but once Oscar had secured the con-tainers away, they called their parents.

Julia's parents asked her to give up the hunt—a request she respectfully denied, and when the request became a demand, she changed tactics.

"Mom? Ca ... ear me? ... ouldn't ... ma ... out ... said. ...base-men'.... later."

"What was that?" Blake asked.

"Oh, she wanted me to give up the chase and come home, but

the phone signal inexplicably went on the fritz. Think she knew I was faking?" She smiled as she turned the device off.

"Probably. Are you gonna be in trouble?"

"Probably, but I assume we're heading to the cemetery?" Together, they bid adieu to Mr. Mayer.

Ever since they'd left the Meagers' rental home, Julia had been absorbed in an internet search, scribbling more notes in her notebook while Blake and Oscar loaded and unloaded the crates. Blake hadn't been as fortunate when he tried to keep his mother away, so he'd caved and instructed her to meet them at the museum with shovels.

"Did you bring the shovels?" Blake climbed out of his car and gave his mother a hug.

"What in the world do you have planned?"

"It's getting dark. Carl Schoeffler is the church elder who oversees all issues pertaining to the cemetery. The man is relentless in his desire to help. We persuaded him to take us to the tunnels, and it's now time to persuade him to help us dig up Great-Grandpa Bloom's grave in the St. Lorenz Cemetery."

"I don't know if I should be proud of your achievements in this mystery or terrified about what you're doing."

"This is what Grandpa wants. And it's the way to find him. Trust me, Mom."

Blake dialed the number in his recent calls list that came from Carl. He reassured the man that he and Julia were fine and then asked him if he still wanted to help them solve their mystery. His yes was immediate.

"Good. Then grab a shovel and meet us at the St. Lorenz Cemetery. I need your help digging up my great-grandpa Bloom's grave."

After a long pause, Carl finally replied. "You're serious, aren't you?"

"You'd better believe it....Hold on. Julia's been doing some research, and she wants to speak with you."

He handed his phone over, and Julia said, "Hey, Mr. Schoeffler. Here's the thing. You're the elder in charge of the cemetery. According to your own cemetery rules and regulations, which I happened to look up, you have the right to request removal

of items from the gravesite. It's fortunate we're such close col-
leagues. I also happened to discover that in order to dig up a
grave, all one needs is to get a permit or letter of permission
from The County Health Department, or—luckily for us—the
local religious organization if the body is buried in a religious
cemetery. So sign us up a permit because we have some items to
remove."

Blake winked at the girl of his dreams and took the phone
from her. "So we have flashlights and our own shovels. All we
need is you. I'm confident you'll take care of the appropriate
paperwork and meet us in say...a half hour at the gravesite."

Schoeffler, on the other side of the line, smiled. "And you
think this is a step in the right direction to get your grandpa
back?" There was obvious excitement in his voice.

"This is the one certain way."

CHAPTER 27

Deborah knew where the grave was, so she directed Blake as close as possible, and then they exited the car, wearing cold weather gear and carrying flashlights and shovels. Schoeffler parked behind them. He stepped out of his car with documents in hand for Deborah to sign. When everything was in order, the foursome made their way to the gravesite.

Schoeffler, who had an armful of gear, kept looking around anxiously, as if he were afraid to get caught in the cemetery at night. He chattered away nervously as they walked. "The burial plot is four feet eight inches by eleven feet, but the monument is centered and placed at the head of the grave. The vault is exactly three feet two inches by seven feet ten inches so we'll be able to easily identify where to dig, but we'll have to dig a bigger area than that to remove the top. That's a pretty big area of frozen ground to cover. Are you up to the task?"

"Yep," said Blake and Julia together.

"Okay...and it'll be eighteen inches down to reach the vault lid. We usually have a machine to do this. Still willing?"

"Ready, willing, and able."

"I still have one question before we start." He threw a blanket to Deborah. "What makes you certain this will help find your grandpa?"

"Let's say it's more than a hunch." Blake stuck his spade in the brown grass, stepped on it with his full weight, and turned up the first shovelful of hard dirt. Julia picked a spot and did the same. Carl measured the area, marking the corners off with small flags, and then without saying a word, he threw himself into the labor as well.

When Julia got tired, Deborah dug for a while, but Blake never slowed. A fierce determination drove him, resulting in more dirt removed than the other three combined. The metallic sound of the spades striking concrete constantly interrupted the silent night air. No matter the amount of progress made, however, the four gravediggers worked away in silence. Either Deborah or Julia shined lights on the work area, depending on whose turn it was to shovel, but silence continued to pervade the sacred cemetery.

The air hovered barely above freezing, yet sweat poured down Blake's face. The entire vault top was eventually exposed except for patches of loose dirt here and there. Julia removed her hands from her giant, padded mittens and began scooping dirt from the cement. There were two raised metal handgrips that were situated at each end of the cover. Again, without talking, Blake went to one end and Carl went to the other. They squatted, and with great effort, hoisted the top and set it aside.

Overtop the wooden casket lay another container almost exactly like the ones hidden in the furniture and in the tunnel. Together Blake and Carl removed the heavy object, recognizing the casket below had deteriorated quite a bit, but the lid remained intact, covering the remains of Joseph Bloom. Blake flipped the hinged end piece and tipped the wooden box so the contents could slide to the ground. What appeared were four flattened canvas duffel bags that *chinked* of metal as they plopped to the ground.

Blake looked at his mother, wrapped in a blanket, her eyes wide with wonder. Julia had a satisfied look of pride on her face. It was Carl's look that surprised Blake. He seemed relieved. No greed. No move to open the bags. No gold fever like he saw with Oscar. No gun pointing his way.

"Open one, Blake," he said. "Is it the missing gold?"

"What do you know about missing gold?" Blake asked Carl.

"The FBI has always believed Detlef Hirsch left behind gold when he killed those two spies years and years ago..."

"And Detlef Hirsch is my father-in-law," a male voice proclaimed from out of the darkness. "That gold belongs to me." He shined a blinding light that left his appearance nothing more than a shadow.

"Who are you?" Blake asked, standing on the edge of the grave.

"That's none of your concern. Throw the bags over, get in your cars, and leave."

"You're not getting any gold until I know my grandpa's safe."

"Listen, punk. I have a gun aimed at your chest right now. I can shoot you and the other dude can throw my gold to me, or you can do it yourself. Makes no difference to me."

"Give it to him, Blake," said Carl.

Blake ignored him. "I need to know he's safe and unharmed. You said if I find the gold, my grandpa will live."

"I have to hand it to you, Nolan. You're pretty smart to find something in two days I been lookin' for for more'n two years, so don't get stupid now. The note said *maybe* he'll live. What do I care about the crazy old dude? He don't even remember his name half the time. If I kill him, I do him a favor the way I see it. So I'll talk real slow this time, so you can follow me....Give me the gold...or I put a bullet in your chest. I ain't askin' again. My patience has already worn thin." They could hear the clicking sound of the gun cocking.

"Where's my grandpa?"

With the question, the gun fired. The shot echoed throughout the graveyard as the world went into slow motion. An *ooff* was heard as Blake's hand went to his chest and the bullet propelled

```

him backward into the grave and on top of the coffin behind him with a crack.

Carl ducked, but Julia leapt to the grave to help Blake. Deborah let loose an insane scream as she ran toward the blinding light where the shot came from. Two steps into her suicidal sprint toward the shooter, two more shots rang out.

The flashlight and gun of the man who shot Blake slipped from his hands. He exhaled an airy *oogh* and dropped to his knees before falling to his face onto the ground. Deborah stopped in her tracks, and out of the shadows stepped Dean Zimmerman.

Deborah's mouth hung open, but she managed to say, "You shot him from behind. What if you would've shot me?"

"It's the fat dude who was gonna shoot you. I was aiming for *him*."

"Call 911!" Deborah yelled. She turned and charged back to the grave where Julia had climbed down beside Blake. Carl hovered close by. Blake lay there moaning, trying to breathe, his hand on his chest. Deborah unzipped his coat as a siren sounded in the distance. There was no blood whatsoever.

"Ohhhh, that's gonna leave a bruise!" Blake moaned.

"You're not bleeding. How could you be hit and not be bleeding?" Deborah asked.

Julia looked at the coat. She discovered a bullet hole on the outside but not on the inside. She unzipped his interior pocket. The package with the relics had a hole torn into the paper on one side, but it too was intact on the opposite side. She felt the bundle, and one of the nails was somewhat bent. A metal spike had taken the force of the gunshot instead of Blake's chest. It had saved his life. She felt farther into the coat pocket and came up with a flattened lead bullet which she held out for Blake to see.

He looked at Julia and smiled. "Just call me the Man of Steel."

"It's a miracle," Deborah said.

"Where, O death, is your victory? Where, O death, is your sting?" Carl quoted.

Blake moaned and stood up. "That's either the Bible or Shakespeare."
```

"Both," said Julia, who seemed to know everything. "You nailed it."

She winked as he rose from the grave, brushed himself off, rezipped his coat, hugged his mother, grabbed Julia's hand, and walked directly to the shooter. Dean had already checked his pulse. The kidnapper who had shot Blake was dead. A police car roared up, siren squealing—blue, white, and red lights flashing. Cristina Bacon stepped onto the scene as Blake pushed the body over.

Leon Hahn lay dead on the cold cemetery grass.

During all the shock and bewilderment, Julia took Blake aside. "Oh, my gosh! I should have known. Hahn said Detlef Hirsch was his father-in-law. But remember when the FBI arrested Hirsch? He'd changed his name to Wilhelm Mueller. When I had to call Kevin's house the day Mrs. Heussner suspended him, his emergency contacts listed his grandma. Her name was Mueller, and she lived with Kevin's parents. She even answered the phone. Your grandpa is probably at the Hahn house right now."

Officer Bacon approached as Blake slipped over and picked up a duffel bag before he and Julia stole away unnoticed in the darkness and commotion. "What's going on here?" she asked.

Two doors slammed, diverting everyone's attention, and two men walked onto the dead cemetery grass. The men had neckties and button-down shirts under blue coats—the initials FBI adorning the front left coat side, each shoulder, and the back. They both displayed their golden badges for all to see.

"What's going on here?" one agent asked.

"Holy cow, Crispy. You have the FBI lingo down pat," Dean remarked.

She glared at him. "I'm Officer Cristina Bacon of the Frankenmuth Police Department. I'm here responding to a 911 call about a shooting. I only beat you here by maybe twenty seconds, so I don't know any of the specifics."

"I'm Agent Miles and this is Agent Miles."

"And miles to go before I sleep; and miles to go before I sleep," quoted the unimpressed-looking private investigator. "Your names strike a poetic chord."

Agent Miles—the one who seemed to do all the talking—pointed a thumb at Dean and asked Cristina, "Who's Robert Frost might I ask?"

Dean ignored the agent completely and spoke before Cristina could answer. "I'm the one who placed the call, Crispy. You'll find two of my slugs in the creep's back."

"Does anyone here notice Agent Miles and me, by any chance?"

"I'm Carl Schoeffler," Carl said, holding one of the duffel bags up for the agents to see. "What you'll find in these bags is the gold the FBI believed Detlef Hirsch abandoned here in Frankenmuth seventy years ago." He focused his attention on Dean, Cristina, and Deborah as an additional police vehicle and a wailing ambulance announced their arrivals. Blake and Julia used the distraction to drive off unnoticed. "After Detlef Hirsch killed those two German spies and disappeared way back in 1945, my father found a gold coin in Hirsch's basement after his house burned down, and he reported it to the authorities. Since that day, both he and I have been the eyes and ears for the FBI. When I saw Blake's gold coin—of the same mint as mine—it was the first real hint I'd ever had that there actually might be more gold. When Mr. Bloom disappeared and Blake began his own personal investigation, I figured the two things were related, and I contacted the FBI."

Agent Miles—the one who had not spoken thus far—said, "It's the Boston branch that's been officially in charge of this case from the beginning—from the time two spies entered America and shot their mouths off about working for the German government. When Mr. Schoeffler contacted us a few days ago, we asked him to find out from Blake as much as he could. But when Matthias Bloom disappeared, we felt as Schoeffler did—that the disappearance was somehow related to the gold we always believed existed. We booked the first flight we could get. While at the airport in Detroit, we got additional word from Schoeffler you were going to dig up Bloom's father's grave. We got here as soon as possible."

"So now I ask again," said the other Agent Miles. "What happened here?"

Deborah spoke up. "Someone placed a note in my house today saying if we found the gold, my father wouldn't be killed. My dad left my son clues..." She hesitated, deciding to leave out information about the artwork. "To find this treasure of gold."

"Who left the note?" asked Agent Miles—one of them.

"Obviously Blake thought I did," said Carl.

"I figured it was Zimmerman," said Deborah, nodding at the private investigator.

"So the man has a name," said the other Miles.

"If you happen to be thinking of recruiting me to the alphabet club for my heroic service to God and country, I'm not changing my name to Miles. Then we'd be Miles and Miles and Miles, and I'd be singing The Who all day long, oh yeah."

Cristina elbowed him in the ribs.

"I figured out," Dean continued while rubbing his side, "that Yosef Bloomberg spent time as a prisoner at Dachau and sailed on the S.S. *St. Louis* that arrived in Cuba in 1939. He changed his name to Joseph Bloom—the inhabitant of that grave over there, I assume." He nodded in the general direction. "When Joseph's son disappeared, I managed to learn the super sleuth and his girlfriend were following clues to find him. I figured if Mr. Bloom hadn't simply wandered off because of dementia, foul play had to have occurred. I followed Deborah, who was the first to figure out something was wrong."

"I found a blue paper clip my dad had in my car before he disappeared," Deborah explained. "It was lying on the parking lot surface next to where he was sitting in my car while I went in for a prescription. He would've never dropped it there. His biggest pet peeve is littering, yet that's where I found it. He had to have either dropped it when he was abducted, or he dropped it on purpose as a clue."

"Apparently Blake followed the clues his grandpa had left him, thinking once he and Schoeffler recovered the gold, Schoeffler would take it in exchange for his grandpa's safe return. But the stiff wanted the gold—not Schoeffler...or me," Dean said, looking at Deborah.

"Hahn's son must've left the note when he broke into the Bloom house today," Cristina said.

"And the coin he had must've come from *his* grandpa too. That would explain how *he* got one," Deborah added.

"So what happened to cause Leon Hahn a premature death?" Cristina asked.

"He shot at my son, and I guess I lost my mind. I don't know what got into me," said Deborah, "but I wanted to hurt him because I thought he'd killed Blake. He would've killed me too if Dean hadn't saved my life."

"Awww! How sweet, Dean. You have a heart after all," said Cristina.

"Nah, I just wanted to shoot someone."

"The point of all this conversation, Agents Miles, is we've *found* the gold in this grave vault, but we don't know the story behind it yet," interjected Carl. "Four bags of it." He still had the one in his hand but when he shined his light onto the others, there were only two on the ground.

"Where's the fourth one?" asked Cristina.

"Where are Blake and Julia?" asked Deborah.

"Gotta love those two," said Dean. "I'd bet three remaining bags of gold, they're on their way to solving a kidnapping."

CHAPTER 28

While the ambulance picked up Kevin's father's dead body to be transported to the hospital for a physician to pronounce the date and time of death, Blake listened to Julia navigate him through town—this time toward the Hahn home.

They had a good ten-to-fifteen minute head start on the FBI, who would confiscate the three remaining bags of gold and allow Schoeffler to ride along. Dean would be hot on the agents' heels—regardless of the fact he'd be instructed to stay put—and Deborah would ride shotgun, worried once again for her son's and Julia's safety.

"You have a plan?" Julia asked when they turned onto Kevin's street.

"How about I bust the door down and complete a heroic rescue?"

"That'd look great in a movie, but this is real life. What if he's not here? Then *you* might get arrested for breaking and entering."

"Lucky for me, you're a voice of reason. What've you got in mind?"

"Let's take the coins, march up to the door, and see if we can get invited inside," Julia said.

"Sounds simple. And once we get in?"

"We improvise."

"Are you sure my bust down the door idea isn't a better plan?"

"Nope."

"Super. Let's try your idea." Blake unzipped the bag and grabbed a few of the doubloons before lifting the duffel bag from the seat and exiting the car, Julia on his heels. He went straight to the front door and rang the bell.

A woman looking to be in her early fifties—Blake presumed it was Mrs. Hahn—answered the door. She opened it but didn't say a word—just looked at the kids, curiosity in her eyes. She had obvious strands of gray slicing through her black hair and icy, fearful-looking gray eyes.

"I'm Blake Nolan. I believe I have the gold you want. I'd like my grandfather back." He shook the bag, rattling the coins.

Her eyes opened in surprise. "I thought...Where's my husband?"

"No question about the gold?" Blake said. "No denial about my grandfather?" He opened his hand, showing the doubloons to the flustered woman. He threw them on the floor behind her, and when she turned to see them, Blake pushed his way inside the house.

"Combination of plans. Good one, Blake," said Julia.

"Here's a whole bag, and there are three more." He threw the bag of coins on the living room floor. He took a quick scan around the empty room. There was no sign of Matthias. "That should satisfy your greed. Now where's my grandpa?"

Mrs. Hahn looked distraught. She seemed frail and scared—confused and visibly flustered. She said, "You shouldn't be here."

"I suppose it's because I'm supposed to be dead? Well, I survived, and now I'm here for one reason. I don't care about the gold. I want my grandpa."

"Blake!" Julia gasped. "Oh, no!"

Blake turned, and his heart jumped. His grandpa stood in a doorway, duct tape around his wrists and over his mouth, a bandage on a cut over his swelled left eye. His eyes had that aware look he often had, however, and he appeared to be happy even under duress. An old woman—probably in her eighties—held a gun to his temple as she led him into the room.

In a gravelly smoker's voice, she hissed. "Where's my son-in-law!" The lady used to be tall, but time had curved her spine and her scrawny frame was hunched. Wrinkles radiated at right angles from her upper and lower lips and the corners of her eyes. Her grayish face was gaunt and bony, and her lips were adorned with red skin splotches. She barely looked alive, but her eyes were sparkling with hate and anger.

"Mrs. Wilhelm Mueller, I assume?" said Julia.

"I asked a question." She cocked the trigger and smirked wickedly.

"We foiled his plan. I guess he wasn't quite the criminal your husband was. But regardless, Mrs. Mueller, I'm here with the gold to make the exchange anyway."

"*His* plan? Hahahahahaaa. The man's greedy, but he's also too dumb to have a plan. It was *my* plan. *I* kidnapped your grandpa. *I* figured out a way to get the gold. It's *my* gold. My husband's gold that your great-grandpa stole." When she said those last words, she pointed her gun at Blake.

Mrs. Hahn cringed as the gun aimed in her approximate direction.

"Why, after all these years, have you shown up here looking for the German spy gold meant for a North American Nazi spy organization?" Blake asked.

Grandpa Bloom's eyes blinked open in curiosity.

"How do you know that? Even your grandpa didn't know that."

"Fritz Duquesne's spy ring, running out of New York, was supposed to be financed by the gold, but your husband never received the confirmation he waited for."

"Metzger and Coleman, the two spies who located your husband, were sent under the assumption he'd ignored a message he received telling him to ship the gold back to Germany," Julia added. "They assumed he stole it instead."

"There was no message!" Mrs. Mueller exclaimed. "Wil—my husband— left a note explaining what he was told to do. He did *exactly* as he was instructed, and he rotted in jail because of *this* man's dad." She smacked the gun against his head. Blake jerked to attention when his grandpa grimaced. "Wil left a note in a safe deposit box that I discovered *after* he died. In it, he claimed he believed the Jew, Joseph Bloom, somehow stole the gold. That's what brought us here. For what he did to our family, we deserve the gold. Get up!" she yelled at Matthias. "And *you* deserve to suffer now."

Blake and Julia...and Mrs. Hahn...all helplessly stared as Matthias Bloom stood, Mrs. Mueller's gun wavering in her shaking hand as she held it against his temple. "Where's the rest of the gold? That isn't all of it," she said, once again pointing with her loaded weapon.

Terrified, Blake didn't know what to say or what to do. He looked at his grandpa, thinking if he didn't do something, she would kill him, but when their eyes met, Matthias winked. The wink seemed to be his way of saying *All is well, Blake. Don't worry one bit. It's a game, and I have the winning hand.*

Even Julia's tongue was tied as the crazed old woman seethed from across the room. Blake put his hands in the air. "I'll get it," he said, forcing her attention on him as he moved away from Julia. Mrs. Mueller turned her head to follow his movements. With her attention momentarily diverted, Matthias twisted his body and unfurled, slamming his elbow across the bridge of her nose so hard she fell to the floor unconscious. Her gun went sprawling.

Julia picked it up and aimed it at Mrs. Hahn. "Don't move!" she said.

Matthias ripped the tape off his mouth, and Blake tore it from his wrists.

They hugged while Julia did her best hot female cop impersonation. She seemed to enjoy it as much as everything else she did.

"It's over, Grandpa. You're safe now," Blake said.

"I knew you'd be here. I knew you'd find everything...you *did* find everything, right?"

Blake grinned.

"I thought so," Matthias said. "I didn't figure you'd have to look so soon though. I was only worried I might forget." He bent over to check Mrs. Mueller's pulse. "I hope I didn't kill her." But even as he spoke, she stirred. Matthias wrapped the duct tape around her wrists as best as possible while blood tricked from a gash on the bridge of her nose and dripped from her left nostril.

"Finally, you get to use some duct tape, Blake." The girl never forgot a detail and never lost her sense of humor.

"I'd like to tape her mouth too; I'm so tired of listening to the old biddy. And her taste in music is awful....and that Leon fella, her son-in-law, is a pig."

"*Was* a pig. He's dead," said Blake.

Mrs. Hahn slumped into a chair and began crying. Blake managed to sit Mrs. Mueller up as both cars from the cemetery came to a stop outside.

"Here's a coat, Mrs. Hahn. It's cold outside," said Julia. "Here's one for you, Mrs. Mueller." She tossed it to Blake while still wielding the gun. "I think the FBI is here, but I'm declaring a citizen's arrest....Ladies, you're both under arrest for the kidnapping of my boyfriend's grandpa."

Blake shook his head and smiled widely at Julia.

"What?" she said. "Haven't you ever wanted to make a citizen's arrest?"

"I can't say that I have. I was more into the whole heroic rescue idea."

"Oh, yeah, but my improvise plan worked flawlessly instead."

Blake wrapped the coat around Mrs. Mueller and paraded the defeated and wobbly criminals out of the house. Julia brought up the rear, the gun still pointed. Blake tossed the bag of gold coins to one of the Miles agents and hugged his mom. "It's over. Grandpa's safe."

With tears in her eyes, Deborah gave her father a tremendous hug.

Dean approached Blake and handed him a card. "Not bad, super sleuth. I couldn't have done better myself. I'm impressed. You ever need anything, don't hesitate to give me a call."

Mr. Schoeffler stepped out as well with a joyous look on his face. "You did it. I'm glad you're all okay."

"Thanks, boss. You mind if I call in sick tomorrow?"

Julia handed the gun to the other Miles and slid her arm around Blake. He turned, cupped her cheeks between both hands, and looked into her eyes. Julia wrapped her other arm around his waist and stood on her toes, reducing the distance between them. After all they'd gone through, it was clear that Julia had become more than just a friend. He leaned down and gently kissed her—a kiss they both felt was long overdue.

EPILOGUE

The clock ticked down...eight...seven...six. A Saginaw High player doubled down on Blake, and a post player slipped across the lane to help as well. Blake stood on the block just outside the free throw lane where he held the ball. Five...four...three...He pivoted, jumped high in the air, and zipped a pass under the basket to Big Ben Smyth. Two...one...the shot banked off the glass and fell through the net as the horn sounded. Frankenmuth had won the final quarter of the scrimmage. Coach Geyer, who had taken over for Leon Hahn, jumped from his seat on the bench and landed with his fist pumping.

The calendar said December 30, but the majority of the past week's questions had been answered by Christmas Eve. Federal authorities had taken possession of the Spanish doubloons. Because of the large amount of gold and the age of the coins, they possessed great value to collectors, so the FBI planned to auction off the treasure. Blake was to get a ten percent finder's fee, which apparently would be quite a lot. Carl Schoeffler's days as an FBI envoy/informant were over.

Oscar Mayer had given Blake an itemized list of the paintings he and Julia had discovered—pictures, descriptions, et cetera. The chairman of the Art Loss Register and the founder of the Commission for Looted Art in Europe promised restitution efforts would be of paramount importance. They promised to work tirelessly to restore the paintings to their proper places.

Coach Geyer's first order of business as the new varsity basketball coach was to gather his players, who voted unanimously to ask Blake to join the team. Blake, the caliber of player who could make everyone else better, meshed perfectly with his new squad. Ben smiled in Blake's direction, knowing without a doubt Kevin Hahn would have never made that pass.

As the players high-fived each other, Julia ran down to the court wearing blue high-topped Chuck Taylor's and Blake's extra-large blue and gold Clarkston hooded sweatshirt. She jumped in the air, and Blake caught her, putting his arms around her waist and twirling her in a circle. His grandpa, mother, and father, who had made it home for Christmas, stood with pride in the stands, faces beaming as Frankenmuth beat the inner-city school on their home court.

Holding hands with Julia, Blake walked to the bleachers where he happily hugged his parents. Things had turned out better than he had ever imagined. "Let's go get some ice cream, Blake," said Matthias. "We need to celebrate."

Once they left the gym and Blake explained to his confused grandpa that he couldn't drive and would have to ride shotgun, he said, "Grandpa, I brought the package like you asked, but it's about time you answered some questions for us first."

Matthias's stomach let out a long gurgle. "Did I eat this morning?" he asked.

"You're still eating those fried jelly donuts we had the last night of Hanukkah," Julia told him.

"I am? Well, I'll be. I don't recall. Go ahead and ask your questions, Blake," he said. "I like your curiosity. Fire away. I'll eat when you get some ice cream."

"Well, first of all, Hirsch couldn't have known anything about the note we found in the nightstand, but I can't help but wonder why he took the gold to Frankenmuth."

"My guess is it was simply a coincidence." His stomach gurgled again. "I should've eaten this morning," he said. "Mrs. Mueller told me her husband's prior instructions were to hold onto the gold indefinitely until specifically instructed what to do with it. He expected instructions by June of 1939, but if he failed to receive them, it meant he was compromised, and he was to move, wait at least a year, and eventually contact a man in New York who would know what to do."

"That would be Duquesne, according to the note we found," said Blake.

"But the FBI had already discovered the spy ring by the time Hirsch would have tried to contact Duquesne," added Julia. "The whole spy network was identified and eventually rounded up and arrested long before Pearl Harbor and the time we entered World War II in December of 1941. Hirsch was sort of stuck with the gold."

"Yep," said Matthias. "But my father discovered the treasure." He paused. "We'll stop and eat at one forty-four, Blake."

"One forty-four? I don't understand."

"There's big ones and small ones. Anything you want." Blake patiently took in a breath. Finding out information from his grandpa would be a challenge. "Hirsch knew my father was Jewish, and as a Nazi spy, Hirsch hated him. But being a Nazi spy happened to be a bigger secret than being Jewish, so Hirsch kept his mouth shut and worked side by side in the mill cellars making fried jelly donuts."

"They made donuts in the mill cellars?" Julia asked.

"No, of course not. Why would you think that?"

"So how did your dad get the gold?" Blake asked, trying to get his grandpa focused again.

"The cellars were a great place to hide the coins, so little by little, Hirsch stashed it all away in an unused storage area. My father discovered both the location of the gold and the tunnel exiting the mill. Since it was barely beyond the basement of our home, he dug his own tunnel, and one night he took Hirsch's gold. Did you bring the package, Blake?"

Blake tried to refocus him. "So how did the paintings end up in the tunnel and the gold end up in his funeral vault?"

"My father's tunnel became the perfect place to store the gold *and* the art, so he moved the paintings there too, but he felt uneasy having both treasures stored in the same place. He hatched the burial vault plan when he purchased his plot at the cemetery. Hardest thing I ever did was to dig that grave back up when I lost my dad."

"So how did Mrs. Mueller and Mr. Hahn end up in Frankenmuth?" Julia asked.

"Detlef Hirsch became Wilhelm Mueller, got married, and had children. According to his wife, until he went to prison, no one had any idea about his past. But when he died, his wife discovered he had a safe-deposit box which held a gold coin and a letter explaining his past. The letter, according to Mrs. Mueller, named my father as the probable thief who'd stolen his gold. Mrs. Mueller lived with her daughter and Leon Hahn at the time, so they hatched the plan to come to Frankenmuth in hopes of one day finding the treasure."

"I remember Mr. Mayer telling Kevin about Mr. Hahn meeting with him several times to talk about the city history," said Julia.

"Yes, he ran a haphazard investigation that went nowhere. He wondered if I might know something, but he didn't do anything about it besides ask questions and watch me occasionally until Kevin saw your gold coin at school, Blake. When Mrs. Mueller decided to kidnap me, she assumed I'd have the answers to her questions."

"One forty-four, Blake." Matthias pointed.

"The exit? Exit one forty-four?"

"There's big ones...small ones...whatever you'd like."

Clueless as to what his grandpa meant, Blake asked, "What would *you* like?"

"Cracker Barrel looks good. That's a big one...but one of my favorites."

"Matthias, you have a wonderful memory." Julia blessed him with one of her sweetest smiles.

"Thank you, young lady."

Blake turned off the expressway and found the restaurant his grandfather wanted. "Will there be ice cream?"

"Of course. But first I have to eat. Haven't eaten all day."

Matthias, Blake, and Julia were seated right away, and talk resumed.

"I have a present for you both," he said. "The pictures you framed and gave me for Christmas are hanging on the wall. Finally, I can enjoy them. To thank you, your parents had these made for me," he said.

A gold doubloon had been cut into two pieces. Julia's left side matched Blake's right side when they put the pieces of the puzzle together. The half coins had a small hole and a chain for a necklace both could wear. Blake put an arm over her shoulder. She wasn't simply pretty; she was beautiful—inside and out. He leaned over and kissed her gently on the cheek, thinking of the adventure they'd shared together. When the brief kiss concluded, they both leaned back in their chairs, smiling at Matthias as their faces reddened.

"Thank you, Matthias. You're still making puzzles, aren't you?" said Julia.

"You're welcome. Kids today should be learning numbers and history...and puzzles and mysteries. I *do* love puzzles, and you two solved my best one. You're a team—a good team—and I want you both to know I approve." Matthias paused and then looked directly at his grandson. "You said you found the whole treasure?"

"We did."

"And the relics? You have them?"

"Yes...The thorns, the splinters, and the nails." He took the bundled package from his coat pocket.

When he unwrapped the items, Matthias noticed one of the large nails was bent. "What happened here?" he asked.

"Leon Hahn shot me." Blake's hand briefly slid up to his chest. "I had the package in my coat pocket." He showed Matthias the hole in the paper and the squashed lead bullet. "The nail stopped the bullet. You can still see the indentation on my chest." He paused. "Are these what we think they are?"

"They sure are. There used to be a document, but it's been more than two thousand years, and it didn't last. Joseph of Arimathea and Nicodemus signed it. When they received permission from Pilate to bury Jesus's body, they removed the nails from his feet and wrists, the thorns from his brow, and the wooden slivers from his back and saved them. They all were touched by the blood of Jesus. Each of those items you have, Blake, is coated with the blood of Jesus."

"I've read of the Crown of Thorns in Notre Dame in Paris, the Iron Crown of Lombardy in the Cathedral of Monza in Milan, and numerous other places claiming to have fragments of the true cross," said Julia. "Those are claimed to be the same relics we have here."

"But what Blake has is real. Disciples of Jesus have hidden and protected these items since his death and resurrection. My father brought them to America with the paintings to keep them preserved. You're now responsible for them, Blake."

"Responsible to do what?" he asked.

"That I can't say. But what I *can* say is I trust you."

"Your note to me said you couldn't risk the secrets falling into the wrong hands. You were talking about these, weren't you?"

"I said you ask the right questions." He smiled at Blake with pride. "They're yours now, so take care of them. And who knows? It's possible one day there may be another mystery and adventure in store for you."

AUTHOR NOTES

Now that my work of fiction is completed, I'd like to share what bits and pieces were real or partly real and what others were totally made up. Let me start with the pieces of information from the World War II era. Kristallnacht happened in Germany on November 9-10, 1938, just like in the book. The destruction was real; the characters were not. Dachau was a real concentration camp and many of the descriptions were obtained through research, including the medical experiments and the releases pending emigration. The S.S. *St. Louis* was a real ship which sailed at the same time in 1939 as in the book. It sailed to Cuba where Cuban President Bru only allowed 29 passengers to disembark. President Roosevelt also wouldn't allow the Jewish passengers into the United States, so the ship returned to Europe, just as in the novel. The ship's captain, the German agent, the men on shore, and the passengers were all made up. There were rumors of a note from German spies that was passed onto the ship, not off.

Adolf Hitler was confiscating evidence of the Jewish culture and history. Yosef Bloomberg, the smuggled art, the artifacts, and the furniture that came to America were made up. Field Marshall van Leeb, Heinrich Himmler, Admiral Wilhelm Canaris, the Abwehr, the Schutzstaffel (the SS), the Einsatzgruppen death squads, and the final solution of the Jewish question were all real. Operation Samland was made up as well as the note that Blake found in the dresser. However, the sinking of *U-1229* in the North Atlantic and the Canadian freighter, *Corn-*

wallis, in the Atlantic by the German submarine *U-1230* were real, and the boats sank on the very dates mentioned in the book. I found evidence of German spies who entered the United States via U-boats, but the spies in my book and their stories were made up (except for rumors concerning the diamonds). It's true that Fritz Joubert Duquesne led the Duquesne Spy Ring, which was the largest espionage case in US history. Thirty-three members were convicted in 1941 of espionage. Their role in my story, however, was made up. It's true that General Franco of Spain was friendly with Hitler, and Spain did not take a side during WWII. It's also true that Spain minted gold doubloons. However, I found no evidence of Franco giving gold to Hitler during the war. That part was made up. Detlef Hirsch/Gunther Metzger was made up as well as the story of the gold, the self-defense killings in Frankenmuth, and the escape, capture, and imprisonment of Hirsch.

Frankenmuth is as real as real can be. The history was reasonably accurate from interviews and research. The streets, business names, parks, covered bridge, river, carriage rides, water parks, etc. were real. The mills, breweries, and restaurants that I mentioned are real. The teachers, coaches, and administrators in the school were made up (as a matter of fact, the school is one part of the town I didn't visit). Bronner's is real and is as incredible as the story suggests. The historical museum is real. The characters from the stores, museum, and church have no resemblance to anyone in Frankenmuth. To my knowledge, there are no tunnels under the city, except for a rumor of one connecting Zehnder's to the Bavarian Inn, but it was that rumor that gave me the idea. St. Lorenz Lutheran Church and many of its descriptions are real, including some of the specific windows, but the two windows used as clues were made up as well as the interior descriptions such as the boiler room. The artists mentioned are real, and the paintings that were specifically mentioned were actual pieces of art, but I have no idea if they were missing or not. The story of the 1,500 priceless paintings, stolen by Nazis and found in a Munich apartment in 2011, was real, however.

The details of Hanukkah, the menorah, and the Maccabees

were researched, and I believe them to be fairly accurate. The Jewish names that Matthias rattled off were real Jewish artists, musicians, actors, and servicemen and women. Dementia is real, sadly, and some of the behaviors that Matthias exhibited were modeled after my father-in-law who passed away after wandering off from his home. Believe me, the emotions and thoughts during the search are real. However, the Saginaw Search and Rescue team is not, to my knowledge.

The story is fiction. The clues, the characters, and the story driving the plot were all from my imagination. I simply wove it around numerous real events in history in an attempt to entertain my readers and give a realistic feel to the story. I hope it was enjoyable to read.

ACKNOWLEDGEMENTS

First, I'd like to thank some amazing people in Frankenmuth who helped me put this book together. Jon Webb at the Frankenmuth History Museum set aside time for me and not only gave me some great information about the town, but he also managed to give me some plot ideas—probably without even knowing it. Lori Libka graciously toured me around Bronner's, helping me to figure out a job for Blake and the whole layout of that huge, amazing store. Mary Porte was crucial to the writing of this book as well. She toured me around the town and shared history and landmarks and was simply a "treasure trove of knowledge." I was thinking of her when I wrote that about Julia.

Secondly, I'd like to thank my beta readers who've had such a positive impact on this novel. Lia Fairchild, Jeannie Fulbright, Joanna Doster, Dawn Rasmussen, and Michelle McCarty, all in their own special ways, have contributed to the growth of this book. It's nice to have honest readers who are willing to share constructive criticism or give suggestions but also are caring friends. I've been blessed to work with such kind, honest, and capable people—authors all, who write terrific books themselves.

Third, I'd like to thank Angie James, Kerri Major, and Renee LaRocque for proofing my book. With all the revisions, I needed capable eyes to find errors and ask questions. I'm grateful for the hours they volunteered and the positive impact they had on this project.

Finally, a huge thank you to my friend, Ashley Fontainne, for all the hours of design work that she put into my book. It was such a relief knowing I had her on my side. She's dependable, talented, and easy to work with, and she writes fantastic books as well. Thank you very much, Ashley.

AUTHOR BIOGRAPHY

Jeff LaFerney is currently a full-time language arts teacher where he lives in Davison, Michigan. After coaching basketball for most of his career, he decided to write books instead and took on his new hobby. Now he spends his free time reading, writing, and editing books. He and his beautiful wife have two young adult children. His Clay and Tanner Thomas series focuses on a father and son team who use parapsychological abilities to solve mysteries. Jumper is a time-travel science fiction adventure. Jeff also has a blog called *The Red Pen* where he usually infuses humor to share about himself or to give inspiration or writing tips. http://jefflaferney.blogspot.com/

OTHER BOOKS BY JEFF LAFERNEY

The Clay and Tanner Thomas series:
Loving the Rain
Skeleton Key
Bulletproof

The Time Traveler Series:
Jumper

Find them all on Amazon and Barnes & Noble.